# AMERICAN PRIMITIVE MUSIC

TETEBAHBUNDUNG

# AMERICAN PRIMITIVE MUSIC

## WITH ESPECIAL ATTENTION TO THE
## SONGS OF THE OJIBWAYS

BY

### FREDERICK R. BURTON

Composer of "Hiawatha," "Legend of Sleepy Hollow," etc.;
Author of "Strongheart," "Redcloud of the Lakes," etc,

KENNIKAT PRESS, INC./PORT WASHINGTON, N.Y.

133442

AMERICAN PRIMITIVE MUSIC

Originally published in 1909
Reissued in 1969 by Kennikat Press
Library of Congress Catalog Card No: 68-8203
SBN 8046-0057-0
Manufactured in the United States of America

## ACKNOWLEDGMENT

The fact that all pioneer work is beset with difficulties, and the conviction that mine have been no greater than those of others who have tried to break new paths in the fields of art, science, or literature, have led me to feel that I should appear to magnify my enterprise unduly if I were to yield to grateful sentiment and mention all persons who, in one way or another, have been helpful to the undertaking of which this book is a record. I treasure many expressions of interest from persons almost or wholly unknown to me in all parts of the country — interest which I recognize as attached to the work itself and not to the personality of the worker; but my own interest in it is so deep that I count as a friend everybody who has given a word of sympathy for it. Acknowledging in this general way, then, my sense of obligation to a considerable number of men and women, I cannot let the occasion pass without a special word of appreciation for Mr. Richard Carden, but for whose disinterested encouragement at a critical period my field work must have been abandoned. I can wish no better fortune for sincere workers in any cause than to find a friend like him.

F. R. B.

New York, September, 1909.

# TABLE OF CONTENTS

## PART I.

## PART II.

# PART I

# AMERICAN PRIMITIVE MUSIC

## CHAPTER I

## GENERAL SURVEY

THE matter contained herein was obtained, first, by personal research while living with the Ojibways in the region north of Lakes Huron and Superior; second, during employment as musical expert in the ethnological departments of the American Museum of Natural History, New York, and the Field Columbian Museum, Chicago; third, by incidental contact with Iroquois and Indians of other tribes, and, fourth, by reading the writings of other investigators. By far the greater part of these pages is a record of my own discoveries and observations, and originally it was my intention to limit the book to a consideration of what may be regarded as my especial field of work, the music of the Ojibways; but the whole significance of Ojibway music cannot be appreciated without attention to and comparison with the music of other Indian peoples, and I have, therefore, undertaken a brief resumé of the general subject. I felt that I could do this with some degree of confidence owing to my unusual opportunities for studying Indian music and the several years during which I have given the best of my time and thought to the work. Moreover, the general subject has begun to

1

arouse widespread interest, and, as infinitely more remains
to be done than has yet been done, it has seemed to me that
a survey of the whole field, coupled with a record of my
individual research, might be stimulative to a comprehensive
organization of effort for the preservation of our primitive
music while it yet lingers in the memory of Indian singers.

If my research contributes in any slight degree to the science
of ethnology, such result should be regarded as its by-product,
for this book is the work of a musician whose astonished attention was attracted to the subject by hearing a party of Ojibways sing a rarely beautiful song, and who followed that "lead"
in the hope, well founded as it proved, of discovering a type
of genuine and useful folksong indigenous to his native soil.
That Indian songs may be useful to civilization, that is, that
they have great art value, I thoroughly believe, and I should be
lacking in the courage of my convictions if I did not make
such demonstration of my belief as lies in my power.   To this
end, in addition to a discussion of scales, rhythm, form, and
other technical and non-technical matters kindred to the subject, I have selected twenty-eight songs from my collection,
adapted to them English verse suggested by the Indian originals, and provided them with pianoforte accompaniments.
Some of the songs I have also arranged for unaccompanied
mixed quartette.   All these will be found in the book in addition to notations of the entire collection of melodies which it
was my good fortune to find.

The foregoing paragraph needs an apparent qualification,
for the disavowal of any ethnological significance may be

hastily interpreted as an expression of contempt for scientific principles and method. On the contrary, although artistic enthusiasm inspired the work of which the book is a result, the spirit, if not the method, was that of the scientist who permits no preconceptions or desires to blind him to facts. The crude and ugly in Indian music has been set down as faithfully as the beautiful, and every possible effort has been made to record an exact expression of the Indian's musical thought.

There is a science of music as well as a science of ethnology; and the science of music is twofold. The subject may be regarded from its material, or acoustical side alone, or from the side that is usually expressed by the phrase "musical theory." The latter has to do with the structure of the art; it concerns itself not with the number of vibrations to an interval, but with the artistic relations of intervals. It is analytical of the æsthetic content of the art, and it is with that phase of the matter that I have to do more than with any other. As will be observed later, the acoustical side of primitive music cannot be ignored even by one who applies himself mainly to the æsthetic, and I shall feel free to dissent from the conclusions of some of our ethnological investigators who have ventured to write on the subject of Indian songs.

### THE FIELD.

To the white man generally it is still matter for surprise that there should be any field whatever for serious study in Indian music. The facts are, indeed, amazing. Archaeologists recognize on the North American continent north of

Mexico fifty-eight distinct ethnic families of aborigines. All
these in the popular view are supposed to speak dialectic variations of the same language, but in reality each language of
the fifty-eight is more distinct from every other than English
is from German. There are common roots in English and
German, to say nothing of common words that differ
merely in spelling, or slightly in pronunciation. The fifty-
eight Indian languages are not linked together by the presence of common roots. The relations between English and
German might, for the purpose of illustration, be likened
to that between Ojibway and Abenaki. The languages of
these peoples abound in common roots, and ethnically they
are the same people, that is, Algonquin, and their languages
at base are the same; yet no Abenaki could understand an
Ojibway, or vice versa, without special study of the other's
tongue. The habitat of the Abenaki was and still is in the
east, where Maine and New Brunswick now are; the Ojibways
live north, west, and northwest of Lakes Huron and Superior.
Between them in the old days were, among other Indian peoples, the Iroquois, and contiguous to the Ojibways on the west
dwelt the Sioux. There is no common root in the Ojibway
(Algonquin), Iroquois and Sioux languages; and this remarkable dissimilarity applies equally to the rest of the fifty-eight
families. Powell summarizes the matter thus (Seventh Annual Report of the Bureau of Ethnology): "It is believed
that the families of languages can not have sprung from a
common source; they are as distinct from one another in their

vocabularies and apparently in their origin as from the Aryan or the Scythian families."

Here, then, is a field for musical inquiry of abundant amplitude and complexity if only it be known that these fifty-eight different peoples practise the art of music to any noteworthy degree. Of that there is no lack of evidence. Sufficient data have been uncovered by travellers and investigators of various kinds to warrant the assertion that music is not only an important but an essential feature of Indian life. Some of these fifty-eight peoples have already disappeared from the face of the earth, but, so general is the use of music among those that remain, it is safe to say that when all were in existence there was no exception in their devotion to music of a kind. Concerning those that are still available for study, it is known that music enters more intimately into their lives than it does into the lives of any white nation. I shall go into this matter in some detail in speaking of music in Ojibway daily life, the observations in the chapter under that head applying very generally to all Indian peoples. For the present it will suffice to state that music is no mere diversion from the Indian point of view; it is not separated from ordinary experience by being classed as an art, but is a feature of daily, homely use and necessity. The Indian has a song for everything—his gods, his friends and his enemies, the animals he hunts, the maiden he wooes, the forest that sighs around him and the lake that glistens before him, the fire in his teepee, the whiskey that excites him, the babe in the cradle, his garments, from picturesque headgear to shabby moccasins—every conceivable thing in which he has an interest becomes the subject of a song. His prayers are couched in song, and no ceremony, public or private, tribal or individual, sacred, mystical or secular, is complete without the music designed expressly for it and treasured in most instances from unknown antiquity. The Indian boy learns the legendary history of his nation coincidentally with its songs, and the vocally gifted youngsters are carefully taught by the old men and women to the end that no song of the tribe or family shall be forgotten. I believe it to be true that among no people, the world over, is music so loved and so generally used as among the North American Indians.

### THE INVESTIGATORS.

Occasional allusions to Indian music in the works of travellers and historians are of little value to the student. In the main they are the expressions of persons who have no special knowledge of music, and are restricted to descriptions of songs that sounded uncouth and barbaric to the narrator. Here and there in the miscellany of history, travel, and ethnological research, may be found what purport to be notations of Indian songs. Some of them may be correct, but if all were correct, and all notations published previous to 1881 were gathered together in one volume, they would not make a total sufficient to justify generalizations, or give any certain impression with regard to the subject. It is remarkable that everything else pertaining to Indians had been the subject of special study at the date mentioned. Not that everything discoverable had been discovered, but that every other phase of Indian activity, mental and physical, had been investigated and the results turned out in numerous volumes, and that music had not been considered even cursorily, is true. It is still more remarkable that the first serious effort to learn and state the truth with regard to Indian music should have been made by a German, and his report published in Europe in the German language. His essay, of nearly one hundred pages, and with notations of several score songs, is always honored with mention in bibliographies of the subject, but I fear that few American students have read it. I myself did not read it until this book was almost ready for the press.

Theodore Baker was a student of music at Leipzig University. He elected to take the music of the North American Indians as the subject of his thesis for his doctor's degree, and he came to this country in the summer of 1880 to gather his material at first hand. His time and means were limited, and the whole field of his personal research included only the Seneca reservation in New York, and the government school for Indians then recently established at Carlisle, Pennsylvania. What he accomplished under such circumstances has aroused my keen regret, first, that his essay was not published in English, so to reach American readers readily and stimulate further research at that period, and, second, that he could not have given his whole life to the work. So far as Dr. Baker went he was thorough, as would be expected of a German student; he fell into quick sympathy with the Indians, a matter that is a *sine qua non* in work of this kind, his mind was free from preconceived notions, and his conclusions were astonishingly sound. He was anything but dogmatic in the assertion of his conclusions, and yet most of what he stated tentatively after study of his few score songs, may now be set down as established facts and principles after observation of the immensely greater quantity of material at the command of the student. By reason, doubtless, of the publication of his essay in Germany, his work had little if any influence in stimulating further research. Several years passed before any other contribution was made to the subject, and then came Miss Alice C. Fletcher's monograph on Omaha songs, supplemented by various magazine articles and her later book, "The Indian in Song and Story," as well as her article, "The Hako, a Pawnee Ceremony," included in the twenty-second report of the Bureau of Ethnology. The monograph mentioned was published among the Archæological and Ethnological Papers of the Peabody Museum, Cambridge, Mass., in 1893.

While Dr. Baker's work, published in 1881, has priority in point of time, Miss Fletcher's marks the real beginning of serious attention to the subject. She is the holder of a fellowship in the Peabody Museum, Harvard University, founded by Mrs. Mary Copley Thaw for the study of American Archæology. In pursuance of her special work, which was not music, she had gone among the Omahas. While there she fell ill and for many months lay helpless in a teepee attended by Indian men and women. They did everything in their power for her comfort and recovery. The medicine men sang their magic songs to charm away her illness, the mothers crooned to their babies within her hearing, old men and women sang for her entertainment. So perforce she heard many songs many times over, and the more she heard them the more they pleased her until at last she came to something like the Indian's point of view with regard to them, and perceived in them an æsthetic value that she had not thitherto suspected. Her own account of this transition from the unappreciative attitude of civilization to sympathetic understanding of the primitive music is so illuminating to the whole subject, that I venture to quote the following from her monograph:

"I well remember my first experience in listening to Indian music. Although from habit as a student I had endeavored to divest myself of preconceived ideas, and to rise above prejudice and distaste, I found it difficult to penetrate beneath the noise and hear what the people were trying to express. I think I may safely say that I heard little or nothing of Indian music the first three or four times that I attended dances or festivals, beyond a screaming downward movement that was gashed and torn by the vehemently beaten drum. The sound was distressing, and my interest in this music was not aroused until I perceived that this distress was peculiarly my own, everyone else was so enjoying himself (I was the only one of my race present) that I felt sure something was eluding my ears; it was not rational that human beings should scream for hours, looking and acting as did these Indians before me, and the sounds they made not mean something more than mere noise.  I therefore began to listen below this noise, much as one must listen to the phonograph, ignoring the sound of the machinery before the registered tones of the voice are caught.  My efforts in listening below the noise were rewarded by my hearing the music, and I discovered that there was in these Indian songs matter worth study and record.

"My first studies were crude and full of difficulties, difficulties that I afterward learned were bred of preconceived ideas, the influence of generally accepted theories concerning 'savage' music.  The tones, the scales, the rhythms, the melodies that I heard, which after months of work stood out more and more clearly as indisputable facts, lay athwart these theories and could not be made to coincide with them.  For a considerable time I was more inclined to distrust my ears than my theories, but when I strove to find facts that would agree with these theories I met only failure.  Meanwhile the Indians sang on, and I faithfully noted their songs, studying their character, and their relation to Indian life and ceremonial.  During these investigations I was stricken with a severe illness and lay for months ministered to in part by Indian friends.  While I was thus shut in from the rest of the world, with the Indians coming and going about me in their affectionate solicitude, they would often at my request sing for me.  They sang softly because I was weak, and there was no drum, and then it was that the distraction of noise and confusion of theories were dispelled, and the sweetness, the beauty and meaning of these songs were revealed to me. As I grew stronger I was taught them, and sang them with my Indian friends, and when I was able to be carried about, my returning health was celebrated by the exemplification of the 'Wawan' ceremony with its music."

In the preparation of her monograph Miss Fletcher obtained the assistance of the late John Comfort Fillmore, an accomplished musician, who not only harmonized the tunes she had collected but contributed some interesting observations of a theoretical nature with regard to a possible subconscious harmonic basis for Indian melody. The publication of this pamphlet came at a rather opportune time. It was nearly coincident with the sojourn of Dr. Dvorak in America and the production of his "New World" symphony, over which there was a considerable controversy among musicians, and no end of misconception. It was rather generally understood that Dvorak had based his beautiful work on the plantation and other melodies indigenous to our soil, and that he sought thus to give American composers an object lesson in the writing of music that should have a distinctively national flavor. The facts are that a fragment of one plantation melody appears as a theme in the symphony, that the rest of it is as Bohemian as anything in Dvorak's long list of works, and that the distinguished visitor had no faint shadow of the intention credited to him.

With all its misstatements the controversy was of value in that it aroused composers, critics and others to some degree of interest in native American music. The main question concerned the possibility of music in this country that should not be a more or less pale reflex of German and other European models, but that should be distinctively American, and speak for our country as our poetry and prose had spoken for generations. There was little dispute over the assumption that such a music, whether desirable or not, must be based upon something analogous to the folksongs of European countries; and, as folksong depends upon an illiterate peasantry, and the United States has no such class among its people, the conclusion was inevitable that the source of thematic material must be sought either among the plantation negroes, or among the Indians. It was natural, therefore, that Miss Fletcher's monograph should come in for much study, and there were not lacking instances of attempts to make use of the melodic material contained in it. The most conspicuous work, the origin of which may be traced to the discussion of nationalism in music, was MacDowell's "Indian Suite." Its thematic material was taken in part at least from Indian songs, and the work has its permanent place in the repertories of the world's best orchestras; but Mr. MacDowell was apparently content to make no further effort in this direction. It might indeed be safe to assume that he was discontented with the results of his single trial, probably feeling that his individual musical nature was not in sufficient sympathy with the melodic expression of the Indians to justify him in weaving their strains into his own pattern.

The influence of Miss Fletcher's monograph threatened not to outlive the controversy with regard to nationalism in music. She was, and still is, an enthusiastic, tireless champion of what appealed to her as a cause; that is, she wrote, and spoke, and pleaded without ceasing for the recognition of Indian music as something worthy of study and that affectionate appreciation in which white people hold the music of civilization. There were reasons, to be noted later, why most musicians failed to be convinced by her arguments, or attracted by the melodic material she uncovered, and presumably there was some sort of reason why the government Bureau of Ethnology, and the several great museums of the country did not institute organized, competent and systematic research in the immense field to which she had drawn attention. Whatever were the reasons for the neglect of Indian music on the part of those whose life work it was to study American primitive man, the fact is that for years Miss Fletcher pleaded apparently in vain—apparently, because the time came when some of the younger musicians began to take the subject seriously, and because improvements in the phonograph made it practicable for the museums to give some incidental attention to music when they sent out their expeditions for field work. By this latter means a vast amount of material has been gathered of which only a small fraction has yet been made available in printed form. Travellers and investigators who have gone among the Indians have been encouraged to include phonographs in their outfits and to induce Indians to sing into them. The records thus obtained are stored in the several museums, and some of them have been reduced to notes for the purpose of giving completeness to articles on ceremonies in which music figured; but I am not aware that any institution has ever set a musician to work on the records with a view to making a comprehensive study of the subject, or of putting in intelligible form such of the material as has æsthetic value. The collection of records is, however, a gratifying step—not quite in the right direction, but something rather better than the absolute neglect of the subject previous to Miss Fletcher's time.

The next specific effort to discover what there might be in Indian music was, I think, my own, begun in 1901, eight years after the publication of Miss Fletcher's monograph and incited by causes quite apart from it. About the same time Miss Natalie Curtis began her remarkable studies among the Hopis and other Indians of the Southwest. She has put a great number of aboriginal songs into permanent form, and has so extended her observations as to include in her chief published work, "The Indians' Book" (Harper's), representative melodies of eighteen tribes. She does not take up questions of theory in her book, and she does not harmonize the songs, but her work is of great value to the student, especially in the side lights it throws on the attitude of the Indians themselves toward music. Another musician to undertake the gathering of material at first hand was Mr. Arthur Farwell, whose research was given to the Indians in southern California. He had previously been an enthusiastic exponent of Miss Fletcher's ideas, having published pianoforte arrangements of several of the tunes in her monograph, some of them retaining the Indian melody in its naked simplicity, others being thematic developments of the material worked out with excellent taste and skill.

During all this period, that is, since about 1882, the Hemenway Southwestern Expedition was at work among the Zuñis, Hopis, and other pueblo Indians, and before the conclusion of that great undertaking music came in for its proper share of attention. The musical study was mainly in the hands of Mr. Benjamin Ives Gilman, whose methods and conclusions will be considered in some detail in the pages that follow. Dr. Franz Boas, now of the American Museum of Natural History, New York, an ethnologist with more than a superficial knowledge of music, has contributed notations and discussions of Esquimo and Kwakiutl songs to the Bureau of Ethnology and the United States Museum reports. There have been, besides those named, various writers who have made brief excursions into the Indian country and brought back tunes, many in the aggregate, which have embellished magazine and newspaper articles, and so contributed a share to general knowledge of the subject.

Finally, the bulletins of the Bureau of Ethnology, and various publications under the auspices of the Carnegie Institution, of Washington, contain incidental allusions to music, sometimes with notations of songs used in religious ceremonies, accompanied by more or less comment on the part of the notators. All these contributions to the subject are fragmentary, and so scattered in papers whose main theme is not music, that they are of little help to any who would take up the study of our primitive music seriously. Adequate study of it can be done only when music is the chief thing to be considered, and not the incident.

### THE POINT OF VIEW.

My work has brought me to pleasant personal acquaintance with most of those who have investigated Indian music, as well as with very many who, while not musicians or investigators, have had intimate contact with Indians and have found much that is admirable in their songs. It has appeared from numerous conversations that my point of view with regard to the subject differs somewhat from that of the others, and as, presumably, that difference extends beyond the bounds of my personal acquaintance, it seems advisable at this time to indicate it briefly.

I have maintained since early in my experience with the Ojibways that their music surpasses that of all other Indians yet known; that they have raised native American music to a higher plane than that attained by any other of our aborigines; and while I am not aware that anybody has disputed my assertion, I have frequently been besought by friends of other tribes to hear, for example, the Hopis, or the Arapahoes, or the Omahas sing, the inference being that, if I heard the singing of these Indians as I have heard the singing of the Ojibways, I might qualify if not reverse my estimate. I should have been glad during the past nine years if circumstances had been such that I could have listened to the singing of the Sioux on the plains, or of the Hopis in the pueblos; but the mere hearing them, no matter how well they sang, would not have tended in the least degree to modify my conviction; for it is the thing sung that interests me, and not the manner of singing it; and the thing sung has been available to me in the notations of Miss Fletcher, Miss Curtis, and others.

Again and again it has come to my attention that few persons make clear distinction between performance and composition. Even men and women who have had the advantage of some degree of instruction in music are often misled by the excellence of a performance into overestimate of the music performed. Caruso could make a cheap, common-place song interesting. So could Tetebahbundung, an Ojibway singer whose tenor voice is of the most appealing timbre, and whose untaught vocal method is well nigh perfection. Not all Ojibway songs are beautiful. Some of them when reduced to notes, as may be seen in the chapter on "Ojibway Songs and Their Stories," are barren of æsthetic value. One of the most barren of Ojibway songs is in Tetebahbundung's repertory, so to speak, and I have heard him sing it many times to white audiences. Often have I seen sympathetic listeners wipe away tears at the end of the song; often have listeners asked me with some degree of indignation why I did not include that song in my harmonized versions. The answer may readily be found by turning to the song I am so frankly berating. It is No. 17 (a) in the chapter named. It was the man's voice that brought the tears, his native art as a singer that made the inquirers imagine they had heard something of value in itself.

I have a comparatively languid interest in the person who

sits at the pianoforte, or plays the violin, or sings. My attention is centred always on that creation of the imagination which has given the performer his excuse for activity. It is the composition that survives and is of consequence, not the performance of it, or the performer. Schubert's songs have outlived three or four generations of singers, and will outlive many more. Those songs of the Ojibways that are beautiful will continue to give their benign service to the world long after the present singers are silent. So, then, no Indian song, no matter how alluring it may be when heard in its native surroundings, can appeal to me as having artistic value unless it proves when reduced to notes to be capable of stirring the emotions under other circumstances. That is the test of beauty, of æsthetic, or art value. The printed notes, read by an entire stranger to Indian life, must reveal to him a beauty inherent in themselves, else the song fails. When the music of any people can be transferred from its place of origin to any other place in the world and there stir the emotions of strangers without the adventitious aid of preconceived romantic interest, then that music is of permanent value; and the measure of its value can be taken only after a lapse of many years from the time of its transplanting.

My attitude years ago toward the Omaha songs collected by Miss Fletcher was doubtless that of many another musician who examined them. Most of them repelled me by their manifest crudity. I saw and felt the rudiments of form in some of them, but they impressed me as incomplete and dull, considered as tunes, and wholly barren of suggestion. I was eager to find thematic material in them and could not do so. My eagerness may be fully appreciated when I explain that I was then at work on the composition of "Hiawatha," and that I wished to give the music a distinctively American color if I could. The best I could do was to use a Kwakiutl song as a theme for the Dance of Paupukkeewis in which I aimed frankly not at beauty but at something bizarre and barbaric. So, when I heard Ojibways sing, I was won to admiration of their songs from prejudice against them. It was the exquisite unity-with-variety in the song I call "My Bark Canoe," that opened my mind to the possibility of real and useful beauty in our primitive music; and from that time to this I have not found on phonographic records, or in the songs published by other investigators, any music that compares favorably with that of the Ojibways in structure and æsthetic value.

It must be clear, then, that my point of view is not that of the ethnologist, for I would not have taken the trouble to collect and record Ojibway songs if they had appealed to me merely as curiosities in human expression; and that it is not the point of view of a friend of the Indian. I hasten to add that my studies have made me a friend of the Indian, and I shall be disappointed if my contribution to knowledge of them does not have its share, however slight, in awakening a more human interest in them on the part of whites, and a better understanding of them as men and women; but that is apart from the present purpose in which I pose merely as the musician, observing certain phenomena in a critical spirit, seeking, if you will, to gain some good from the Indians for my own people rather than, primarily, to do the Indians a service.

CHAPTER II

SCALES

WHOEVER undertakes to give information concerning Indian music is met at the outset by an inquiry that has often taken this form when addressed to me: Do Indians use the quarter-tone?

The quarter-tone is a loose expression for a division of the octave into more and, therefore, smaller intervals than are recognized in the chromatic scale. It is well known that certain Oriental peoples recognize and adjust their voices to minute intervals that are in some instances less, and in some instances greater than one quarter of what we call a full tone, or whole step, or interval of the second. The music of such peoples is insusceptible of harmonic relations, and it cannot be expressed in terms of our five-line staff. If the Indians employ such subdivisions of the semitone, that is, if their scale is adiatonic, the main question concerning the serviceability of their melodies to art is answered at once in the negative. Civilization, in its present stage of musical advancement, cannot make use of motives insusceptible of harmonic treatment and inexpressible in the present scheme of notation. The question, therefore, is of vital importance, and it deserves to be met without prejudice, with an eye single to the truth. Its bearing on the integrity, or aboriginality of the Ojibway songs that I have adapted to the

20

uses of civilization will be appreciated best by indicating the attitude of most inquirers.   They are good enough to take for granted the intellectual honesty of the notator, and also to credit him with a considerable degree of talent in the composition of music; for they suggest, when he sets forth a coherent, beautiful Indian melody, that he has unwittingly written into it a finish that really is not there; that, being a musician trained in the diatonic scale, he has instinctively, nay, unavoidably chosen the nearest diatonic interval to express what, in the Indian's singing, was adiatonic; that he has been misguided by his æsthetic sense into correcting the Indian's false (adiatonic) intonation, and that he has, therefore, presented a garbled report of the Indian song.

One of the fairest statements of this attitude that I have seen is to be found in a monograph issued by the Smithsonian Institution, "Contributions to the History of Musical Scales," by Charles Kasson Wead, of Washington, D. C.   Discussing stringed instruments, he says:

"All musicians know that this number of notes, twelve, is found confusingly great for ordinary playing, and know the principles by which the player selects certain notes for any tune.   But this multiplicity of notes has an important bearing on all studies on nonharmonic music made by harmonic musicians.   For every sound within the compass of the instrument comes very near to some one of the twelve notes and may readily be represented thereby, owing to the difficulty the hearer has in estimating deviations from the familiar series and in noting them down.   The results of this approximation are to mask all deviations from the twelve-tone piano scale, whether intentionally or accidentally made, and to make it appear to musicians that nearly all the music in the world is performed substantially in our scale."

I have considered this matter with all the candor that lies in me. My answer, so far as the Ojibways are concerned, will appear in due course. With regard to the music of other tribes I conceive it to be incumbent on me, after examining the evidence, to lay before the reader a digest of it with such conclusions as have been expressed by other investigators.

Everybody who has undertaken to reduce Indian songs to notes, whether from phonographic records or from the lips of singers, confesses frankly to the bewildering difficulty of the task. There is much vagueness in the Indian's frequent slurring from one tone to another, the intervals are often, to say the least, unexpected, their scale relationship hard to determine until long familiarity with both style of songs and performance enables one to listen in much the same spirit with which the song is sung. These difficulties are heightened when notating from phonographic records by the foreign noises which accompany the operation of the machine, and, when taking from the singer's lips, by the clamorous thudding of the drum, without which the Indian usually declines to sing. There is, therefore, abundant room for error, and, in instances where the singing was probably out of tune, that is, from our conception of scale relations, it is undoubtedly the tendency of the civilized musician to correct the apparent error by writing the chromatic or diatonic note that lies nearest to the one doubtfully intoned.

It is this tendency that leads most writers who speculate concerning the origin and nature of music to discard as evidence all notations of primitive music, holding that the notes on our staff that purport to represent the primitive song can be but approximate statements of the facts. Thus discredited by those who pose as authorities in matters scientific, the musician who has toiled hard to grasp and retain primitive song finds himself in a position of peculiar embarrassment. He cannot well assert that his sense of hearing is so acute that he can infallibly detect deviations from diatonic pitch to the extent of an eighth, or less, of a tone, and if the man of science asserts that such deviation is accomplished at will on the part of the aborigine according to a conception of scale relationship of which the civilized musician is ignorant, he must be a bold investigator who would insist that his notations were absolutely correct. If he replies that this is the tune as he heard it, the man of science tells him that, because he is civilized and a "harmonic musician," he has not been able to hear correctly; that certain tones sung by the aborigine inevitably escaped him; and that what he put down in notes may be beautiful but is not what the aborigine sang.

There is a good deal to be said, nevertheless, on the musician's side of the controversy, for such the discussion really is, and that he is by no means defenceless has been proved to my satisfaction by the latest and most striking statement from the purely scientific point of view. In all that follows, the dual nature of musical science should be borne in mind. The composer who is so far advanced in the science of musical structure that he thinks in counterpoint and dreams fugues, need know nothing whatever of acoustics. It is no concern of his whether the A has 490 vibrations, or 49000. His work is securely grounded whether or not he is aware that in true pitch relations certain full steps in the scale are larger than others. His science is based on matters of which usually the physicist is blandly ignorant, and he is entitled by his knowledge of such fundamental matters to doubt the validity of the physicist's conclusions when the physicist presumes, as he often does, to invade the province of musical æsthetics.

### THE ACOUSTICAL TEST.

Now it happens that one who is as competent to discuss music in one scientific aspect as the other, Mr. Benjamin Ives Gilman, has studied certain Indian songs from the acoustical viewpoint and, by resort to a modern mechanical device, has come to a close understanding of the exact intervals used, and, further, has invented a method by which very minute deviations from diatonic pitch may be graphically expressed. Mr. Gilman's book, Hopi Songs [Houghton and Mifflin, 1908] is not only the most recent publication with regard to Indian music, but the most valuable in that it points the way to answering the vexatious quarter-tone question, although, as will be indicated, he has not yet answered it convincingly even with respect to the precise Indians whose music was the subject of his observation. I may add here that his method points the way to something of more importance to art than the determination of anything connected with primitive song. We may discover through it a great deal about the relation of tones in the music of civilization that is not now suspected. Through it even may come such a reconstruction of musical theory as to make the compositions of Richard Straus appear to conform to sound canons of art.

Mr. Gilman was connected with the Hemenway Southwestern Expedition which had to do with the Zuñis, Hopis, and other Pueblo Indians. This scientific expedition, to the credit of its founder and members be it said, did not neglect music as a feature of Indian life worthy of special inquiry, and Mr. Gilman, a profound student of music, devoted himself to an examination of Zuñi and Hopi songs from the acoustical point of view. In a paper contributed to the Hemenway archæological reports published some years before "Hopi Songs," he expressed the conclusion that the Zuñis have no sense of scale relations:

"What we have in these melodies is the musical growths out of which scales are elaborated, and not compositions undertaken in conformity to norms of interval order already fixed in the consciousness of the singers. In this archaic stage of the art, scales are not formed but forming."

Mr. Gilman proceeded along this line in examining Hopi songs, and undertook to test the accuracy of the notations he had made in the terms of the staff by ascertaining the exact pitch of every tone in every song. He first reduced the songs to notes on the standard staff, relying only on his sense of hearing, thus following, of course, the procedure of other investigators. The songs were recorded on phonographic cylinders, and his next step was to establish beyond reasonable doubt the faithfulness of the phonograph as a reproducer of its contents. This required a long series of experiments, and, when he was satisfied of the phonograph's integrity, a much longer and more arduous series followed in connection with an instrument designed to register the exact pitch of a sound to the hundredth part of a semitone.

Without going into the details of the operation, which Mr. Gilman describes fully in his book, it must be evident at once that the question of the quarter-tone would be answered unequivocally in the case of every song subjected to this method of inquiry. For the sake of convenience in expressing the results graphically, by means of an amplification of the five-line staff, Mr. Gilman restricted his considerations of deviation from diatonic intervals to the one-fourteenth part of a tone. That is, his scheme of notation provides for a graphic representation of fourteen different degrees of pitch between, for example, A and B, which, it must be admitted, is variety enough for the present inquiry.

Working out his songs by this method, he found that the phonograph caught and reproduced some sounds that he had failed to hear, and that many of the intervals as expressed in his own standard staff notations were radically incorrect. In other words, when depending on his unaided sense of hearing he believed he heard, or made himself believe he heard, tones on, for example, G, which in reality were some fourteenths of a tone above or below that pitch. The melodic line of the song touched here and there notes of the diatonic scale, but for the greater part it wandered with astonishingly irregular approach to regularity among intervals that were adiatonic, that is, between the pitches represented by two successive chromatic steps. The inference seemed to be inevitable that the singer sought and touched these intermediate intervals by conscious effort, and that, therefore, any expression of his song in the terms of the standard staff would be misleading.

Taking the results of this study in bulk, it would seem at first glance that Mr. Gilman had established the adiatonic character of Hopi music beyond question; and inasmuch as Miss Curtis, who approached the music of the same people from the other viewpoint, and notated a great number of their songs in which she found exquisite beauty, also found qualities that defied her ability to express graphically, it will be well to see what she says. She does not enter upon theoretical discussion, or mention the quarter-tone question directly, but the following paragraph appears in her introduction to the pages in "The Indians' Book" devoted to the Hopis:

"To seize on paper the spirit of Hopi music is a task as impossible as to put on canvas the shimmer and glare of the desert. Hopi music is born of its environment. The wind sweeping among the crags and whirling down the trail has carved upon the rocks in curious fashion the record of its presence. Its echo is heard in the song of the Hopis yodelling through the desert solitudes. There, in that wide land, under the blaze of the Arizona sun, amid the shifting color of the tinted sands and the purple-blue of the sharp-shadowed rocks, must the songs be heard to be heard truly."

If I interpret this paragraph aright it is an admission on the part of Miss Curtis that Hopi songs fail under the test outlined in "The Point of View," Chapter I; that is, they will not, when transplanted, stir the emotions of men to any degree comparable to their performance in their native surroundings. To persons who have heard them there the notations may revive the mood they then induced, but if others cannot "hear them truly" when sung from the printed notes, then their limitations in serviceability to musical art are very sharply drawn.

### EXAMINATION OF THE ACOUSTICAL TEST.

I would not appear to disparage either the accuracy of Mr. Gilman's results, or the worthiness of his method, and yet I must raise a question or two concerning them.  On his evidence and that of Miss Curtis, I am inclined to think that the Hopis habitually sing intervals that defy statement in the terms of our staff, but Mr. Gilman's patient labors have not yet proved so much.  There are seventeen songs in his collection to which he applied the acoustical test, a rather small number on which to base conclusions with regard to the music of a people. It is clear from an examination of his notations that the singers either did not utilize the minute subdivisions of the intervals with any consciousness of system, or that they were incapable of directing their voices with certainty to the intervals they desired.  In other words, if the Hopis sing according to an adiatonic system, the singers whom Mr. Gilman heard, sing out of tune with respect to it. Their failure to touch the intermediate degrees of pitch with certainty and regularity may have been instances of individual error. The only way to decide whether this was, or was not, the case, would be to get as many Hopis as possible to sing the same song, and reduce every sound in every separate performance to its exact pitch, or within the one-fourteenth part of a tone according to Mr. Gilman's staff. In this way one song would serve much better than seventeen as a basis for generalizing concerning the music of the whole people; for if all the singers touched the intermediate intervals alike, nothing more could be said against the supposition that the Hopis recognize and sing according to a system of adiatonic intervals.

Let us look at this matter in another way. I have conducted choruses of civilized singers, all the members of which understood something of the rudiments of music and were accustomed to singing. All knew the scale and were familiar with the facts of modulation, little though most of them may have comprehended the theory. Time and again when conducting such a body of singers in an unaccompanied rehearsal or performance of music in which the chorus had been drilled for weeks, I have heard the pitch descend slowly until, at the end, it would be a semitone and sometimes more below the initial pitch. This is a common experience. It is unhappily not altogether uncommon to hear solo singers who avoid the correct pitch from beginning to end of an aria or song. Again, students of singing who are required to sing a moderately long piece without accompaniment, plume themselves proudly if they come to the end precisely in tune.

Now let us suppose that the music of civilization had no scheme of notation, and that the only evidence of its character available to, say, an investigator from Mars, consisted in phonographic records of choruses that flatted, opera tenors who sharped, and soloists generally, with their multitude of sins. Suppose the erudite Martian subjected his records to a specially tuned harmonical and notated the exact pitch of every tone in every piece. Would he not be likely to conclude that Earth's choruses had an amazing conception of pitch relations in that they were able to descend from a given tone by minute gradations, sometimes only one one-hundredth of a semitone, to a point fifty or more hundredths below the starting point? The argument to this conclusion would be invincible, for he would observe that, although the chorus was divided into separate choirs, each with its own harmonic part, all descended together, the sopranos arriving at as relatively low a finish as the basses; and, therefore, these singers, one and all, must have proceeded upon a well-established system, which proved clearly, to say the least, a conception of adiatonic intervals. Then suppose the Martian wrote a treatise to that effect, who could controvert it? What damage suit against him in behalf of Earth's slandered art would lie?

The foregoing is intended merely to be suggestive. Seriously, I should be glad if some physicist would test the singing of civilization according to Mr. Gilman's method and record the results on the Gilman staff. It is a fact that the singer who maintains absolutely true pitch is rare; nevertheless our music is based on the diatonic scale, and he is a rarely bad singer whose false intonation can deceive a well-equipped musical theorist as to the melodic contour of his song. Mr. Gilman's experiments lead me to wonder if the line of a song, so to speak, that is, a graphic representation of the exact pitch touched from tone to tone, might not properly be likened to the edge of a sharp razor. Under a powerful microscope the razor edge proves to be an irregular line, worse than a worn-out saw, marked by ragged indentations and extensions, utterly unlike the straight, even line that it appears to be to the naked eye. The microscope undoubtedly tells the truth and yet the razor cuts. It would not be surprising if a graphic representation of a good singer's performance proved that he avoided the diatonic intervals by a few hundredths of a tone here and there, thus projecting a "line" for the melody as uttered by him that would be misleading to one who regarded music merely from the viewpoint of the physicist. If this should prove to be the case, the singing of civilized persons would be only approximately correct, and the staff notation of their performances would not be an accurate representation of what they do.

### THE INTERPRETATIVE METHOD.

In view of the fact that most choruses do fall from pitch unless sustained by instruments of fixed intonation, and the further fact that highly trained singers do on occasion, and in some distinguished instances, habitually avoid the key, there is no need to take my suggested parallelism between the melodic line and the razor edge as a bit of harmless fantasy. I believe that an application of the Gilman method to civilized singing would necessitate the use of the Gilman staff to record the exact performance; but the stability of the art of music would be undisturbed thereby. The æsthetic value of the song represented by the notes would be undiminished. It might be well, and, indeed, very exact, to say that the notes penned by the composer represent an ideal to the expression of which man bends his vocal efforts without always, or perhaps often, attaining accuracy. It does not follow and nobody would suggest that composers should cease to express their ideals in the rigid terms of the staff, or that we should try to conform our scheme of notation in accordance with the imperfections of the human voice.

"In this archaic stage of the art, scales are not formed but forming," says Mr. Gilman, which, I think, is the same as saying that the Zuñis are groping for a satisfactory system of interval relations. This is precisely my feeling with regard to Indian music generally, although I believe that some tribes, among them the Ojibways, have groped their way out of the confusion of adiatonic music. Here is primitive man, conscious of the beauty of modulated sound, stirred by the tunefulness of tones uttered, one after another, at different pitch. With no knowledge of acoustics, with no instrument of the string type to suggest to him the nature of vibrations, he gropes vocally for such tone relations as shall satisfy him. Now it is certain that among the meagre contributions which

Nature has made to the art of music, one of her gifts was the relation of tones in the scale as discovered by Aristoxenos six centuries before the Christian era.   It took the white race unknown centuries to find so much of certainty and stability in the science of music.   Sixteen centuries after Aristoxenos the white race was still groping for its next step forward.   It had not even then settled upon what we now call the major scale as the basis for its musical art; it was even then only beginning in a crude way to experiment with harmony.

We whites, then, have come to rest on the intervals of the diatonic scale only in modern times.   The Indian is still groping—for what?   Some difficult, unnatural scale such as the comparatively sophisticated peoples of the Orient have succeeded in mastering to a very limited degree?   Unlikely.   It seems to me that they are groping for the Greek intervals, and that if they could fully express their melodic aspirations they would utter melodies as susceptible of representation on the staff as are the melodies of civilization.   It is worth while to discover that the Pueblo Indian does not sing in our scale; it is admirable to invent a method of indicating to the one-fourteenth of a tone just what he does sing, but let no details of that material kind forefend the champion of that other science of music from discovering and interpreting the beauty of Indian song in such terms as the standard staff makes available to him.   We may not thereby get a faithful reproduction of Indian song; for the purposes of art we do not want it.   We want what there is that is lovely and suggestive in it; we would approximate to its spontaneity, if it has any, to its simplicity,

if that be its general character; we would be drawn by it closer
to nature to the end that our music eventually should be the
expression of subconscious sympathy with our country, and
not a laborious effort to square our original thought to European models.

This is no fantastic dream; neither is it in conflict with any
science.  The ethnologist, naturally, will have none of it, and
properly, for it is his business to store up obvious facts, but he
cannot object to this other work, this search for the facts that
are not obvious, this research for the spirit of things, the results
of which tend to enliven as well as inform a people.  The two
kinds of work may go hand in hand.  The properly equipped
musician may not only set down the bald facts of the Indian's
imperfect musical utterance, and thus contribute to exact
knowledge, but he may apply his knowledge and perception
as an artist to correct their utterances, expand them even, and
so dress them with the devices of civilization that they become
capable of a wider influence than is possible when they are
preserved merely in their primitive form.

It is this double work that I have tried to do—the presentation of exact record of Indian song, and the interpretation of it
in terms of music as understood by civilization.  I shall have
occasion again to discuss the interpretative method briefly in
relation to Ojibway songs, where more enters than a consideration of scales and intervals.  The foregoing excursion was
induced by what seems to me the incompleteness of Mr. Gilman's examination of Pueblo Indian music.  It goes far
enough to confuse the general subject, for the extraordinary

care bestowed upon seventeen Hopi songs, added to his paper
on Zuñi songs, gives an appearance of great weight to his
"belief that aboriginal American music is a type apart, whose
essential remoteness from the music of Europe and Asia may
be symbolized, as it doubtless was conditioned, by the physical
isolation of the Americas."

It is gravely to be doubted whether Mr. Gilman expressed
exactly what he meant to say in this sentence found on the
first page of "Hopi Songs." It is not, to be sure, the assertion of a scientifically established fact, but, viewed in the light
of the author's distinction and his painstaking work, the inference is likely to be drawn that the music of all North American Indian peoples is structurally similar to that of the Pueblo
tribes. Presumably Mr. Gilman would not justify such an
inference from an examination of a few Zuñi and Hopi songs.
Granting, for the sake of argument, that Pueblo Indian music
is adiatonic and "a type apart  .   .   .   from the music of Europe," it does not follow that the music of a single one of the
more than fifty other ethnic families is of the same character.
The fact is that, judged by such tests as musicians usually employ, the songs of the Ojibways are diatonic, and a considerable
part of the songs of other plains and forest Indians are unmistakably expressed according to a scheme of intervals recognized by civilization.

### THE MUSICAL TEST.

Presumably every musician who has notated Indian songs
has undertaken in one way or another to test the accuracy of

his notations. Dr. Baker's method consisted of singing his notated songs to and with the Indians from whose lips he had taken them. His conclusion was that the Indians whom he heard, sang according to the intervals established by Aristoxenos. It may be worth noting that I expressed this conclusion with regard to the Ojibways in a paper written some years before I had read Dr. Baker's essay, my phraseology being close enough to that of Dr. Baker to pass for a translation of it. Miss Fletcher and Miss Curtis pursued much the same method, and Mr. Fillmore, Miss Fletcher's associate, conducted some interesting experiments at the pianoforte, the Indian singers listening to his harmonized arrangements of their songs. Miss Curtis's indirect evidence as to the adiatonic nature of Hopi songs has been quoted. Miss Fletcher makes but casual allusion to the subject, but she says [Omaha Monograph, page 11], "The Indian's management of the voice, which is similiar in singing and in speaking, make Indian music seem to be out of tune to our ears conventionally trained to distinguish between the singing and the speaking tone of voice. Although the Indians have no fixed pitch, yet, given a starting note, graduated intervals are observed; not that any Indian can sing a scale, but he repeats his songs without any material variation."

Mr. Fillmore and Miss Fletcher both observed that grace notes in several songs "were struck by the Indians about a quarter of a tone above pitch." The essential tones of the melodies, however, appealed to them as in tune and were so notated. In one case, Mr. Fillmore observed that the second part of a song was sung in a key a semitone lower than the first part. There was an upward skip of an octave and the singers fell short of it. They proceeded, however, from their false start and sang the second part relatively like the first; but when Mr. Fillmore played the song to them on the pianoforte and carried through the second part, as they had sung it, in a lower key, his Indian listeners were displeased. He had made a mistake. When he played the piece throughout in the same key, they were satisfied.

I have been at some pains to present all the evidence there is of adiatonic singing by Indians, and it should be added that the writings of Dr. Franz Boas concerning certain Indian peoples on the north Pacific coast indicate that deviation from diatonic intervals prevails among them. Against this evidence must be set not only my own observations, but the presumption that so appreciative a musician and so distinguished an archæologist as Miss Fletcher would not have persisted in notating the songs of the Omahas, Dakotas, Pawnees, and other tribes, on the standard staff if she had not been convinced that the notes penned were a correct statement of the musical facts. Further, aside from her confession of doubt about Hopi music, Miss Curtis has complained of no difficulty with regard to the interval relations of the hundreds of songs notated by her. She is a thorough musician, and her sense of hearing is extraordinarily fine. It is preposterous to suppose that she would continue to reduce the songs of tribe after tribe to notes of the standard staff if there were such deviations from the standard intervals as to make those songs "a type apart from the music of Europe."

It might be fair to say, then, that from our present knowledge there are three general kinds of primitive music on the continent north of Mexico: that of the Pueblo Indians, that of the north Pacific coast, and that of the Indians of the plains and forests. A complete investigation of the subject, which, I fear, will never be made, might reduce or add to this classification. The Indians of the forests and plains far outnumber the other two classes together (there are upwards of 30,000 Ojibways alone) and as a great part of their music is diatonic, the proper conclusion seems to be that, generally speaking, the North American aborigines developed music to a stage where the so-called true intervals prevailed.

My own method of testing notations was that of the other musicians. The unfamiliar nature of the work led me at first into many errors, some of which were ludicrous in the light of further experience, but I was far more hampered in determining rhythm than intervals. During one summer that I passed in Ojibway land I had a pianoforte in my cabin, and I often had the Indians sing their songs to my accompaniments on the instrument. This in addition to singing with and to them without accompaniment. All musicians know that the pianoforte scale is a compromise; that our harmonic music is possible only by tuning our intervals so that every key is slightly out of tune; and no musician need be told that anybody who sings according to the Greek intervals can and does unconsciously adjust his voice to the tempered scale when there is a harmonic accompaniment. It was thus with the Ojibways. If singing out of tune had proved to be universal among them, I should have suspected that their apprehension of intervals was different from ours; but there are Ojibways, like Tetebahbundung, who sing in tune. I have often accompanied him on the pianoforte, and never has there been the slightest sense of disagreement between his voice and the pitch of the instrument. He is a full blood and uneducated; he is exceptionally fond of music, but I never heard him sing other than Indian songs which, he tells me, he learned from older Indians, most of them from a great-uncle still living on the north shore of Lake Superior, but too feeble to sing now.

Tetebahbundung is by no means the only Ojibway who sings always in tune, but there are others who sing persistently false. If these latter constituted a large class, and if their deviations from pitch were committed according to a recognizable system, we could admit the argument that they represented the true Indian manner, and that men like Tetebahbundung either were exceptions, or that unconsciously they had adapted their intervals to our scale after having had some contact with the music of civilization; but they are not a larger class, relatively speaking, than the palefaces who annoy chorus conductors by a tendency to flat; and their deviations from pitch are not consistent. That is, these singers seldom or never depart from the apparent pitch at the same place, or to the same degree. Moreover, a faulty singer will seldom err twice in just the same way in a song. Again and again I have noticed that an Ojibway who appeared to reach unsuccessfully for a major third, for example, the first time he sang a song through, would hit it right the second time, and fail to get some other interval in tune that he had sung correctly the first time. Finally, in the majority of Ojibway songs, the intonation, from our point of view, is correct throughout; and the same song may be intolerably out of tune by one singer and perfectly in tune by another. I must conclude, therefore, that the faulty intonation of the Ojibway is an individual error and not a racial peculiarity.

### OJIBWAY SCALES.

It is proper to speak of scales in connection with Ojibway music, because scales are deduced from and do not precede the development of melody. The Ojibway is not conscious of scale relationship; he would not understand the nature of a scale if it were explained to him. Music to him is not a science, so far as conscious knowledge goes. He knows nothing of acoustics, he has no instrument of the string type. He has gone far, as will be seen later, in the development of pure, formal melody, his progress in this direction being due not to knowledge, but taste. No Ojibway, so far as I know, has ever undertaken to analyze the art of which he is so remarkable an exponent; none has ever advanced the crudest beginning of a theory of music; yet he has come to an apprehension and appreciation of the fundamental principles of melodic structure, and so fashioned his songs that they conform to the canons of civilized art. In his centuries of groping for satisfactory tone relations, he has come to couch his melodies in certain scales which the civilized musician has no difficulty in deducing from the songs themselves.

An examination of the songs in this collection shows that the Ojibways recognize all the intervals of our major diatonic scale, but the fourth and seventh rarely occur in the same song. Most of the songs indicate a scale relation that differs from ours in its point of rest; that is, the melodies do not come to a conclusion upon the tone *do* that with us is the logical and satisfactory end of the series. In view of this fact it is not surprising that these Indians do not perceive the peculiar value of the leading tone, the seventh of our major scale. When this interval occurs it is in the nature of a passing tone, never as the last step before conclusion.

When I began to study Ojibway songs I felt a dual tonality running through most of them. They appeared to start in one key and end in another five degrees below the first. This rule has its beautiful exceptions, as "Her Shadow," and "Morning Tryst," wherein the major key is perfectly distinct and the tonality unmistakable, but it is a rule, nevertheless, and from it is deducible a five-note scale that is logical and that the civilized musician has little difficulty in learning to appreciate. This scale is not what is generally known as the pentatonic, although it consists of the same tones. It should go without saying that there can be more than one pentatonic scale, but the dictionaries, general and musical, recognize only one; they speak of it as "the" pentatonic scale, and describe it as consisting of the following notes in this order: *do, la, sol, mi, re, do.* I have written the scale downward because it will be convenient in making comparisons to follow the general Indian tendency to downward steps. The Ojibway scale begins and ends with *sol,* so that it would syllabize thus: *sol, mi, re, do, la, sol.* That there is a vital distinction in this order of intervals hardly needs asserting, and if there be any doubt, it will be resolved by analysis of the songs. Note, for examples, "My Bark Canoe," "Winter," "The Naked Bear," "Morning Star." This may be regarded as the major scale in Ojibway music, the songs comprised in it being bright in character (from our point of view) and harmonizing inevitably in the major mode. Corresponding to it is a minor scale, also pentatonic, which reads downward as follows: *mi, re, do, la, sol, mi.* In this scale the final note of the song is more often *la* than *mi,* which gives it a semblance to our melodic minor, the seventh *(sol)* in the Ojibway scale never being sharped. Examples are "Parting," "The Coward," "The Lucky Trapper," and so forth.

Each of these scales is developed by the addition of one tone which brings about a scale relationship closely analogous to the ancient hexachord. The Ojibway hexatonic major scale reads thus: *sol, mi, re, do, si, la, sol;* and the hexatonic minor: *mi, re, do, si, la, sol, mi.* Examples, major—"A Song of Absence and Longing," minor—"Lonely," "In the Forest."

There are also Ojibway songs that appear to be based upon the diatonic major scale of civilization, notably "Her Shadow," a remarkable example of spontaneous, spirited melody that comes to a normal conclusion on *do.* This song is noteworthy also as an example of the variety that may be attained with a very limited number of diatonic tones. Examination of the song will show that only four scale intervals are employed— *do, re, mi* and *sol*. Following is a comparative view of the several scales referred to, grouped under signature of one sharp. for convenience in writing:

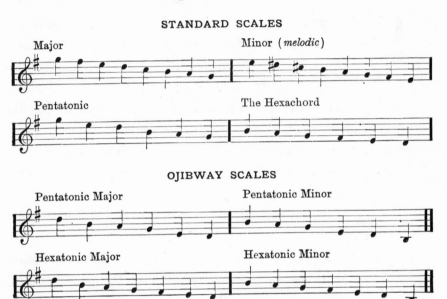

**STANDARD SCALES**

Major — Minor (*melodic*)

Pentatonic — The Hexachord

**OJIBWAY SCALES**

Pentatonic Major — Pentatonic Minor

Hexatonic Major — Hexatonic Minor

## CHAPTER III

## RHYTHM

IN the spring of 1904 I examined a large number of Pawnee songs for Dr. George A. Dorsey, curator of the Department of Ethnology, Field Columbian Museum, Chicago, who was preparing a work on the religion of the Pawnees under the auspices of the Carnegie Institution, of Washington, D. C. The report I made of my observations covered some of the ground that is to be considered here, and I have incorporated in the pages that follow such portions of that report as bear on the topic.

By far the most difficult subject in a study of Indian music is its rhythmic structure. We meet here phenomena that appear to be in defiance of ordinary human intelligence; we seem at times to be confronted with the unaccountable, even with the impossible. The phenomena are so bewildering that scholars otherwise sane have been led to declare not only that the primitive red man has developed rhythm to a plane higher than that attained by civilization, but that he has a conception of rhythm wholly at variance with ours.

When this latter observation was first brought to my attention I was so staggered by it that a long time passed before I recovered. It had been uttered by a scholar of world-wide repute and in a tone of finality that banished dispute from

44

his presence. What had led to the oracular deliverance were some remarks I ventured to the effect that the puzzling phenomena of Indian rhythm indicated not the red man's superiority in this regard, but on the contrary his inferiority; that he had, instead of a higher sense of accentual relations, a lower; and that his disturbing performances in so-called irregular and conflicting rhythms were but manifestations of a helpless groping for the truth which, rhythmically speaking, is order, and regularity, and simplicity.

In the outer darkness to which I found myself and my heretical ideas condemned, I came to something upon which I could take firm hold when I realized that if the Indian's conception of rhythm were different from ours, it would be vain to discuss the matter because our musical symbols are incapable of expressing any conception of rhythm other than our own. We should have to content ourselves with admitting that the Indian had acquired perceptions of rhythmic relationships that are beyond our ken, and make imperfect effort to show the nature of his advancement by pointing to the general belief that he drums in one rhythm and sings in another.

On the heels of this thought came the query: Can there be more than one conception of light? Yes; as many as there are blind men; but besides all these there is exactly one possible for those who see. Rhythm is a fact, not a hypothesis. It is patent to those who are capable of perceiving it, and it underlies not only life itself but all forms of art. That a universal fact should be imperfectly grasped by most persons the world over, that it should have been recognized in music

at a late period in the evolution of the art, that no adequate
treatise on the subject has yet been written, are matters that
suggest a volume of philosophical speculation. For the
present it will be proper to consider merely a few elementary
propositions pertinent to Indian music.

RHYTHMIC PHENOMENA.

Let us see, first, what is the nature of the phenomena that
lead observers to different conclusions; second, let us come to a
common understanding of rhythm; and, third, let us see what
actually happens in Indian music so far as that can be made
known through my studies.

The prime purpose of the drum in music is to mark the
rhythm. It has been observed repeatedly that the Indian's voice
has little or no regard for the rhythm strenuously established by
his drum. Travellers have often brought home accounts of
Indian music, and embellished their accounts with examples
in our notation, that told of a drum beat steadily in 4-4, for
example, and the accompanying song in 3-4. I am so far
from discrediting any report of this kind that I will say at
once that I have heard Indian music wherein the conflict between drum and voice was much more marked than is the case
between 3-4 and 4-4. What I shall object to, with even then
no disparagement of the notator's sincerity or ability intended,
is the use, actual or implied, of the word "steadily." The
presentation of an example in printed notes, with no qualifying
explanation, implies that the relation between drum and voice
expressed in the printed measures was maintained indefinitely,

or for as long as the performance lasted. This I gravely doubt, and the reason for the doubt lies in my own experience as an investigator, and the discovery of errors on my own part early in my work.

Perhaps I cannot quote a better example of conflicting rhythms than the Indian song that formed the basis of my first attempt to utilize the music of the red man for the purposes of art. At that time I had heard few Indians sing, and knew Indian music only through the writings of other investigators. Two measures will do to represent the rhythmic scheme:

This scheme, four beats in the voice part against six in the drum, with the confusing omission of the first of every three, continued for seven measures, which was the extent of the song as printed, and the implication naturally was that the Indian, repeating his song *ad infinitum,* held firmly to that all but unthinkable relationship to the end. Maybe he did. I ventured to develop the theme, giving the fantastic drum beat to the tympanist, and have found that by strenuous endeavor on the part of the conductor, chorus and orchestra can be held to the scheme for the two minutes during which it is maintained.

The piece referred to is "The Dance of Paupukkeewis" in

my cantata, "Hiawatha," composed long before the origin of the Indian play of the same name, and long before I had heard Ojibways sing. The theme is a Kwakiutl song. It may be of interest to know that circumstances have led to the performance of the piece before many Indians of various tribes, all of whom become greatly excited when they hear it, recognizing doubtless the native character of the theme, and stirred by the incessant thudding of the drum.

I cannot help suspecting that if the original notator had counted time during the Indian performance for the same period, he would have found lapses in the voice part analogous to those described in the Pawnee song discussed below.

Other phenomena that have puzzled investigators are concerned with the distribution of accents without reference to the drum, that is, in unaccompanied singing. It sometimes happens that two strong pulses will occur without a weak pulse intervening. The execution of such an effect by a civilized singer is almost impossible, and, when accomplished, is grotesque in the extreme. Not so puzzling as this, but still foreign to our manner, are the numerous abrupt changes from one rhythmic scheme to another, as the injection of a 5-4 measure into a series of 3-4, or vice versa.

### THE NATURE OF RHYTHM.

So much for the nature of the phenomena. An attempt will be made presently to reconcile them with our "conception of rhythm," but preliminarily it is necessary to arrive at an understanding of rhythm which Frederick Corder, Esq., writing in Grove's Dictionary, calls a "many sided term," and defines as "the systematic grouping of notes with regard to duration." Later in the same article, he says: "Rhythm, considered as the *orderly arrangement of groups of accents* . . . naturally came into existence only after the invention of time and the bar lines." Here we have two definitions by the same writer. They do not necessarily conflict, but they are not in absolute agreement, and I think the general understanding with regard to musical rhythm is that it applies to the orderly arrangement of accents. But that rhythm, the universal fact, was not recognized as a factor in music until something else had happened, is deeply significant.

Here are two quotations from the Standard Dictionary definitions of rhythm: "Movement characterized by regular, measured, or harmonious recurrence of stress, or impulse, beat, sound, accent, or motion;" "The musical property dependent on the regular succession of accents or tone impulses." Other dictionaries that I have consulted agree with the Standard in making accent the basis of rhythm, and all regard orderliness, regularity, or recognizable system, as essential to it. Duration has much to do with the matter, but duration alone, without accent, would not establish rhythm; and duration may enter either to conceal one or more accents, or to introduce a number of secondary accents. For example, suppose a piece that consists rhythmically of a regular recurrence of four pulses, the first strongly accented the third a little less strongly, and the others without perceptible accent; that is, a piece that would naturally have the time signature 4-4.  Fill a measure with a whole note and the accent on the third beat disappears; break the measure into eight equal parts, and not only does the accent on the third beat remain, but there are introduced secondary accents to mark the relationship between the eighth notes comprising each group of two.

The diagram of notes is but a suggestion of the well-nigh infinite variety that may be attained in a rhythmical scheme of the simplest character.   In Indian, as in civilized music, we find that the duration of notes representing the voice part often differs from the notes that represent the accompanying instrument, be it drum, or pianoforte; but in civilized music the notes of the accompaniment, be they few or many, are in an orderly proportion with regard to duration to those of the voice; in Indian music there is often no possibility of orderly proportion, so that there appears to be, and often is for a limited period, a concurrence of rhythmic schemes that are in violent conflict. If this conflict could be maintained with perfect steadiness in each part, voice and accompaniment, indefinitely, it would be incontestable that the Indian is capable of conceiving unrelated rhythms at the same time. It is impossible for me to prove that this is not the case, for I have studied but a fraction of all the Indian music that exists; but close observation of the music of several tribes leads me to infer that the appearance of sustaining unrelated rhythms coincidently is appearance only and not fact.

### POSSIBLE CONFLICTING RHYTHMS.

The phenomena that justify this inference are similar in general character to those discussed in the chapter on scales, the Indian's own deviations from his scheme in the course of several repetitions of a song. Let us observe in approaching this part of the discussion—the third in the plan outlined above—that not all civilized singers are gifted with a clear perception of rhythm. The average chorus must be reminded frequently that bar lines in written music are drawn as a guide to time and accent, and that the first note in every measure deserves a special stress. In other words, the rhythmic structure of familiar music often fails to manifest itself in the work of the chorus, the reason being that the singers are not conscious that

133442

there is such a thing as rhythm.  Again, solo singers, left to their own sweet wills, delighting perhaps in the sound of their own voices, are prone to dwell unduly on some tones and give scant attention to others until melodic contour is all but destroyed and rhythm is lost utterly.  It will do no harm to remember these things when we come to glance at what the Indian does.

More essential still to a sane view of the subject is it to remember that from the days of the earliest measured music until the present, educated composers have been capable of sustaining conflicting rhythms in the imagination, and educated singers and instrumentalists have been capable of executing them.  It requires a certain effort of the will to conceive of two rhythms at the same time, a greater effort to execute them; and to both it is essential that there should be some definite proportion between the pulses of the rhythms if they are to be sustained beyond a few pulses of either, the tendency of each being to force the other into correspondence with itself.  For example, every pianist has to learn to play double rhythm with one hand against triple rhythm with the other.  There may be three notes for one hand and four for the other, but the time given to the group of four is the same as that given to the group of three, so that at regular intervals there is a coincidence of pulse that enables the performer to take a fresh start.  We will now analyze an Indian song in which there is no coincidence of pulse between drum and voice, and no conceivable proportion between the drum beats and the natural accents of the vocal part.  It is a Pawnee song about a boy who was turned into an eagle, one of the series I reduced to notes for Dr. Dorsey from phonographic cylinders. That series was remarkably fruitful in examples of rhythmic oddities, and "The Boy Turned to Eagle" was the most striking of all in its coincidence of unrelated rhythms. For the sake of throwing all possible light on the subject I shall venture to detail the process by which the song was reduced to notes.

### EXAMINATION OF A CONFLICT.

There are several repetitions of the song on the cylinder from which I took it, and no two are exactly alike, rhythmically speaking, in the vocal part, but the drum remains perfectly steady throughout. In recording music of this type, my attention is given first to the drum in the hope that it will be found to be rhythmically proportionate to the voice; for, if such proves to be the case, the time value of the voice notes is immediately established. Perceiving, in this instance, that the rhythms were dissimilar, I ignored the drum until I had set down an outline of the melody. This was not difficult, so far as pitch was concerned, for the singer's intonation was true, but the matter of establishing the time value was distressing. I was not disturbed by the drum, considerable experience in this manner of work enabling me to forget its presence; it was the fact that the singer not only distributed his accents according to no recognizable plan, but broke up measures that should have corresponded with each other in a way that no arrangement

of dots and stems could express.    Moreover, in the repetitions
he frequently mutilated measures that previously he had constructed with firmness and regularity.

Eventually I had on paper, as a result of observing all the
repetitions, the notes that may be seen in (a), of the following.
The accents are indicated by the sign > over the various
notes.    This, in a way, was striking an average to obtain a
correct statement of the song, and the division of the piece into
measures followed readily.    It may be seen in that form
under (b) and I hazard the opinion that if the Indian had
sung without the drum, he would have sung according to
that scheme.    But it must be understood that in no instance

did he sing the whole in that way. What he did do was
to present every measure at least once in the way indicated.
From the viewpoint of detail, therefore, I have not "fixed up"
the Indian's work for him. Taken as a whole, the piece as
expressed in (b) is at least comprehensible and perfectly

singable. It ought to end three measures before it does, but the prolongation of the real finish in nowise affects the consideration of rhythm.

My next effort was to set down the drum strokes just where they occurred beneath the voice part. It was impossible. One measure could be done, but not another. After much fussing over the task, I made the arrangement shown in (c) which indicates approximately where the drum beats fell in relation to the voice. To the eye they appear to have fallen irregularly, but that is an illusion. The strokes were as steady as a metronome, and at only one spot in any of the repetitions was there exact coincidence with the voice, (d) in (c).

Now, the voice part in (c) not only shows where the accents of the song would logically fall, but where they did fall, and it is also a correct presentation of the Indian's rhythmic scheme in the terms of our notation. Counting the beats, we find that there are 48 in the voice part (omitting the initial note which, according to the custom of writing music, is supplied in the last note previous to the repeat sign) and there are 35 in the drum part. If only there had been 36! There then would have been a proportion—four to three—which would have brought about either regularly occasional coincidence of pulses, or a regular distribution of them which would have enabled a strong-willed singer to sustain the rhythm of the song. But no end of counting would make any more, or less, than 35 strokes.

I think no human being could drum and sing this piece and keep both rhythms intact. The Indian certainly did not. It would take pages to put into notes my attempts to express the variants of those measures in which a dotted quarter note occurs as the logical symbol. I found that what the Indian actually sang could not be written without some mechanical device to measure the length of each tone in the minutest subdivisions known to the printer's outfit. In fact, a little figuring of an arithmetical problem will show that it would be impossible. I believe the one-hundred-and-twenty-eighth note ♪ is sometimes used, but there is no perfect mathematical relation between 48 and 35 in 128. For example, the Indian had great difficulty with the fifth measure. On one occasion he managed to sing what is written at that point, but at other times it was neither ♩♪♩, nor ♩♪♩, nor ♩♩♩. The difficulty of indicating what he did might be evaded by this device: ♩♪♩ ; but that is merely a confession that the phrase is incommensurable, and this device: ♫♫ ♫♫, or something like it, would still fail because 48 and 35 and 128 have no common factor.

### THE INDIAN'S PERSISTENCE IN ERROR.

I could multiply examples from my note books, but this one is sufficient for illustration. It follows that in songs of this type it would be misleading to draw bar lines. In the first place, we should be in doubt as to whether the voice or the drum should be regarded as establishing the measure. In the second place, the Indian speedily breaks his own arrangement of accounts through sheer inability to maintain his scheme. I find that the Indian usually keeps time when the drum is in correspondence with the voice, or in no more violent conflict than 3–8 against 2–4. When the conflict is worse than that he never keeps his vocal measures in order. He will start his drum in 9–8, for example, and begin bravely to sing against it in 4–4; but after a few measures of success he breaks away, and from then on the value of his notes can be expressed only approximately.

The inference is inevitable that the Indian singer's "conception of rhythm" is so exactly like ours that the drum disturbs him and draws the voice away from its special movement. That it is the voice rather than the drum that weakens is readily explainable through the fact that melody, as distinguished from chanting, is a comparatively recent development of music. The Indian has not attained a high plane in the invention of music; his perception of the melodic relation of tones is weak; the definite, forceful pulse of the drum, appealing directly to his ear, overwhelms the sense of rhythmic pulse in his imagination, thus bringing about a distortion of the vocal part that depends upon the imagination for its form and character.

It is pertinent now to inquire why, if the Indian has any perception of rhythmic relations, as is indicated by the corrected version of his melody, he permits himself to drum in such a way as to obscure or destroy it. It seems to me the answer should be obvious to any who know the Indian well enough to appreciate the immense importance to him of the dance. For untold centuries the dance has been his vehicle for the expression of his deepest feelings. It is common knowledge that the warriors of the tribe are stimulated by it to undertake deeds of desperate valor; it is not so well known or realized, rather, that the Indian dance is a form of prayer. Dance and song almost always go together; the Indian's prayer is couched in song, and through the dance that accompanies it he gives his petitions and aspirations more obvious expression than could be attained by song alone. Add that the Indian is, up to his lights, very religious, and it will be seen that he has inherited tendencies of the most powerful kind which impel him to respect the drum, for upon that instrument the dance depends. To drum is instinctively with him to set the tempo and mark the rhythm for a dance. Habitually, then, nay, irresistibly he drums with steadiness, according to a set plan, varying the stroke only when some uncommon feature of the dance calls for a change of step or tempo.

Slowly, insensibly with him as with the race of whites, grew a perception of beauty in melody. Born somewhere within the recesses of the soul, melody will often fall within the rigid rhythmic lines marked by regularly recurring drum beats, but sometimes it leaps beyond them and demands a rhythm of its own. The simple-minded Indian could not possibly perceive that his incessant double rhythm, as uttered by the drum, was in conflict with the occasional demand of his spirit for triple rhythm in his song. He must have been a self-analyst equal to civilized man if he perceived the conflict and rectified it consciously. Melody, therefore, became distorted; it was hindered in its normal development, struggling always to assert its spontaneous freedom, and always restrained by the habit of the drum which the Indian would abandon no more readily than he would abandon any other of his numerous traditions. But, so great is the inherent strength of melody that it developed measurably in spite of untoward circumstances, and, among the Ojibways at least, overcame at last the obnoxious, disturbing drum stroke, the Ojibway himself, meantime, being blindly, childishly unaware of what was going on within him.

So it appears that the conflict is a radical one, as deep-seated as life itself; a struggle between truth and error; on the one side, the sense of beauty in tone which in all races has led to the making of some manner of music; on the other, traditional regard for the dance and its obvious rhythm; vague groping for melodic form on the one side, a familiar, easily comprehended habit on the other. The truth in this conflict is the artistic union of spontaneity and symmetry. That, the Ojibways have obtained. Among some other tribes habit still overcomes spontaneous melody to the extent of warping it, or keeping it confined in narrow, rigid lines.

The foregoing answer to the query is an attempt to reason backward from knowledge of present conditions. It would be simpler, and might be more satisfactory, to summarize the speculation in one word which agrees with known facts, and attribute the Indian's persistence in error to ignorance. He who has never stepped outside civilization cannot comprehend the Indian's devotion to his drum, but I cannot remember that I have met one white man who has lived with Indians who will not acknowledge frankly that he learned to like the instrument. I think I can enter appreciably into the Indian's interest in it. Perhaps it is the savage in me, latent from long past ancestry, that is stirred by its resounding clamor. But while I have no ancient superstitions associated with the instrument, the Indian has, and he is not aware that the drum beat is in conflict with the scheme of accents he invents for his song. Both, drum beat and song, are ingenuous expressions of his nature. One is extremely primitive, the other comparatively advanced, and, as he is still primitive, he clings to his cheerful noise, understanding it, aroused by it, while his musical soul toils darkly on toward an expression that aims ever at, and sometimes attains, symmetry. All of which is to say that he drums as he does because he knows no better.

When I began to study. Indian music seriously, I did so with the conviction, learned from the writings of others, that the Indian had developed rhythm more highly than had the white man. I have come to exactly the opposite conclusion through observation of many songs like "The Boy Turned to Eagle." It should need no saying that the highest development of rhythm is that which is most orderly; and if no order can be recognized in a given piece of music, it would be fair to speak of it as without rhythm. Better this dictum than the assertion that the Indian has accomplished more in this field than have all the civilized peoples in the world. But that, also, would be misleading, for it has been shown that the application of rudimentary principles of musical art makes it possible to discern and set down the Indian conception of melody even when it is distorted by an unwitting attempt to link it to a complex rhythmic scheme that is impossible of execution.

RHYTHM AMONG THE OJIBWAYS.

If the Indian really had a highly developed sense of rhythm, he would modify his drum beat and bring it into correspondence with the accents of his song. When, in a preceding paragraph I spoke of the Indian's perception of the melodic relation of tones as weak, I made a mental reservation in favor of the Ojibways. These people have a remarkably strong perception of melodic relations, and their sense of rhythm is indicated by the symmetrical character of their songs. It is emphasized by their use of the drum which, in the hands of a good Ojibway singer, ordinarily performs its proper musical function, that of marking the rhythm. I have come upon examples of conflicting rhythms in Ojibway music, and in every instance the effort to sustain them resulted in a mutilation of the scheme, but, as compared with other tribes, there was this significant difference: the drum part weakened quite as often as did the voice. Time and again I have heard an Ojibway singer interrupt the accompanying drum beats to bring the accents into at least temporary correspondence with his voice. The inference, of course, is that, his perception of melodic relationships being keen, he was sensitive also to the interference of the drum accents; and that he was highly enough developed musically to seek to adjust his accompaniment to the scheme of the song rather than sacrifice the melody. Another manifestation of the singer's sense of discrepancy might be indicated by drum notes in the following order:

 and so forth

On all such occasions the quick strokes were injected with evident irritation. Something was wrong; the singer hardly knew what had happened, presumably, and likely enough condemned himself for having forgotten how to drum. The fact was that the scheme of accents in his imagination was strong enough to overcome the mechanical, purposeless pounding on the deer skin.

It is worth noting that instances of the kind just described were always in connection with ceremonial songs of undoubted antiquity. In the old days, before the appreciation of this people for pure melody had fully developed, it is probable that the ceremonial songs were as little related to the drum as they are still in other tribes; and anything connected with tribal ceremony would be less subject to change than, for example, lyric songs, the expression of the individual. In all Ojibway songs other than ceremonial, I have always heard the drum beaten consistently with the vocal accents.

It appears, then, that if the discussion had been limited to rhythm as expressed by the Ojibways there would have been little to say; but it seemed proper to make comparative observations and through the musical superiority of the Ojibways to other tribes to dispose of the fallacy that the savage Indian had outdone civilized man in grasp of rhythm. As for the minor phenomena referred to in the foregoing as offering difficulties to the investigator, it is to be said concerning the distribution of accents in unaccompanied singing, first, that the Indian, like the white man, is fond of the sound of his own voice. He enjoys, as we do, the effort of producing modulated tones, and he dwells pleasurably on those tones that are most congenial to his throat, or on syllables that, from his viewpoint, are most pregnant with meaning. Second, if we will but recognize that the Indian is primitive in music as in other things, we will cease to look for an abstruse conception of rhythm in his songs and will give our mind no further concern with the matter.

The grouping of measures containing different numbers of beats in the same melody is interesting, but, so far as the Ojibway songs are concerned, calls for little comment. Sometimes it appears that the injection of an odd measure is due to basing the rhythmic accents on the natural pronunciation of the words, but quite as often the words are transposed from their usual order for the sake of the musical measure. I am inclined to think that these irregularities should be regarded as manifestations of the groping for simplicity and directness of expression which is attained only in the perfectly balanced period. On the other hand, as so many of the songs indicate a firm grasp of periodic structure, it may be proper to look upon them as the normal expression of a people who have passed the bounds where appreciation of music is confined to the simple period. The songs are here, and each student may form his own conclusions from them.

### THE OJIBWAY SYSTEM OF NUMERALS.

Before closing this chapter I wish to direct attention and a query to one rhythmic feature of Ojibway music that has been

highly interesting and troublesome to me from the beginning:
the frequent occurrence of songs consistently in quintuple
rhythm throughout. This is by no means unknown in civilized
music, but it is not common, and it appeals to most persons as
abnormal. It has been troublesome to me because of the confusion made on my note paper in the work of recording it,
the five-beat measures not always appearing to be such until
attempts to express them in three- or four-beat measures have
failed. So often is this scheme of accents found that it might
be regarded as an idiosyncrasy of the Ojibways, and I have
wondered whether it may be connected with their system of
numbers? They have the decimal system, but examination of
their numerals from one to ten shows that it was based upon
five, the suggestion being that in the old days five was the
greatest number the Ojibway could grasp. He counts to ten
thus:

| one, | bayzhig | ningotwasswe, | six |
|------|---------|---------------|-----|
| two, | neezh | neezhwasswe, | seven |
| three, | nesswe | neshwasswe, | eight |
| four, | newin | jangwasswe, | nine |
| five, | nanan | midwasswe, | ten. |

The first five Ojibway numerals are independent words, the
second five, compounds. *Bayzhig,* one, in certain grammatical
relations, becomes *ningo.* It will be seen, therefore, that the
words for six, seven and eight are clearly compounded with
the words for one, two and three, respectively. I cannot ex-

plain the formation of the words for nine and ten, but they are clearly compounds, also. That is, the Ojibway counts as far as five and then takes a new start. After ten there are compounds analogous to those found in the languages of all peoples who use the decimal system. The question, a curious one, merely is, whether the Ojibway's grasp of numbers was to any degree responsible for, or connected with his predilection for five-beat measures in his music?

## CHAPTER IV

## HALF-BREED MUSIC

THE reader cannot have failed to notice the vein of controversy running through the preceding chapters. It was unavoidable, for I could not forget the reception accorded to my reports on Indian music when first I came from the region north of the Great Lakes and sang the songs I had heard there. There was nothing unkind in the reception. On the contrary, the interest evinced was plainly genuine, and the encouragement of kind words was generous. I was given to understand, among other things, that I was in a fair way to contribute something of value to ethnology, a view of the matter that surprised while it gratified me, because, as stated heretofore, my aim was artistic and not scientific. But when I fell in the way of men of science, I discovered that my notations were held in doubt; that the artist in me gave grounds for discrediting the results of my research.

This was quite right, although it was hard to believe so at the time, for I knew the care I had taken to set down the melodies exactly as the Indians sang them, and in subsequent visits to Ojibway Land I took even greater pains to collect my material in such form that, if I erred unwittingly in my notations, anybody so inclined could detect the errors and cor-

67

rect them.  To this end I went armed with a gramophone, and had all the songs I had heard recorded on its cylinders, and these cylinders I deposited subsequently in the American Museum of Natural History, New York.

But even this was not enough.  There was still a point of difference between me and the men of science that troubled me greatly, and that still gives me food for thought.  Satisfied that my notations were at least substantially correct, some of my scientific friends made light of the matter by presuming that the music of the Ojibways had been influenced by contact with civilization, and was, therefore, not properly to be called primitive.  Now, when there is a difference between a scientist and a layman, the natural presumption is that the scientist is all right and the layman all wrong.  Nevertheless, I must venture to dissent wholly from this view of Ojibway music. From the viewpoint of art, music is music wherever it is found. A beautiful melody appeals to us whether it be the composition of a full-blood or a half-breed.  A type of folksong that is distinctive is no less distinctive because it happens to be the product of a mixed race, or of one that has taken measurable steps toward civilization.  To such observations as these, my scientific friends have responded in effect that there can be no possible objection to the attempt of a musician to find artistic material wherever he chooses to seek for it, but that such work is none of theirs, as they have to do with the study of actual primitive life; they will welcome anything that throws light on it, but they cannot be expected to take interest in phenomena that have been modified by the influence of civilization.

It has been very difficult for me to understand this, and if I misrepresent the scientific attitude it is because I state briefly the substance of what several ethnologists have said to me. I can quite understand that a student who has set himself the task of discovering and informing the world what was, for example, the religious doctrine of the Ojibways before the advent of Europeans, should thrust aside as negligible and untrustworthy evidence what an Ojibway born and reared on a reservation might tell him. Such an Ojibway could hardly fail to confuse the misty traditions of his people with Bible stories learned from missionaries. I can understand that men of science have not the time to bestow on subjects other than those in which they have chosen to specialize. The trouble lies, as I apprehend it, in the general attitude of scientific men, who appear to ignore that which is not of undoubted antiquity, that which is not unmistakably and purely aboriginal. This attitude is open to criticism, so far as the study of primitive music is concerned, on two grounds: first, that it tends to obstruct the study of primitive music; second, that it is in itself unscientific.

As to the first criticism, from the time of Dr. Baker to the present, it is the unqualified opinion of every musician who has sought to learn of our primitive music at first hand that it is a subject to which a great deal of attention and effort should be given. We who have worked in the field know the immensity of it; we know how comparatively little can be accomplished by the sporadic efforts of individuals; we know something of the material cost of such work, and that it cannot and ought not to be borne by the enthusiasts alone. It is work that needs and deserves support, a difficult matter to arrange under the best of circumstances. How much more difficult when men of distinction in ethnological science manifest indifference! Those persons who might take an active interest in the preservation of such primitive songs as still may be found, are readily deterred if Science utters the disparaging remark that the beauties of Indian song are merely the results of contact with civilization. Let it be admitted for the moment that the musician's work is not germane to the general pursuits and purposes of ethnology; is it not clear that an attitude of reserve, if not of hostility, on the part of men of distinction is bound to have a deterrent influence on those who might otherwise be aroused to an interest in the musical work for its own sake? I cannot, to mention but one instance, account for the persistent refusal of the Carnegie Institution to aid and sanction musical research on any other ground than that, the matter having been referred to scientific men, a report has been made that minimized the value of such investigation.

As to the second point, is it possible that there is no room in the science of ethnology for the observation of living phenomena? We know that there is. We have only to recall the recent death of William Jones at the hands of Philippine savages whose customs he was studying, to know that Science sacrifices much to learn what there still is of primitive life in the world; but when it comes to the evolution of a primitive people to or toward civilization, should Science turn aside her

eyes? Holding the argument strictly to the line of musical
inquiry, it seems to me that Science misses an exceptional
opportunity of observing the process of evolution when it neglects to equip competent musicians to go among the Indians
and report how these people with their unformed or doubtful
scales and their faulty rhythm, gradually slough off errors,
gradually adapt their melodies to the canons of art, gradually
improve their mode of melodic expression, come to knowledge
of harmony and, in other ways recognizable by a musician,
give evidence of progress. It is a fine thing to dissect a corpse
for the benefit of students; a finer thing, it seems to me, to
study a growing child. Surely there are lessons to be learned
from a well conducted observation of the progress of a race
toward a higher plane of life. So far as music offers opportunity for such observation, and on the North American continent the offer is of gigantic proportions, Science has stub-
bornly, I had almost said stupidly, ignored it.

There is no doubt in my mind that the music of most if not
all the Indian peoples on the continent has been influenced
by contact with civilization, and that the process of change
is still going on; but that does not compel us to abandon the
term primitive in characterizing a system of music the beginning and end of which is melody uttered by the human voice.
It cannot make the music any less interesting to a musician;
on the contrary, it is likely to be more interesting than the
unaffected primitive music, for, under the influence of advancing knowledge, the Indian will tend to refine his utterance

and do away with whatever is grotesque, inartistic and useless.

This is precisely what has happened with regard to the Ojibways, as I shall show in subsequent chapters, and the point I wish to make with all emphasis is that it is still Indian music. No white man has taught the Indian to correct the errors in his music, no white man has even called the Indian's attention to the errors. No deliberate effort has been made by anybody, Indian or white, to improve the red man's music. Such change as has come about is due to the Indian's own sense of melodic beauty. Having heard the white man's periodized tunes, he has consciously or unconsciously instituted comparisons with his own music, and, as his taste developed, he has lopped off here and there a conventional ending, a needless introduction, and omitted numberless excrescences in the shape of crude appoggiaturas that deformed his native melody. The Ojibway has done this in considerable measure, but observe, it is the Ojibway who did it. Probably the same could be said of the music of the Sioux, the Omahas, the Hopis. It is the primitive man himself who effects the changes, and, in advancing his art to a higher plane, he does not copy from civilization; he grafts no white-man tunes upon his native stock. What he does is to improve and refine his own. No layman could display an unscientific spirit more obviously than by ignoring the wonderful opportunity afforded by our aborigines to observe an art in the process of transition; for the Indians, advancing rapidly toward civilization, are making strides in generations, so far as music is concerned, that the white race crawled over in centuries.

## A GLANCE AT IROQUOIS MUSIC.

As I deal with this matter in some detail in chapters that concern the Ojibways more especially than other Indians, I will try to indicate at this point some of the effects of civilization on primitive music. A brief consideration of Iroquois songs will serve the purpose. These people have had more intimate contact with civilization than the Ojibways, and they are much more sophisticated. In fact, the Iroquois are so far advanced in civilization on their reservation in Canada that it is remarkable that they retain any features of the ancient life. They are Christianized, most of them can read and write, they are nearly all skilled laborers, they were born and brought up in houses, they know more of canned meat than of the chase. Yet they still sing many of their ancient songs, a proof in itself of the inherent strength of Indian melody.

There are certain earmarks of civilized music that a musician recognizes readily. Among them are tonality; that is, unmistakable relationship of the tones in the melody to a keynote; and form, which is the subdivision of the melody into contrasting phrases of equal length; and the interval of a half-step between the keynote and the tone next below it; this interval, technically the major seventh, is represented usually in primitive music the world over by the minor, or flat seventh. Let us now examine the structure of a popular Iroquois song called "The Mosquito." I am not conversant with the Iroquois language and have never undertaken to set down the original words of this song, but my daughter, who has given me considerable assistance in my song-hunting, patiently extracted the meaning from several singers, and our Iroquois friends assure us that her "translation" is quite correct.

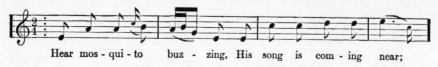

Hear mos - qui - to    buz - zing, His    song    is    com - ing    near;

Oh,    he    is    fond    of    gos - sip - ing,    The    lat - est    news    I'll    hear.

'Skeeter saw me drinking,
    Saw me acting queer—
Oh! then he went and buzzed a tale
    Unto my sweetheart dear.

'Skeeter made his story strong,
    Made me bad appear,
So when I went to call on her,
    She boxed me on the ear!

The tonality of this quaint little song is unmistakable, and it is as regular as a square. There is more than a suggestion of civilization in the obvious modulation to the relative major in the closing the first half of the period; that is, the end of the second line. Traces of Indian characteristics are found in the ornamentation indicated by grace and sixteenth notes, and in the flat seventh. If the grace notes were omitted, and the seventh were sharped, it might well pass for a product of civilization—not of a high order, but distinctly non-barbaric.

What happens in the singing of the song by the Indians is interesting and instructive. The old men sing it as above

notated; many of the younger who have been familiar with
the white man's ways since babyhood, not only omit the orna-
mentations, but, at the conclusion of the song, sharp the seventh.
The young fellows, for example, sing—

Hear mos - qui - to    buz - zing,

lat - est   news   I'll   hear.

When old and young sing together there is a blurring at
the points where the sixteenth notes occur, and strident discord
at the next-to-the-last note, some singing G, others G-sharp—
as if, indeed, a whole swarm of mosquitoes were gossiping.
It is impossible, of course, to fix the time when this song was
composed, but, while it may be a modernized version of an
ancient Iroquois tune, its mechanical regularity inclines me to
think it the product of a period subsequent to the advent of
the whites.   In either case it retains to-day certain characteristics of both civilized and uncivilized music, and its treatment by the younger generation indicates how native musical
art may be influenced by contact with civilization.

A more interesting example of Iroquois music is the song
that accompanies their snake dance.   The significant words
in this song are very few, meaningless syllables being used
for the most part.   The general sense, as I am told, is an
invocation to the snake.   Voice part and an indication of the
drum- or rattle-beat follow.

The barbaric effect of this song, when given by a good leader and from a dozen to twenty strong-lunged men, is thrilling. I have heard it hundreds of times and, bare though it seems on paper, I never fail to be stirred by it. The almost unbroken succession of two-bar, or four-bar phrases suggests the influence of civilization in polishing the ancient original, but the modern Iroquois has retained the flat seventh in the first part (to A), throughout which the underlying harmony is obviously E-minor, and the duality of key so often observed in Ojibway and other Indian music, as evidenced by the obvious A-minor harmony under the second part. Moreover, in performance the Indian characteristic of indefinite repetition is manifested by reduplicating at will the last four bars before A, as well as the last bars of the second half.

This is one of the few Iroquois songs that I have heard that retains so much of the ancient atmosphere. Most of them go much further than "The Mosquito" in the employment of features identified with the music of civilization. The largest Iroquois reservation is at Caughnawaga, near Montreal. To anybody who might be inclined to make a study of Iroquois music at first hand I would recommend as a preliminary work, consultation of the Annual Archæological Reports to the Minister of Education, Ontario, for 1898 and 1899, and an article on the subject by A. T. Cringan, Mus. B., in the Report for 1902.

# CHAPTER V

## STRUCTURE AND MEANS

SONG is the beginning and end of Indian music. The means to its production, therefore, are limited, with one almost insignificant exception, to the human voice and simple instruments of percussion. So far as vocal gifts are concerned there is no essential difference between the Indians and the whites. Their voices may be classified in the same way, that is, there are tenors and basses among the men, but the great majority are barytones; there are contraltos among the women, but the great majority are sopranos. I am inclined to believe that the compass of the average Indian's voice would be found to be greater by several tones than the voice of the average white man. The opinion is based partly on observation, partly on logic. So far as I know there has been no attempt to gather definite information on this point. It would be a difficult thing, even if it were worth while, to establish the precise compass of an Indian's voice, for he cannot sing up and down the diatonic scale to the end of his capacity in each direction, as a white man can. We can estimate his compass only by his songs and by hearing him sing them. Every Ojibway whom I have heard had a command of at least two octaves without recourse to the falsetto. Under certain circumstances, as in cries of joy, and in the warwhoop, every Indian uses the fal-

78

setto, but it never occurs in singing until the song proper is ended, when there often is a coda, or flourish, usually an inarticulate yell, an octave or more in falsetto above the highest tone of the song. Music teachers are pretty well agreed that the average civilized man's voice covers about an octave and a half. Observation indicates the red man's superiority in this detail, and logic strengthens the indication. For the Indian sings much more than the white man does. As faculties grow by exercise, it follows that the Indian will naturally be able to produce more and bigger tones than can civilized man.

Concerning quality of Indian voices, let me quote a line from one of the very earliest books written about our aborigines. William Wood visited the Plymouth and Massachusetts Bay colonies not long after their settlement, and wrote an account of his observations under the title "New England's Prospect," which was published in London in 1634. In the course of a chapter devoted to Indian women he says:

"Their musick is lullabies to quiet their children, who generally are as quiet as if they had neither spleene or lungs. To hear one of these Indians unseene, a good eare might easily mistake their untaught voyce for the warbling of a well tuned instrument. Such command have they of their voices."

My own testimony would be that there is nothing whatever in the Indian's voice to distinguish it from the white man's. Much singing in open air and frequent forcing of the voice to sound extremely high tones, combine to produce a rather harsh, generally nasal quality that is especially apparent in the upper register, but in the medium and lower registers the quality is much more agreeable; and when the singing is of the quiet sort that goes on in the tepee or wigwam, the harshness disappears altogether. The nasal quality is much less noticeable among the Ojibways as compared to the plains Indians. I have heard many individual voices of exquisite beauty in Ojibway land. One of the purest, freshest sopranos I ever heard anywhere was the possession of an ungainly, elderly, almost repulsive-looking squaw. In this instance I agree with the observer of three centuries ago, above quoted. Her voice, herself unseen, heard in meaningless vocables would have seemed like a rarely sweet flute. In general, if differences in language could be ignored, the unseen Indian's singing would readily pass for a white man's.

### INSTRUMENTAL OUTFIT.

The Indian's meagre outfit of instruments was not designed for the production of music for its own sake, but either to assist the voice, or to take the place of it in certain rare contingencies. His one important, essential instrument is the drum. This is made of a frame, or hoop of ash across which is stretched untanned caribou or deer skin. Its size varies from a few inches to more than two feet in diameter, and the depth of the frame varies also, the average distance between the skin surfaces being somewhere from four to six inches. It is held in the left hand by a thong attached to the frame, and beaten with a short stick held in the right. Among the Sioux and other tribes the drum usually has only one surface, and the instrument is often as large as a washtub, in which case it is set on the ground, open side down, and two or more players pound upon it at the same time. Every Ojibway drum that I have seen in actual use had two surfaces, each decorated with crude designs in color, and provided with the thong handle so that it might be held free before the singer while he accompanied himself.

This instrument when well made and played enthusiastically has extraordinary force. One was presented to me by an Ojibway friend, Wabena Obetossoway, with the earnest injunction always to warm it before using. The Indian invariably holds his drum over a fire before playing upon it, and he is keenly distressed when the humidity of the atmosphere prevents the skin from remaining perfectly dry. I have myself become sensitive to the difference between the sound of a warmed and perfectly dry drum and one that has not been properly prepared for performance. The skin surfaces absorb moisture from the air and, in damp weather, respond to the stick with dullness that is the reverse of inspiring. In fact, the drum is a good barometer. Its tone will foretell rain many hours in advance of its coming.

### AN EXPERIMENT IN ART WITH A DRUM.

I had occasion to test the power of the drum in the winter of 1903 when some of my Ojibway friends were giving entertainments in New York. I had written a set of variations on one of their favorite songs—"Old Shoes"—and conceived what seemed to be the happy notion of substituting the aboriginal instrument, with an Indian player, for the conventional tympani; for the Indian's drum, though it generally has recognizable pitch, does not enter into any harmonic relation with his melody. In the song as given by the Indians in their own way, the drum is beaten in a perfectly regular alternation of strong and weak strokes, and as in my variations I had not departed from the original time or tempo, it was evident, theoretically, that all the Indian drummer would have to do would be to pound his instrument in his accustomed manner, the white musicians undertaking to follow him.

We rehearsed the piece first without the drum, and when the orchestra had "got the hang" of its somewhat disconcerting rhythm, I sent for Tetebahbundung, about whose charming personality and unusual musical gifts I shall speak later. I explained to him what we were about to do and told him to drum "Old Shoes" as slowly or as fast as he liked, and that we would join with him after he had made a start. The orchestra was of the conventional symphonic make-up, strings, wood, horns and brass, numbering forty-two pieces. Tetebahbundung began placidly, and in the first statement of the theme all went well. The succeeding variations naturally introduced more and more complexity and increasing volume of sound. As the volume increased, so did the reverberations of Tetebahbundung's drum. He was not disturbed in the least by the many transformations through which the familiar song passed, but he was considerably excited as the shrieking of wood and the blare of brass rose up in waves to overwhelm him, and he increased the force of his strokes concurrently until, when we were about half way through I seemed to hear little more than the thundering of the drum. There was a confused roar from the band, but not a shred of theme was distinguishable. We tried it several times, Tetebahbundung patiently agreeing to hold himself in check, but he was not equal to the demands of the occasion. His enthusiasm got the better of his judgment every time to the end that the piece sounded like a drum solo faintly accompanied by forty-two instruments played at random. We had to give it up, and when the variations were presented to the public, the tympanist marked the rhythm on the comparatively subdued bass drum.

The Indian drum is usually supplemented by rattles of various shapes and sizes. The commonest type consists of a gourd partly filled with pebbles or shot. Horns of animals are sometimes used for this purpose, and there are many quaint contrivances like tiny shallow drums provided with wooden handles. The rattle is shaken in rhythmic unison with the drum.

### THE SO-CALLED FLUTE AND ITS USE.

Besides these two instruments of percussion there is one other, improperly called a flute, for it is of the flageolet type. It consists of a straight cedar stick, about as long as an ordinary flute, that has been split in half, both portions grooved the entire length, and then glued together to form a tube. One end is whittled away for a mouthpiece. A few inches from this end the tube is partially stopped, and just beyond the obstruction there is a longitudinal opening partially closed with a wooden block fashioned usually to represent an animal. This is slightly movable and is held in place by a thong wound around the tube. Six finger holes, at approximately equal distances from one another, are burned along the length of the tube, and just at the further end the tube is encircled by five holes to provide for the freer emission of air. I cannot find that there is ever any attempt to place the finger holes scientifically, and the result is that the instruments are ludicrously out of tune and no two are ever alike in fundamental pitch, or scale. The example in my possession, which I found and bought after weeks of search, for the instrument is rare among the Ojibways, has a soft, rather melancholy tone that would be agreeable if the intervals were in accordance with any recognized scale. Its lowest tone is approximately D in the bass clef.

So far as I can learn there is only one use to which the flute is put. No tunes are composed expressly for it, but it always serves as a substitute for a bashful lover's voice. If the young man has not the courage to declare himself openly to his sweetheart, he hides himself in the bushes near her family teepee at sunrise, knowing that, according to Indian domestic custom, she will be the first to rise and go to the neighboring spring for water preliminary to preparation of breakfast. When she appears he plays a love song on his flute. This is his declaration. It must be understood that words are associated in the player's mind with the melody. The maiden may not know what they are, for the song may have been composed expressly for her, but she knows that it is a love song and that it comes from an eager suitor. In all probability the concealed lover will repeat his serenade many consecutive mornings, for the maiden's endeavor will be to find out who he is before she gives him any sign whatever. She will discover his identity—what maiden in any nation or clime would not?—and if she favors his suit she will make her feelings known, whereupon the lover will forego the flute and join her at the spring. On the other hand, if she disapproves, she may tease the hopeful swain by giving no sign, thus compelling him to repeat his serenade day after day until discouragement overcomes desire.

The flute, therefore, does not figure as a means to instrumental music, which was wholly unknown to the aboriginal Indian, but as a substitute for the voice; and in the making of love songs care is often taken that they shall be capable of reproduction upon the flute. In view of the custom described it is not surprising that very many Indian love songs contain references to sunrise and the spring, or fountain.

Coming now to consideration of the structure of Indian music, I must make perfectly clear, what has been implied previously, that the aboriginal Indian had no conception of harmony, and that the modern Indian never employs it in his songs. There is, of course, the relation of voices in the octave, for men and women sing together; and now and again there is momentary harmony in certain ceremonial songs where two singers alternate in stating the theme. The second sometimes begins before the first has finished—after the manner of the stretto in contrapuntal writing—so that for a measure or so there seem to be two individual parts; but this is to be attributed either to accident, or the solemn enthusiasm of the singer, and not at all to any perception of harmonic relationship. I have heard one Ojibway who undertook occasionally to add an independent part to a chorus. He called his effort "undertones," and it consisted in singing the melody a minor third below the other voices. The effect was barbaric in the extreme and so disturbing to the other Indians that the song usually broke up in confusion when far from the end, or the others changed their pitch and sang the conclusion in unison with the innovator. It is fair to presume that this abortive attempt at part singing was due to the individual's desire to make music in white-man fashion.

### PRIMITIVE CONVENTIONS.

Study of the music of any primitive people has a special value in that it brings us in touch with the very beginnings of the art; and the music of our North American Indians offers unusual advantages for observation inasmuch as it includes several stages in the process of evolution. We find in it perhaps not the rudest music of the world, but a type of song wherein speech melts insensibly into singing, so that the notator is puzzled to find where declamation ends and song begins; and from this crude suggestion of musical expression we pass in review rudimentary melodies wherein the art principle of form manifests itself only in the slightest degree, then others which betray clearly a groping after formal expression, until, in the songs of the Ojibways, we come upon examples of perfect tunes, periodic in structure, æsthetically interesting, in brief, a type that marks the last step in purely melodic music. If the Ojibways had been so situated that they could have proceeded with the development of their music uninfluenced by contact with civilization, the next step would inevitably have been harmony. Whether this step would have been taken in one or twenty centuries is matter for useless speculation. In order to arrive at their comparative advancement in music, the Ojibways have had to break away from certain traditions or conventions of the red race. We are not concerned at present with how they came to do so, or why they are musically superior. The fact is that, having in mind the songs of such other tribes as are now available for study, Indian music is the all but hopeless victim of conventionality. It is possible to classify the songs according to various categories, but in so doing we are guided by the words rather than the melodic structure, for though an Indian never would mistake a ceremonial for a love song, supposing the tune were sung to meaningless words, yet after all, the songs melodically considered are of pretty much the same type. A great proportion of them begin with an introduction that is rudely analogous to the *recitativo secco* with which the elder masters preceded their arias. This introduction may be melodic in character, or a monotone; it may be brief, or as long as the song proper that follows; it may have words, or meaningless syllables, or simply the vowel sound *ah*.  A Pawnee once sang for me eight love songs and every one of them began with the following:

The song proper then started on the fourth beat of the second measure.

Oftentimes the introduction is barely distinguishable from declamation, and the more earnest the singer the less like music is his utterance.  The song proper, which may consist of no more than one word, will have at the least a melodic impulse; that is, it may be recognized as the beginning of a possible tune, but though there may be repetition, and even some sort of imitation, there is anything but a logical development of the musical idea.  On the contrary there is a speedy lapse into conventional phrases, or fragments of phrases, leading generally to a conventional ending far down in the gamut.  Time and again in notating songs of this type I have had my interest genuinely stirred by the melodic impulse only to come swiftly to a sense of keen disappointment because the promise of beauty was not fulfilled.  This is another way of saying that civilized man demands that music shall be not only fluent but symmetrical.  He may not insist upon the eight-bar period, but he does crave some manner of proportion, and in this respect the Indian generally fails to satisfy him.

A less number of songs, but still a large proportion, begin without introduction, but, as in the others, the melodic impulse is lost in conventional phrases almost as soon as the listener

becomes conscious of it. Very rarely there are found songs
that have neither introduction nor conventional ending, and in
these there is the closest approximation to periodic structure.

## MONOTONY.

The familiar reproach of Indian music is its monotony, a
characterization that has abundant truth and yet that is somewhat misleading. Remove the drum, and listen patiently, and
it will be found that no little variety is infused into the conventional introductions and conclusions. Let us see, then, what
it is that gives the appearance of monotony. There are the
conventional introductions and endings, conventional in that
they work over and over a few brief fragments of melody that
in themselves have little significance or appeal to the sense
of beauty in tone. Again these same fragments reappear in
many of the songs proper, slightly expanded at times but
seldom so modified as to come to us with an impression of
novelty. There are two groups of three notes each, so similar
in form and effect as to be regarded as the same motive—
one a variation of the other—that crop out in the majority of
the songs of all the tribes whose music I have examined.
These groups are:

They occur in all parts of the scale, often varied in the
relative time values of the notes, but manifestly the same
melodic impulse always; and, speaking of them as one and the

same, it might properly be regarded as the Indian's leading motive. It will be found in most of the Ojibway songs presented here, and it forms part of the principle melodic idea in "My Bark Canoe."

Proceeding with the discussion of monotony, it is evident that a rather high degree of constructive skill would be required to infuse grateful individuality into tunes that harped well nigh incessantly on one motive. Further than the points enumerated is the fact that the majority of Indian songs have at least one rather long passage of absolute monotone, or chant, and that the prevailing tendency is to begin as high as the singer can sound a tone and descend gradually to rest on a tone an octave or more below. I have heard the Ojibways themselves utilize conventional endings that compelled them to whisper the final words because the required tone was below the range of their voices. This continual reaching for the depths necessarily gives an impression of sameness, as if all Indian songs were cut from the same piece, or constructed upon a rigid formula, an impression that is deepened by their lack of structural proportion. It is not enough to say that form is essential to beauty in the art of tone, for form, as the musician understands the term, is boundless in its variety; let us say, rather, that civilization demands resting points, or punctuation in its music, and that without them the civilized ear finds difficulty in grasping a melody In the early days of Wagner's "infinite melody" how many were they who decried the master because of his monotony! To the uninitiated his music was meaningless noise because he ignored convention and would not condescend to cast his melodies in periodic form. The mind does not perceive a melody as a whole in the same way that the eye takes in a statue, or a painting, at a glance, and the reason for this lies in the fact that music is not stationary. The very essence of music is motion, not merely in the sense that it depends upon vibration, but that it consists in a succession of tones that have relation to one another in the order of their coming to the ear. While we are in the very act of perceiving the relationship of two tones, a third relationship is making, and so on to the end. The possibility of making an art out of tones depends upon the capacity of the mind to hold the impression of several succeeding relationships as a whole, this whole constituting but a fragment of an entire melody, or period. This fragment may be called a motive, or a phrase, and the end of it is marked by a pause of some kind, usually the sustaining of the final tone, which thus becomes a new point of departure for the next phrase. If the following phrases were wholly dissimilar to the first, the agreeable impression made by the first would not, could not be retained, and at the end of the last phrase the average person of musical intelligence would not remember the first phrase sufficiently to reproduce it. So it will be found that in the construction of those melodies that appeal most strongly, the succeeding phrases are modifications of the first, the composer seeking to reinforce the initial impression until, when it is securely fixed, he introduces a phrase in contrast, of entirely different relationship; and that contrasting phrase he is at pains to re-introduce literally, or with slight variation, before the melody as a whole is complete.

Let no layman infer that the composer is conscious of the process described. Given a sense of proportion, in other words artistic feeling, and creative talent, and the entire tune sings itself so far as the composer is concerned. Cold analysis subsequently proves the symmetry of the melody and indicates the subtle process by which it came to being.

Mention of Wagner was made for the purpose of illustration, not to institute any comparison between his marvellous creations and the ingenuous musical utterances of the Indian, but it is well to bear in mind that many were they who had to listen repeatedly to Wagner's music and study hard before they could receive it gratefully. It needs no saying now that there is ample deference to form in Wagner's compositions. We were staggered at first by his vaulting genius which compelled us to grasp and retain melodic relationships grouped in long successions of tones. The Indian, deficient in sense of proportion, neglects necessary pauses, and rambles on, to our perceptions incoherently, until the end; and after all my observation of his music I am at considerable loss to understand how he himself can retain a permanent impression of his melodies—that is, how he can remember them sufficiently well to sing a given song always in the same way, which he seldom fails to do.

### STANDARDS OF COMPARISON.

There is this further to be said before we leave consideration of monotony: our own popular songs are steeped in convention.

It is impossible to survey the art of any foreign people without instituting comparisons. We may not be conscious of it, but in listening to the Indian we are forever gauging his efforts by the standard of our own. There is nothing wrong in this, and it is so self-evidently a necessary part of our observation that mention of it is sufficient; but we may fall into error by setting up an unfair standard. The standard I try to maintain in my own mind is suggested by the term used above—"popular songs,"—for the music of an uneducated people cannot properly be compared with the creations of geniuses, or talented men who have had every opportunity for the cultivation of their gifts. Consider for a moment the matter of conventional endings. Civilized composers have devised a considerable number of endings, but they are incalculably few in comparison with the total output of songs; and in our popular songs of the day the endings are limited to a still smaller proportion. And how much real variety is there in the melodic impulse of the annual avalanche of "new" songs? It has been my painful duty on several occasions to examine some dozens of new songs, and the utter absence of originality, of any recognizable departure from the safe, beaten track which the public is supposed to enjoy, has been depressing in the extreme. It has come nigh to making me a pessimist so far as our musical possibilities are concerned. I am no prude in this matter. I do not despise popular songs but, on the contrary, try to find good in them. Sometimes I am rewarded. In its day I rather like "Bedelia," and my blood stirred to the swing of "Annie Rooney." After this confession I am sure I shall not be misunderstood when I affirm that the white man's popular song outdoes the Indian's in its appearance of construction according to a rigid formula.

These things depend upon point of view, that is, education and environment. I am inclined to think that the Martian investigator suggested in a previous chapter would find our hymns cast pretty much in the same mould, and our secular songs well nigh indistinguishable one from another. Speculation aside, I once sent two exceptionally musical Ojibways to a song recital in Carnegie Hall, New York. It was given by one of our most distinguished vocalists, and the programme consisted in the main of choice songs by Schubert, Schumann and Franz. Business unhappily prevented me from going with the Indians, but I had a friend accompany them to observe the effect. Poor fellows! I fear the experiment was rather cruel, but they sat like statues throughout the performance, never manifesting by yawn or restlessness anything but the most studious attention. They made no comment to my friend and were extremely reticent in discussing the event with me. When the Indian frees his mind, he is the most outspoken person in the world, but he is also most polite and considerate of others' feelings. My friends were reluctant to tell me how they enjoyed the treat I had set before them, and they would not lie. At length one of them, urgently pressed, said: "It was undoubtedly very fine. It was a beautiful hall and the man had a great voice. But it seemed to us as that he sang the same song over and over, only that sometimes he made it long and sometimes short." Which is to say that the Ojibways were ineffably bored by the lack of variety in Schubert, Schumann, and Franz.

The Ojibways to-day are musically in a period of transition. We cannot tell when the movement began, or why; we can only guess that it was subsequent to the coming of the white race, but, in spite of the neglect of music as a subject for scientific research, it is possible to trace its progress for sub-stantially a century and establish some significant facts. One is that the Ojibways, in refining what was and is their own, have not discarded anything that was essential to a distinctive style. Their music still stands the test of analysis and is in-dubitably Indian. What they have discarded consisted not in original melody, but in ineffective mannerisms. Many of their songs still have conventional endings; some of the oldest singers still begin with a conventional introduction; the line of monotone still appears in the majority of the songs. What might be the eventual result of the gradual change of ex-pression will unhappily never be known, not because they will not continue to refine their songs, but because, under the influ-ence of civilization they will forget them; but that result may be inferred safely from what has been accomplished, and that is clearly indicated in the songs that accompany this volume.

In selecting songs for publication I have included some that are distinctly in what may be called the ancient Ojibway style, for example, the "Visiting Song," "A Song of Faith," and others.  They show not only that the Ojibways had the musical mannerisms common to other tribes, but that such melodic impulse as was hidden in the mannerisms was superior in form and æsthetic value.  How progress has been made toward a more artistic expression may be demonstrated by an example which also illustrates the gradual decay of the native art through neglect.  For this purpose I choose the song known in its English version as "The Lake Sheen."  It is one of the most popular songs among the Ojibways themselves, more widely known, I think, than "My Bark Canoe."  I may say at this point that not all the songs I have collected are known throughout the length and breadth of Ojibway land.  Many appear to be known only in special localities, but "The Lake Sheen" must be in very general use for I have heard it from a dozen different Indians representing as many places.  That this is not a modern song is attested by the fact that School-craft, writing more than sixty years ago, made a versified translation of it.  Its extended distribution, too, is suggested by an episode in one of Mr. Stewart Edward White's charming stories where he tells of an Indian girl singing a sweet song and quotes a line,

"Mahng o doogwin nindenendam."

When I first heard the song, the Ojibway words and music were as follows:

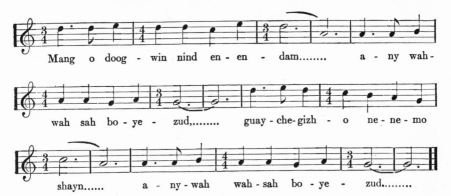

Mang o doog - win nind en - en - dam........ a - ny wah -

wah sah bo - ye - zud,........ guay - che- gizh - o ne - ne - mo

shayn...... a - ny - wah wah - sah bo - ye - zud.........

In this form I heard it many times from men, women and children.   That was early in my acquaintance with the Ojibways, when I understood not a word of their language, and I had no doubt that I had obtained the entire song.   The Indian of whom I sought a translation spoke English very imperfectly, and such words as he could master were all but unintelligible.   I gathered as much as this: that the text was in the first person, that the singer was seeking for his sweetheart, and that he was in doubt about the significance of a distant flash upon the surface of the lake.   It was clear that he connected the flash with his sweetheart, and at length I asked the Indian if the general meaning was this: "When I see the flash of the sun upon the lake I think it is my sweetheart beckoning to me."   With politeness that I have since found to be undesignedly misleading, he replied that that was about it.   In his attempt at interpretation he had used the word "loon," but what he meant by it he could not make me understand.   I had forgotten my Schoolcraft and never dreamed that I was dabbling in verse that he had preserved.   So, quite convinced that I was on the right track, I made the verses that accompany the harmonized version on other pages of this book, and to this day nobody, Indian or white, has called me to task for misinterpretation. As I came to some knowledge of the language, I saw that I was in error, but then, as now, the music was my first interest, and that was unmistakably correct.

Some two years after the first publication of the song, the Indian who had tried to translate for me, announced a discovery. He had met an aged Indian who told him that he left out more than half the song. From the old man my friend had learned the entire song in the following form:

The words mean: "I have lost my sweetheart, but I will leave no place unsearched and will find her if it takes me all night. As day breaks I think I can see her in the distance, but as I draw near I find that what I saw was the flash of a loon's wing on the water." It will be observed that, though much of the verse had been forgotten, nothing melodic had been lost, expansion of the song being effected by literal repetition. Inasmuch as the compression of the song to the form in which I first heard and notated it is quite general, and not the freak or carelessness of a few individuals, I am inclined to believe that the change from the older to the modern version was due to the Ojibway's groping for formal, that is, artistic, expression. Musically the song is far better in the modern version because there are fewer repetitions of the leading phrase. It appears that the Indian singers felt the tendency to monotony in the older version, and as they were not educated in music and knew nothing of thematic development, they solved the art problem by discarding some of the repetitions, thus evolving at last a perfectly made tune that happens also to be exquisitely beautiful. This speculation as to the reason for the compression of the song may appear to be vain at this moment: but it will be more convincing when we have given some consideration to the nature and structure of Indian verse.

Still another version of "The Lake Sheen" is necessary to a complete view of the process of transition. It was sung to me by a very old man, one who clings so tenaciously to the ancient ways of his people that the younger men complain that they cannot sing with him because "he does not get the songs right." I have heard his disturbing voice in choruses and know, what perhaps the young men do not realize, that he is harking back to his boyhood when shakes, and grace notes, defiance of measure and devotion to conventional phrases were established features of song, and when the essential portion of "The Lake Sheen" ran in this way:

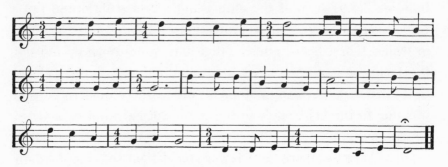

A SONG UNINFLUENCED BY THE PROGRESSIVE MOVEMENT.

Let us now glance at the structure of a song in which there is no trace of the influence of transition. It is a "Visiting Song," a class of which there are many examples still lingering in the memory of the older Ojibways. The ancient Indian was greatly given to visiting. It was common not only for an entire family, but an entire village to pack up necessary utensils and tramp or paddle long distances to pass some days with friends. When the visitors came within earshot of the homes where hospitality was expected as ingenuously as it would be extended, the leader of the party lifted up his voice in song for the purpose of giving intimation that visitors were approaching. In this instance he begins with a long introduction with meaningless syllables in which he states the theme, so to speak, of the song proper, and all, presumably, join in when he comes to the words that convey a definite message. There follows then a long, meaningless passage similar to the introduction. This leads to an imperfect conclusion and to recurrence to the song proper when the meaningless passage is repeated with a perfect close. Sometimes, and I think it would prove to be generally, if we could get back to the old days and observe the songs in actual use, there is a second recurrence to the song proper before the conclusion. This would make three separate statements of the song, which would be in accordance with a rule of Ojibway music that certainly was observed in former times. The song which I employ for illustration was used in winter, when the visitors had to tramp over the snow and ice, and when the prospective hosts would either be snuggled within their dwellings or occupied near by. As the Indian is inured to cold to a degree that amazes the paleface, it is quite presumable that the hosts would be seated on the ice and snow by the wigwam door, smoking their never neglected pipes. Under such circumstances the queer words of the song take on a shadow of meaning to us. Their literal significance is, "Who sits on the ice will hear me singing." By implication there is an added significance—"and know that I am coming, and you can guess how many are with me by the sound of our voices." It may be that the Indian had a subtler meaning in mind to the effect that if the hosts were indoors they might not receive courteous warning of the approaching party, but that if any one were sensible or lucky enough to be without, he would know all about it. Be that as it may, the song was a serious one to the Indian, and no faint suspicion of humor entered into his conception of the situation or the expression.  As the singer did not maintain a fixed time value I cannot arrange the notes in measures, but the accents are indicated by the grouping of notes and by the sign >.

It will be seen that the notes grouped under A in the introduction are a substantial statement of the notes eventually used for the song proper—that is, the fragment sung to intelligible words, "Ogit ko nemadabit ninganomdog." What follows under B is a rude imitation of the last part of A, and the rest of the meaningless passages might be regarded as rudimentary thematic development as far as C, after which the notes comprise a conventional ending. There is manifest here no high degree of melodic invention although the leading phrase has distinctive character, that is, it seems like the beginning of a possible tune; but there is a trace of form, a faint perception of the art principle of imitation; and the tonality, consistent throughout, is clearly established by the final notes.

Songs of this type constitute a link that binds the Ojibways not only to their own past, but to many other Indian peoples. It may be said to be the crude material out of which they have developed their shorter and perfectly finished tunes. When that process of development began never can be known. I have tried in vain to trace these tunes to their origin. Once I thought I had succeeded. I was assured that Chief Shingwauk composed both the words and music of the song he sang on the occasion of the Prince of Wales's visit to Canada. That was only about forty years back, and yet the melody, as sung into the gramophone by the chief's granddaughter, was of decidedly ancient character. I inferred that the great chief had not been close enough to civilization to acquire its musical manner, but it was my method, whenever possible, to verify the songs by asking different Indians to sing them. When, as was often the case, an Indian declined to sing a given song on the ground that he was not sure he could get it right, I would ask him to listen to the phonographic record of it.

More than once this led to further information of value. Some weeks after the "Prince of Wales" song was recorded I was working with an old Indian, John Squaguan, a citizen of Michigan, who remembered the occasion of Chief Shingwauk's journey and the song that was made for it; but Squaguan doubted whether he could recall all the "tones" of the song. He was sure he would know it if he heard it. I put the cylinder in the machine and he listened with a smile of delight. "Yes," he said, "that's it. It was an old, old war song that our people used when they started out to meet the enemy. Shingwauk used the tune but made new words for it when he went to meet the Prince." The song and further information about it may be found under Songs of Travel and Death, in Chapter X. It is not in common use at present, but it represents a large class of tunes that have persisted after the original words were forgotten. By unconscious selection the Ojibways have preserved many melodies that would have become extinct with the passing of their ancient ceremonies. An instance is the "Morning Star," once a sacred song, but now used as a love song to three different sets of words that I know of, and quite likely to a dozen more.

In discussing the structure of Ojibway songs, I have not dipped into analysis of the melodies that I have harmonized because they will speak for themselves to any student of theory. The contrasting and balancing phrases cannot escape attention, but it may be well to point out the comparatively rare occurrence of the eight-bar period which has come to be the standard form of the music of civilization. It occurs, but rather more frequent is the period of six bars, subdivided into phrases of three bars each, and often with a concluding phrase of three bars. There is a noticeable tendency, too, for structure in which five is the unit. This sometimes brings about a ten-bar period, but instances of the eight-bar or four-bar period comprised of measures having five beats each are more frequent. The five-beat measure is substantially a three-beat followed by a two-beat, and, for the sake of readier grasp of the songs I have sometimes arranged such melodies in a regular alternation of three- and two-beat measures. It will be observed, further, that in some instances, like "Hiawatha's Death Song," and "The Song of a Coward," there is a glorious freedom from the restraint of regular bar lines that yet does not result in unsymmetrical structure.

## CHAPTER VI

## MUSIC FROM THE OJIBWAY POINT OF VIEW

THE Ojibway's respect for music is profound. It means more to him than it does to us, for it implies verse also. He has no word for poetry. Whatever departs from plain prose is *nogamon,* song, which means that his poetry is not only inseparable but indistinguishable from music. Even in his oratory the voice is modulated to a manner of utterance that is beyond the pale of declamation, and a long step toward singing. Among all civilized peoples the art of expression through verse is one thing, and the art of expression through modulated tones is quite another, linked though they often are by the deliberate intent of the composer, and always associated, though they are, in the popular mind; in the Ojibway conception the two arts are not merely linked inseparably, they are fused in one.

If there is any difficulty in grasping this conception, let us recall for a moment the attitude of uneducated whites toward music. I have often observed a confusion in their minds with regard to song that, before my acquaintance with Ojibways, was quite incomprehensible to me. This was once expressed by an amazed inquiry as to how I could make music for words written by a man who died years before I was born. Sometimes I have hummed a tune, or sung it to meaningless syllables, and asked the listener if he knew it. On receiving a negative answer I would sing a line or two with words, whereupon the listener's face would lighten. Yes, he knew that song, and immediately would proceed to sing it to a wholly different tune. Having had his attention called to the melodic difference, he would appear to be deeply puzzled, and it would take some measure of patience to explain to him that the tune I hummed was not the same as the one he sang; and at the end I have never been sure that the discrimination was well established in his mind.

Of course I was dealing with a low, or rather, undeveloped order of intelligence, but it is fairly clear to me now that the confusion was due to a mental association of words and music so firmly fixed that the music as such made no impression upon the man's mind, and was merely a half unrealized vehicle for expressing the words. The contemporary Ojibway has taken one step beyond this, as is evidenced by his conversion of ancient ceremonial songs to love and social songs; but his difficulty in apprehending music as a distinct, separate creation, is still apparent. Time and again, after I had come to intimate terms with the tribe, a man would come to me saying he had thought of a new song. My music paper was always at command and the pencil sharp. The Indian would sing his "new" song through only to reveal to me a set of words that I had not heard before, the melody being substantially, and often exactly the same as I had taken from his lips on a previous occasion. Some of the Indians could not be made to perceive that under these circumstances they had not contributed a new song to my collection. The tones might be "very like," yes, but the *nogamon* was different,—and yet *nogamon* is a form of the verb that means I sing. This was brought out in a most interesting way in the course of special search for the original of the lines in "Hiawatha" beginning,

"Ewayea, my little owlet."

I had already heard and notated the song from which Longfellow derived the line,

"Hush, the naked bear will get thee,"

a literal translation of which would run thus: "Hush, little baby, go to sleep: do not cry or the naked bear will eat you." One after another I tried the squaws who came my way with suggestions and direct inquiries intended to revive memory of "Ewayea, my little owlet." They shook their heads. They didn't know "ewayea;" it was not Ojibway, some other language, Sioux, perhaps, but not Ojibway. I may note in passing that the Sioux are traditional enemies of the Ojibways, which may account for the presumption of the squaws that this strange word was of the Sioux tongue; and I have been told recently that the original of Longfellow's charming quatrain is actually to be found in the songs of the Sioux. I hope some musician will hear and reduce it to notes before it is forgotten.

Of course I explained patiently to the Ojibway squaws that "Ewayea" meant nothing in any language, that it was merely a make-believe word like those that abound in Ojibway

songs to fill up when real words are lacking, but still I made
no progress.   Then I concentrated attention on owlet.   Did
they never playfully call their papooses owlets? or little owls?
They seemed to see a grim humor  in the question but denied
knowledge of owlet as a term of endearment.   So, reluctantly
I was forced to accept the dictum of a chief, who lent the
sanction of his interested presence when I was questioning a
number of squaws at one time, to the effect that "we Ojibways
do not know owlet," but incidentally I had every squaw sing
every lullaby or cradle song she could remember.   I hoped
yet to trace in one or another a suggestion of the quatrain,
and failed not only in this attempt, but also in getting a new
song.   Every single lullaby sung to me by the Ojibway squaws
on that occasion was but a direct repetition or slight variation,
so far as the tune went, of "Hush, the naked bear will get thee."

### SINGING CONTESTS.

Whenever you come upon a party of these Indians, be it a
whole village on a journey, or a scant half dozen, you may
be sure that at least one among them has his drum with him.
Unless he is thoroughly familiar with palefaces that chance
his way, he will keep the instrument concealed, but when night
comes and the party is secure from intrusion, it will be produced
from its bag and long hours will be filled with music.   The
drummer always sings.   The others generally listen with apparent interest and satisfaction.   Now and again they add their
voices to the song, and more rarely the drum passes from the

first singer to some other member of the party, but by no means every Ojibway would presume to take his turn at drumimng. It is not only a skilled art, and not only do the Indians recognize the fact that some are musically gifted, and some not, but there enters also a certain jealousy, with which white musicians are not unfamiliar, to keep the accompanying instrument in the hands of one performer. I have many a time had to repress my smiles at sight of the offended dignity of an Ojibway musician when I have loaned my own drum to another that I might induce the latter to sing.

In olden days this rivalry in music led to friendly contests that lacked only pageantry and a judge, or jury, to be quite analogous to the tournaments of song in the times of the Master and Minnesingers of Germany. It is likely that such contests are held to-day in the remotest wilds of Canada, but it has never been my good fortune to witness one. An old man told me of a contest at which he was present when a small boy. His father was the chief of the village, and to him came another chief on a friendly visit. The second chief brought a number of his people with him. In the evening the chiefs sat by a campfire, the sub-chiefs, warriors and other members of the tribe being seated at appropriate distances. One of the chiefs was a visitor, and some of his people were with him. The host took his drum and sang, all listening intently. At the end he passed the drum to the visitor who sang in his turn. After several songs had been exchanged, and enthusiasm had risen, the host asked his guest if he knew a certain song. Yes, and he would like to hear his host sing it, whereupon the

host complied on condition that the visitor would sing it afterwards.  This was done, the visitor making some changes on
the ground that the host had not sung the song aright.  Then
followed a long series of comparatively unfamiliar songs, each
taking his turn, correcting the other, singing better if he
could, while the audience applauded in characteristic fashion,
the partisans of each singer trying to out-yell the others.
There was much laughter as impromptu jokes were interpo-
lated in the songs, and the contest ended only when day broke.

As a rule the leading voice, as the drummer is often called,
is respected only second to the chief because, I suppose, he
is the repository of so much that the tribe venerates, for it is
certain that the leading voice learned his songs from some
older singer who was great in his day.  I have observed another link in this that helps to bind us and the red men in a
common humanity, i e., the singer of the shadowy past was always a great man, a much better singer than any who lives
to-day.

### PAGAN IDEAS AND IDEALS.

There could be no finer exemplification of the Ojibway's
respect for music than the experience I had in the summer
of 1903 with a venerable pagan.  He was a visitor to the camp
where my actor friends were giving open air performances
of their play, "Hiawatha," his son-in-law being an inconspic-
uous member of the company.  One day this actor came to
me.

"I thought mebbe," said he, very slowly, "you like to see
an old gentleman.  She is my wife's father."

Yes, I answered, it would give me pleasure, and the Indian added, "She is a great singer, she knows many old, old songs, for she is not a Christian like us."

He went on to explain how the old gentleman—the Ojibway seldom says man or woman; it is always gentleman, or lady—had resisted every attempt to convert him. Wearied with the appeals of missionaries and the members of his family to forsake his ancient religion, he had once consented to be baptized, but he had gone on worshiping Gitche Manito and the four winds and never had given any further recognition of the strange faith.

"She was baptized," said my friend, to "stop her wife from too much talk."

At the time of this conversation the old gentleman was absent from the camp picking berries, but in the early evening I called on him at his son-in-law's birch-bark wigwam. A light but severely persistent rain was falling. The women and children had gone inside and closed the door, before which, seated on stones, smoking their pipes and serenely indifferent to the downpour, were the actor and the old gentleman. Never, it seemed to me, was the designation, gentleman, more aptly applied. I saw a man whose emaciated frame, white hair and quavering voice proclaimed that he had attained at least the span of three score years and ten. After the manner of the modern Indian he had allowed his sparse beard to grow so that his dusky face was framed in white. He wore the most ill-fitting, shabby garments I had ever seen upon human being, but his face was a fine picture of benignity, and his manner dignified without affectation, or that somewhat characteristic pomposity of the Indian that is apt to provoke amusement. Our conversation was conducted mainly by the aid of his son-in-law as interpreter, for he knew nothing of English and I was timid in Ojibway. We talked first of the play, which interested him greatly, though he ventured to protest mildly against Longfellow's perversions of Ojibway traditions. "It is not all just as we understand it," he said, and added with fine graciousness, "but it is very hard for the white man to understand the Indian's thought and feelings. It does very well, it is very good."

In due course I brought the conversation around to music. I had heard that he was a great singer, that he knew many songs. He gravely acknowledged the tribute. Would he let me hear some, or one of them? "Not on the stage," he replied quickly, but gently, and went on to explain that the band of actors had their singer and it might hurt his feelings if another were put in the work beside him. Here was delicacy of feeling, it seemed to me, that might shame some of our white vocalists, and I promptly disclaimed any intention of subjecting him or his rival to comparison. I told him about my desire to learn the songs of his people partly that I might inform the palefaces about them, and partly to preserve them; and his son-in-law explained at length how I had a way of making signs on paper by means of which I could remember any song I heard, and by which, too, other persons who never had heard the songs could sing them.

The old gentleman nodded from time to time and eventually

expressed approval of the plan. "It is good," said he, sadly, "for the young men are forgetting our songs." But he modestly doubted whether he knew any songs that would serve my purpose. I assured him that I would be glad to hear any song that pleased him, and, to stimulate his memory, suggested a hunting song. "The Indians have hunting songs, have they not?" I asked. He bowed gravely and replied that they had many, one at least for every animal; he supposed he knew most of them. Then he relapsed into thought and I knew that I had gone as far as could be gone on that first occasion, for the point had been reached when the Indian must be allowed to commune with himself. He is a remarkable silent debater. So we said "bozho," shook hands, and I left him to his thoughts, and tobacco, and the rain. Next day came his son-in-law.

"The old gentleman," he began diffidently, "she cannot sing you a hunting song."

"What's the matter?" I asked. "Can't he remember any?"

"Yes."

I let this answer stand for a moment to call attention to its ambiguity. Apparently nothing could be more direct and unmistakable than a plain yes, or no; but time and again I have been momentarily confused by the Indian's affirmation. Ask him a question in the negative form and invariably he answers, yes. Take a weatherwise glance at the clouds and remark, "It won't rain to-day, will it?" and the Indian reply will be, yes, by which he means that it will not rain. Ask him, sympathetically, "Aren't you feeling well to-day?" and his yes will mean that he is feeling ill. In this instance the actor's yes

meant that the old gentleman could remember as many hunting songs as need be. There was a different reason for his
inability, or refusal, rather, which came out on further inquiry.
"It is not the right season," explained the actor.

So, then, I had blundered. I did not comprehend fully the
meaning of "out of season," as it appeared later, but it was
clear that I had erred in suggesting to the old gentleman that
he sing me a hunting song. However, there was hope still,
for the old gentleman, with that courtesy that is characteristic
of the Indian, wished to return my call, and an appointment
was made for him to spend the evening at my lodge. He
came and devoted the first half hour to fluent speech explanatory of his refusal to sing a hunting song. It was apologetic,
regretful, the very refinement of courtesy, but firm; and this
was the substance of it—that the hunting song, be it the caribou, the red deer, the partridge, or any other, was a prayer;
it was sung only when the hunter set forth to seek game;
and this devout worshiper of Gitche Manito could not profane
his ancient faith by singing such a song for the mere purposes of entertainment, or to gratify commendable curiosity.

It seems to me that comment is unnecessary, but I suggest
to those who despair of the Indian, and there are many, includ-
ing some missionaries, that they take this fine old gentleman's
honest piety into prayerful consideration. How many palefaces are there upon whom their religion has taken such a hold
that they would regard it as profanity to sing a hymn to please
a stranger? Does not the episode convey this further, practicable suggestion: that if we superior whites endeavor to make

something of the Indian, it behooves us with all our might to get within and behind his point of view to the end that we may understand the material that we try to mold to our own ideas and purposes?

Needless to say that I yielded the point but I besought the good old pagan to sing something for me. He was reluctant still, and, at the risk of another blunder, I suggested a love song. The idea at his age of indulging in such sentiment was so manifestly amusing that again I retreated, and another half hour of speech-making followed. I was beginning to despair, though intimate contact with the red man's method of thought sustained me in patient endeavor, when at length it occurred to the old gentleman that he could, with entire appropriateness, sing me a visiting song. And this he did with much gusto, though, oddly enough for such a stickler as to the proprieties, he sang me the winter visiting song reproduced on one of the foregoing pages, forgetful, perhaps, as we sat by a blazing log fire, that it was mid-summer.

The song found its way to paper in a hurry and with a sense of long deferred triumph on the part of the note-taker, but I was not content. In the matter of songs I was forever wanting more, and on this occasion I resorted to a daring experiment. I made a speech of my own to the effect that the old gentleman's courtesy demanded a return in kind, and if he would be pleased to listen I would sing him an Indian song. He manifested lively pleasure at the suggestion, and forthwith I sang two of the Omaha songs in Miss Fletcher's collection that I had memorized years before. The language was strange to him, but the downward progressions, the startling grace notes and the exaggerated portamento that I had learned to imitate, evidently awoke a responsive chord and stirred his blood, for his eyes glowed with almost fierce joy, and the calm benignity of his face was transfigured to something well nigh ecstatic.   It was a most successful experiment.   Thereafter songs of love and war came from his trembling lips until it was I who had to cry enough and bring the long night's session to a close.

The old gentleman's name is Innéquahung Shawanibenayse, which the whites have turned into John Shawan.   He was born somewhere on the north coast of Lake Superior and now lives on Drummond Island, Michigan.

### DISTRUST VANQUISHED BY HARMONY.

Further light on the Ojibways' regard for music may be had from their attitude toward me and my self imposed work. At first they were distrustful and put every obstacle in my way except physical violence.   For a long time I could not persuade man or woman to sing for me in private.   Indians whom I approached for this purpose developed sudden and unaccountable difficulties with the English language; or they discovered sore throats a half hour after a performance of the play in which I had heard them singing; or they were too busy. When I came upon them singing by themselves, they stopped abruptly.   Some of them strolled away, the others sat staring at the ground, or out upon the lake.   In the course of time I had memorized a few songs, having heard them daily in the play, and I wished to verify my notes, for having caught them through the noise of the drum I was doubtful as to their entire accuracy. After nearly three weeks of persuasion I induced a singer and an interpreter to spend an evening at my lodge for the purpose of going over these few songs. The work went smoothly enough for a time, and then there was rebellion. The singer made a speech to the effect that he would be accounted a bad man by his people if he should give me the songs. I asked for a frank explanation, and there was another speech which the interpreter reproduced substantially as follows:

"Sir, we do not understand it. We like you, but we do not understand what you are doing. We ask what has the white man done to us? He has made us live in reservations, forbidden us to hunt in the forests, taken away our land. He has taken from us everything Indian that we possessed except our songs, and now you come and would take away those, too. You will have our songs sung all over the world where white men live, and when that has been done you will turn upon us, like the white men who came before you, and say, get out! I have no further use for you."

We had a long argument. I tried to show them that I left behind all that I took away, and that I was trying to save their songs from being forgotten. So far as the two men who heard me were concerned, the argument was convincing, but there lingered even with them a reluctance to help me to certain songs because they belonged to other persons. Nearly all the Indians of my acquaintance recognize this proprietary interest in songs. A has no right to sing B's songs; B did not compose them, but they came down to him through his family, or from some chief who taught him, and B alone should say whether they might be given to another. To this day there are some Ojibways who refuse to sing for me, still influenced apparently by that well founded distrust of the paleface that was voiced so frankly in my lodge.

The confidence of those Indians who were concerned in the play was won by a rather hazardous experiment. I made a four-part arrangement of "My Bark Canoe" and gave it to a quartette of white singers who chanced our way. This was in the afternoon. In the evening the Indians were called together and I told them that I would show them what I was doing with their music. I said that if they would sing "Chekabay tebik" in their way, my friends would sing it in the whiteman way. After characteristic hesitation the Indians complied. The quartette, taking the pitch from the Indians, immediately repeated the song in English. The excitement of the Indians knew no bounds. They yelled as if they were engaged in fierce combat and, surrounding the startled quartette, demanded a repetition of the piece. Several repetitions were given before the Indians were satisfied, and then they crowded about me, asking eagerly if they could learn to sing like that—meaning in parts.

My adoption into the tribe followed not long after this episode. They named me Negaunneekahboh, the man in front, the significance of the name arising from the fact that the first time this group of Indians saw me I was conducting an orchestra.

In answer to a question that is often asked I will say that the Ojibways seem to be very appreciative of the harmonized versions of their songs.  There was a piano in the hotel near the Indian playground, and the company of actors would gather at the windows whenever I undertook to sing the songs of the play to visitors.  Often when the music room was deserted one or more of the Indians would go in and try to pick out the songs and find those elusive effects that came from striking more than one key at a time.

## MUSIC IN INDIAN HOMES.

Many of the more prosperous Ojibways have parlor organs in their cabins at the reservations.  In some instances there is no one in the family who can play, but there are children growing up who some day may be taught, and the instrument is provided for them.  At Garden River, where most of my Ojibway friends live, there is a music teacher from whom several of the younger Indians have learned to play simple pieces. I have listened to them with mixed feelings.  It savored of romance to call Tecumseh Bukwujjinini in from his hayfield and hear him, in overalls and shirt-sleeves, play voluntaries. He is the organist in the Episcopal church at the reservation. I grieved when he turned from his church music and played the trivial stuff that had run its brief period of popularity in the cities a few years before.  In default of access to anything better, he was accepting the white man's trash; and the exquisite melodies of his own people were not available because they had not been put into notes.  In his house, and in others, I have sung Ojibway songs in the Ojibway language with harmonized accompaniments, and the result has always been a hurried gathering of such neighbors as were within call; and sometimes the people have overcome their shyness sufficiently to join with me in singing their own songs.  The men and women who take part in the Indian play may often be found of an evening going over "My Bark Canoe," or "Absence and Longing," or the "Death Song," and trying to put in the various harmonic parts.  Most of these long ago recognized the value of my work to themselves and cheerfully put themselves out that I might record their unwritten melodies.

The attempt to arrive at an understanding of the Ojibway's view of music has been made thus far by consideration of obvious evidence.  There is possibility of more complete understanding by inference from the music he has composed and preserved.  I call attention elsewhere to the fact that the words of some Ojibway songs are archaic, so long out of common use, indeed, that the modern Ojibway does not know what they mean.  He nevertheless sings the songs with manifest satisfaction.  I note also the fact that I have often heard Ojibways sing songs in which every word was meaningless, that is, the vocables were made up exclusively of nonsense syllables which are employed conventionally to piece out lines which are too short for their respective tunes.  The inference is inevitable that, in respect of these songs, the Indian is appreciative of music in precisely the way that the cultivated man of civilization is appreciative of it; that is, he is stirred by music purely and simply, without any association of the melody with tangible ideas; in other words, the Indian has risen high enough to appreciate absolute music, a plane that he might not have been expected to reach in view of his linguistic failure to distinguish between music and poetry.

It is the fact that civilized man finds pleasure in humming or whistling melodies that linger in his memory that makes the Indian's procedure especially striking and significant. We take it for granted that civilized man will do just this, and the phenomenon calls for no special comment or analysis. It is different with the Indian because he has no notation for the preservation of his music. Words of some sort, therefore, are essential to him as pegs for his tunes. Having in mind his generally backward condition in comparison with our race, we are inclined to infer that his appreciation of melody should be measured by his words, and that, words lapsed from memory, the tune also would disappear. Presumably some of the wordless songs I have heard were originally composed to words of precise meaning, but I do not know that to be the fact. It may be they were the invention of melodies on the part of some musical Ojibway whose tunes came too fast for joining them to significant words. In either event, the preservation of a tune of this type has been on its own merits, so to speak; the significant words lost, the singer treasures the tune and hands it down to the next generation as a thing of absolute beauty that ought not to be neglected. Can we imagine civilized man going to such pains to preserve his favorite tunes from oblivion? It is not, of course, a conscious process on the part

of the Ojibway singer; that is, I doubt if he sings his wordless song for the precise purpose of keeping it alive in the
memory of himself, family and friends; he sings because he
enjoys the music, and he is far enough advanced in musical
development to be indifferent to the presence of words in connection with his art.

Thus it has often appeared to me when, after hearing a
song given with great vigor and earnestness, I have sought
to get the words and have discovered that they meant as little
to the singer as they did to me.    From the manner of the
singer one might have supposed that he were uttering senti-
ments of the profoundest import.    In fact, his earnest manner was his ingenuous tribute to the beauty of modulated tones,
to the art that inspired him.

# CHAPTER VII

## MUSIC IN OJIBWAY DAILY LIFE

I AM often asked whether the Ojibways have industrial songs. In the general acceptation of the term, no; but we must take into account the nature of Indian industries before leaving the answer there. Before the Ojibway came in touch with civilization he had no conception of factory life, or of systematized labor. Contrary to popular belief, he was not improvident; he had thought for the coming winter and dried his meats and laid in his cereals accordingly. He knew that the birch tree yields its bark best in the moon of strawberries—late June—and he did not neglect then the making of the canoe that might not be needed till the summer had passed. When he chanced upon medicinal roots he gathered them against the illness that happily might never come. In other words, he provided for his simple needs with such diligence as was necessary, but he was not possessed of greed to the end that he must work for more than he needed. Accumulation of property was limited substantially to furs and garments. Therefore, the word industry, standing in our commercial age for systematic toil, lay outside the pale of his experience. When he wanted anything, he hunted for it, or made it. In some things, the manufacture of canoes, for example, the Ojibway excels all people; but canoe-making could

124

not be called an industry, for he did not strip a thousand trees in June that he might have stock for the making of canoes throughout the entire year.

This conception and manner of life is not conducive to the making of industrial songs.    Man sings of that which interests him.    His interest may be aroused by religious aspiration, human love, the beauty of Nature, the excitement of conflict against man or beast, or the very joy of idleness; and it may also be aroused by the force of circumstances, as when he is habitually engaged, day after day, at some manner of occupation not in itself interesting.    The sailor, tugging away at a windlass, finds in the rhythm of arduous exertion an incentive to song, and in the song a stimulus to renewed labor. The Maryland negro, "shucking" oysters in a dismal cabin, relieves his pent up soul in melody through sheer necessity for something brighter and more wholesome than his environment.    The peasant's foot on the treadle that keeps the spinning wheel a-whirring, stirs the spinner's soul to rhythm, and song issues from the lips as readily as breath itself.    Man would not be human if, under such circumstances, the words of his songs were not suggested, occasionally at least, by the nature of his toil; and thus industrial songs come into being.

### DEPENDENCE ON THE DRUM.

There is little analogous to this in the Ojibway's daily life, but he does have songs characteristic of, or applicable to his few occupations.    He has a multitude of hunting songs, secular as well as sacred.   Not as many, but still a great number, are the canoe songs, that is, songs whose appropriate place and time are in the canoe while paddling.   There are also corn songs, which are religious rather than industrial, although applicable to planting and caring for the grain, and inasmuch as 'tending the baby is an occupation with the Ojibway as it is among all peoples, there are cradle songs.   Furthermore, the Ojibway is so much given to visiting that this might almost be regarded as an occupation, and there are social songs and songs of hospitality without number.

The modern, or reservation Ojibway, who has learned something of carpentry or agriculture, does not employ song at his civilized labor as freely as does the plantation negro, though the tendency to sing while at work is very noticeable.   I have often heard a dozen or more men, busy with their saws and hammers, burst into a roaring chorus, some one among them having started a song alone.   But work halts while the song is in progress, and the diversion is not long continued.   The early cessation of music under such circumstances, is to be accounted for partly by the fact that the Ojibway is a conscientious workman, devoting himself to his appointed task with rare faithfulness; but more by reason of his own regard for music and his dependence upon the drum for the expression of it.   When he sings he is disposed to give himself up to song and to that alone.   He is absorbed at once in his music to the exclusion of all other considerations.   His dependence upon the drum for entire satisfaction is the feature of his art that separates him most widely from the musical manner of civilization.   The Ojibway can sing without the drum, but he misses it.   Even those who have grown up in semi-civilization prefer the thumping accompaniment, and when an Indian sings for me without his instrument he usually marks the rhythm by patting the table, or his knee with his hand.

Perhaps it will add no interest to these observations and speculations, but I cannot refrain at this juncture from stating that this part of the book is being written, and the accompanying music prepared, in Ojibway land.   Around me is the wilderness but recently and slightly broken by Canadian pioneers. From my cabin window I look upon the western waters of Lake Huron where Nature has outdone herself in loveliness. Ojibways are my daily companions; I visit them in their teepees and log houses, and they come of an evening to smoke their pipes by my fire and cudgel their brains to revive memory of songs they heard when they were children, their interest in my attempt to preserve their songs being a mighty stimulus, if one were needed, to its continuance.   So, what I reduce to writing is as near as can be a series of snap-shot impressions of daily occurrences intensified and corroborated by their reduplication of experiences in years past.   It was but yesterday —I was discussing dependence upon the drum—that I called at the Ojibway dwelling where for convenience I store my phonographic records.   While I was busy with them an aged man sat on the floor taking care of his chubby, eighteen-months-old grandson, his wife and daughter engrossed at the time in preparation of dinner.   The white-haired old man sang to the baby, songs of war, of the chase, of love, and cradle songs; and while he sang he drummed incessantly upon the floor with a stick of firewood. Now and again the soft treble of the child's voice rippled across the wavering, uncertain tones of the song, sometimes in the inconsequential remarks of babyhood, often in faulty attempts to join in grand-pa's singing. I wish that whites who regard the Indian as a stolid brute could look in on such a scene!

### TETEBAHBUNDUNG, "THE SWEETEST OF ALL SINGERS."

Let me pass to another instance, almost as recent, where drumming played a part in music necessary to the Indian but at odd variance with our conception and habit. I was working at the Garden River Reservation and set forth one evening to call upon Tetebahbundung, the finest Indian singer I have heard anywhere. Allusion has been made to him before, and several of the best songs in this collection were taken from his lips. He is about forty-five years old, a full-blood and extremely sensitive upon that point. It offends him deeply when palefaces who hear his superb tenor voice and note the exquisite grace with which he sings, jump to the conclusion that his superior gifts are due to a strain of white blood.

"It is not so," he says quietly; "I am all Indian."

Tetebahbundung usually appears in the drama, "Hiawatha," as Chibiabos, the sweet singer, his son, Adamosa, taking the part of Hiawatha, the boy. Longfellow never visited Ojibway land, and his personal acquaintace with Indians was very limited, facts that impress us who haunt the region as remarkable tributes to his poetic imagination, for his lines reflect the beauty and character of the landscape with unerring accuracy; and in nothing did the prophetic vision of the poet arrive at truth with more certainty than in his delineation of Chibiabos. This personage in the poem might well have been drawn from Tetebahbundung. All the superlatives in Longfellow's description fit him as a well made garment. His voice is pure tenor with that human quality that can be suggested only by the word luscious; it is so powerful as to be heard distinctly over a chorus of fifty men with the drum banging fortissimo, and yet, so keen is the man's unwitting artistic insight that when he sings in a small room, like a concert hall, or a parlor, nobody dreams of his power, for he modulates his volume of tone to the demands of the place and occasion. Furthermore, though he never has had other than Indian instruction and knows nothing of written music, his tone production is the despair of professional white tenors who have heard him, and he sings with such a wealth of feeling that no audience fails to be stirred in spite of the fact that his words are meaningless to the listener, and sometimes to himself, for I have heard him repeatedly sing entire songs that had not one intelligible word in them.

This tribute to the Ojibway singer may read like enthusiastic exaggeration, but if so I must be content, for I know the truth and I am not alone in my estimate. Tetebahbundung is, indeed, all Indian, with the shortcomings of his race, but he is a musician from the ground up, and, as a man, singularly attractive; quiet, unassuming, absolutely honest and faithful to his promises, gentle and affectionate.  His relations with his little son are those of ideal parental and filial companionship. Altogether Tetebahbundung appeals to my heart with special force, perhaps because he was the last Indian to become my friend.  For a long, long time he held aloof, resisting me with stubbornness that was the more difficult to meet because it was so deathly quiet.  No need to dwell on that now, for he has become a firm friend and one of the most valuable collaborators in the work of recording the songs of his people.

I knew that Tetebahbundung was at home when I was yet at some distance from his house, for I heard his drum.  He was not pounding hard, but the night was still, and the instrument evidently had been thoroughly warmed, for its tone was resonant and penetrating.  I paused at the door, unwilling to interrupt, fearing to make an ill timed intrusion.  He was singing a love song, and in true Indian fashion he sang it many times over without stopping.  At length the end came with disaster, for he beat with added vigor, and of a sudden the tone was dull.  Drumming and singing ceased abruptly, and I heard Tetebahbundung mutter a low "Ah!"  Then I knocked.  He came slowly, and the open door revealed a room dark save for the dying embers in the fireplace, empty save for himself.

"Come in," said he, by way of greeting, and I responded that I had heard him singing.  "Yes," he admitted ruefully, "and now my drum is broke.  I heated it too hot, I suppose. My wife and boy she gone, visiting.  I was lonesome.  So I

got my drum and sang.    No more song now," and he laughed
a little.

Is comment necessary? simply to point out that the white
musician under such circumstances might betake himself to the
pianoforte to ease his soul.    Should the strings snap, he would
no longer sing, failing of instrumental support.    To this musical Indian, the tuneless drum was as the responsive keyboard,
and without it his diversion was unthinkable.    I asked him how
he would manage now that his drum was broken, and he replied simply that he would make another.

Tetebahbundung is an exception among Ojibways only in
that his gifts in and love for music are greater than the average.    The men, it seems to me, sing much more frequently
and more freely than the women do.    Gentlemen who go to the
Canadian forests for game return with tales of the taciturnity
of their Indian guides, and the casual visitor at a Reservation
finds little response to his questions.    If he should speak of
songs he would probably get no answer whatever, and might
go away with the conviction that self expression through music
is unknown to the Ojibway.    Such, certainly, was the case
with a distinguished gentleman whose scientific studies have
taken him among the Ojibways of Canada for the past forty-
eight years.    He learned their language and, incidental to his
main research, made a special study of their myths and traditions.    Coming upon me in the midst of my work in the summer of 1904, he frankly expressed amazement that I found
anything to do.

"A few years ago," said he, "a wealthy Bostonian who con-
templated a season in the wilds of Canada for his health
thought of taking along a phonograph for the purpose of
recording Ojibways songs, and he asked me for 'points.' I
told him that I could give him one that would be of great value,
and that was to leave his phonograph at home, for the Ojibways
had no songs. Of course I had heard the Indians howling to
the drum now and then, but I never had heard sounds that appealed to me as music."

The gentleman's amazement was equaled by my own at this
revelation, for, with me, it is the commonest experience to come
upon an Indian singing softly to himself as he sits idle and
alone after the day's work. I follow the unseen bark canoe
across the lake at night by the melodious voice of the paddler.
By the campfire—at their social gatherings—beside the dead
—wherever they are, alone or in familiar company, I hear them
sing. "He that hath ears to hear, let him hear!"

### MUSIC FOR THE DEAD.

It is said that the early missionaries won the attention of
the Ojibways more by hymn tunes than by exhortation. This
is entirely credible, but I have evidence that the Ojibways
adapted themselves to the white man's melodies with no little
diffiulty. My first hint of this fact was conveyed to me
through hearing part of a touching ceremony at a house where
one lay dead. It was in the Garden River Reservation.
Somewhat remote from what might be called the centre of the

long, straggling village, is a cabin where four aged sisters lived.  One was blind, another lame, the third had been a helpless paralytic for years, and the fourth was afflicted with the feebleness of old age, if by nothing more acute.  With no assistance save that a man hauled their winter's supply of wood to their door, they attended to their cow and their acre of vegetables, splitting the wood, fetching the water, weeding the garden and gathering their crop.  Two of these women were Episcopalians, the others Roman Catholics.  Of the latter was the paralytic who was the first of the four to join the majority.  Long had glowed the embers of her life; long they smouldered after the darkness gathered upon them.  Her mind was the last to flicker and go out, and while the end delayed, her sisters cheered her by laying upon the table and calling her attention to them, the clothes, the finery, the favorite articles that would faithfully be placed in the coffin and buried with her.  She died at sunrise.  During the day the kind offices of neighbors were administered in much the same fashion as would have been the case in a community of whites.

At sunset came Megissun, "the singer" as he is called, a staunch Episcopalian and older by a long span than she who had departed.  He brought with him his Protestant hymnal, a collection of hymns translated into Ojibway, but with no note of music between the covers, and sat beside the dead.  The surviving sisters took their places near.  No word of greeting had passed, no comment of any kind was uttered, no moan of grief escaped the lips.  Upon the table at Megissun's elbow was a lamp, and beside it a saucer of lozenges and a plate of

plain cakes. Shortly after Megissun's entrance three neighbors, a man and two women, drifted in, more silently, more
unobtrusively than if they had been autumn leaves impelled
by an idle wind. By not so much as a nod, or a glance from
the eyes, did they recognize the presence of the singer or the
bereaved sisters. Megissun stirred not, neither did the mourn-
ers. Presently another silent figure blotted out the doorway
for an instant and joined the expectant group, and then still
others, till the narrow room was full. All these, Christians
every one, were there to go part way with their friend upon
her long journey to the land of the hereafter. In the presence
of death, sectarian differences were forgotten, the new faith
itself faded and fluttered before the persistence of ancient
custom.

Megissun did not wait for the room to fill. In his own good
time he opened the hymnal and began to sing. Through
nearly the whole of the first line his wavering voice bore the
tune alone; then one and another joined in unison and sang
the hymn through all its slowly toiling stanzas to the end.
A pause ensued while Megissun turned the pages of his book.
Presently he selected another hymn and began. As before, the
assembled neighbors joined as soon as they recognized the tune.
Now and again a single voice stumbled over the words of an
ill remembered line, but nobody was disturbed or abashed
thereby, least of all the person who committed the error. While
yet the hymn was sounding, other neighbors drifted in. Some
of them had walked miles from the far end of the Reservation.
Silently, unobtrusively, recognizing nobody, they found their

places.  Between hymns the clatter of crickets beat noisily upon the ear, and the sudden hoot of an owl shocked as might profanity before the altar.  There was no uneasy rustle of garments or shuffling of feet to indicate that the unbidden visitors had wearied; they seemed not to breathe.  Only Megissun stirred, and he all but inaudibly turned the pages of his oft-thumbed hymnal.

Some time between ten and eleven o'clock, two of the guests arose and, without word or glance of parting, drifted out into the darkness and came not again that night.  By midnight others had gone, but the places of a few were filled by late comers.  At rare intervals as the night wore on with its succession of hymns, Megissun relieved his throat with a lozenge, and such guests as were so minded sought the table for a piece of cake.  When the sun rose, the room was no longer crowded, but a loyal handful of neighbors yet remained singing a final hymn for the comfort of their friend upon her journey through the darkness.  With the full light of day Megissun closed his book and went home, and the others, with no word to him or the sisters, departed also.

### THE CONFLICT OF STYLES.

To the wondering Yankee who observed and heard this ceremony, the musical interest lay in the unwitting perversion of the tunes by Megissun and the older singers.  So dominating was Megissun's voice that at first I did not realize that some of the others were not keeping strictly with him; and at that time I was hard put to it to know whether the tunes were aboriginal, or the product of civilization. The occasion was well calculated to befog critical observation, but presently, when the human interest could be subordinated, I perceived that the fresher, younger voices were inclined to shorten the phrases, and that they followed, as if with some timidity, the shakes, turns and slurs with which Megisssun crowded every line. Fixing attention upon what the younger voices actually did, and eliminating as much as possible those instants when they followed the leader with hesitation, I began to perceive the outlines of a civilized melody, and eventually recognized it as one that is to be found in many hymn books. Regarding Megissun's voice alone, I might have persuaded myself that he was singing the Christian words to an ancient Ojibway tune, so completely did he cover and disguise it with the mannerisms I had become familiar with as characteristic of ancient Ojibway song. The older people kept with the leader easily, for he harked them back to childhood when, perhaps, to every one the Christian faith and its music were unknown; but the others, who had learned their hymns from the lips of a white missionary while they were young enough to receive and retain strange impressions, found the old leader's manner disconcerting.

I can give no more than this indication of the mixed style that resulted from Megissun's perversion of the civilized tune, for I could not introduce a phonograph into the scene; I could not take notes in the darkness outside the house, nor profane the occasion by note-taking within; and my memory would have

been an insecure guide.  But I looked into the matter at another time and, mainly through the coöperation of William
J. Shingwauk, phonographed several hymns sung in the manner of a bygone age.  This man, a lineal descendant of that
Shingwauk who was the greatest chief the Ojibways ever had,
tells me that in the early days the Indians, finding that they
could not express their emotions freely through the white man's
melody, either abandoned it altogether and adapted tunes of
their own to the words of the new faith, or deliberately modified the missionary's tunes so that there resulted what Shingwauk characterized with humorous gravity as "half breed
music."  The printed notes do not give a satisfactory representation of this mixed style.  There is no doubt about the
melodic outline, but there lacks the tone color, the infinite
slurring and dragging that no type can set forth and no civilized singer reproduce unless he has heard the Indians many
times and is good at imitation.  Nevertheless, I give one of the
hymns on page 233, partly because it has a certain historical
interest, and in the hope that the reader can deduce from the
bald symbols an approximate conception of the older Indian's
manner of singing.


### DEATH SONGS.

This was Chief Bukwujjinini's favorite hymn, and the Garden River Indians still sing it occasionally.  Shingwauk,
grand nephew of the chief, and other well informed Ojibways,
believe that the tune is aboriginal.  "It is very old," they say,

"and was made over for this hymn by Chief Bukwujjinini himself." I think they are mistaken in this. Up to the present I have not been able to identify the tune with any in the hymn books, but it appeals to me as a white man's tune made over rather than an Indian's. Whether or no, it was sung at Bukwujjinini's bedside by the members of his family while he lay dying, the incident illustrating another conventional use of music among the Ojibways, for every Indian has his death song, one that he will sing himself, if possible, at the very moment of dissolution; and if voice fails him, his friends sing it for him. In the old days the words of death songs befitted the occasion, being expressive of courage, faith, doubt, defiance, as the case might be. I am thinking of the non-Christian Indian when I use the term "old days," the fact being that the pagans of the present adhere to the custom. United States Army officers have told me that when it is necessary to excute an Indian, the victim marches to his place before the firing squad singing his death song, and that his voice never falters till the bullets stop it forever. The Christianized Ojibway tends to modify this striking custom as he does all else that belonged to his ancient life, but not infrequently he preserves the poetic atmosphere. A good old friend of mine fell fatally ill in a foreign city far away from his home. Sympathetic whites sent flowers to him in the hospital, and these he appreciated with pathetic joy—I fancy they symbolized the forest home that he was never to see again. Death lingered for hours at the threshold after his unmistakable knock on the door. The old man knew the signs.

"I should like to hear a song," he whispered.

They understood, those who stood around, and asked him if there were some particular song he would like to hear.

*"Gayget; 'Chekahbay tebik ondandayan,'"* he replied, lapsing into his native tongue: "Yes; 'Throughout the night I keep awake.' "

These are the first words of the love song to which I have given the English title "My Bark Canoe." Possibly the dying man, who was one of the most truly devout Christians it was ever my good fortune to know, imagined a symbolism in the words appropriate to the occasion. The shadows of his long night were upon him even then; the song tells of a stream that must be crossed to gain the happiness desired by the singer. Possibly it was associated with the dearest romance of his youth; it may have been the song he used with voice or flute when he went hopefuly a-wooing. We can but speculate, but the gratifying fact is that those around the bedside knew of an Ojibway resident in the city; that they sent urgent word to him; that he came, knew the song and sang it; and while yet the sweet strains were throbbing, the old man died.

### OLD HUNDRED AT SOCIAL GATHERINGS.

There is one of our hymn tunes that the Christianized Ojibways north of the Great Lakes have adopted without mutilation and made their own to an extent that is manifested with striking frequency. Most of us know the tune as "Old Hundred." To the Ojibway it is the "Doxology," their words being a translation of "Praise God from whom all blessings flow," and so forth. My first encounter with it in this form was at a wedding supper early in my acquaintance with the Ojibways. It was not an Indian function, but a social gathering organized by Mr. L. O. Armstrong, friend and employer of the bride and groom, to which a half a dozen whites and nearly a hundred Indians were invited. The wedding, according to the Church of England rite, had taken place in the open air at four o'clock in the afternoon. It may throw a little light on the Indian's attitude toward civilization if I explain that the bride and groom were the "Minnehaha" and "Hiawatha" of the Indian play to which reference has been made heretofore. Theirs was a charming romance while it lasted, sadly brief, for "Minnehaha" died within two years after the wedding. Tekumegezhik Shawano, a young man of modest demeanor, great physical strength and handsome face, had been promoted from the ranks to play the principal part at a time when circumstances made it advisable to reorganize the cast, and, at the same time, Miss Margaret Waubunosa had been assigned to the part of "Minnehaha." Both, I think, were selected for their looks, and both justified the choice. It was not suspected that a real courtship was in progress every day when "Hiawatha" made his visit to the lodge of the "Ancient Arrowmaker" and laid a deer at the feet of "Minnehaha," but the revelation came when Shawano asked for a day "off" in order to get married. He was persuaded to continue playing his part even on the day of the wedding, and the Garden River missionary, Rev. Frederick Frost, journeyed to the playground and officiated at the marriage ceremony immediately after the performance. Of course there was a great to-do about it. Hundreds of persons, paleface and red, came from great distances to witness the event, and it was suggested to the bride and groom that it would add to the general interest if they would keep on the picturesque costumes worn in the play. This they politely but firmly refused to do on the ground that it would profane the new faith if they should wear the ancient costumes of their race in one of its most sacred ceremonies. And all the other members of the Hiawatha "band," as the Indians call the dramatic company, coinciding in this view, hurried to their teepees when the play was over to don the habiliments of civilization before presuming to assist at the ceremony in the humble guise of spectators.

In the evening, too, the Indians preferred to go to the white man's supper in white-man clothing. There was manifest much of the traditional shyness of the race at first, but the ice was broken by abundance of good food and a succession of songs and stories until all except Mr. and Mrs. Shawano were quite at ease. Presently a monster cake was brought in. Two men, Tetebahbundung and Obetossoway, carried it on their shoulders all around the room, meantime dancing as grotesquely as the safety of their burden permitted and singing a most lugubrious tune which, from the Ojibway point of view is a joyous festal song, until at length they deposited the cake on the table before Mrs. Shawano. She was then told that she must cut the cake so that every person present might have a piece, and there ensued an awkward pause. All eyes were turned upon the bride who, doubtless, never had heard of this paleface custom, and was painfully embarrassed.   None of the whites present saw just what to do to relieve the situation, but it was taken in hand by an aged Indian who stood up and, using his native tongue, spoke substantially as follows:

"My friends, this is a very large cake and it will take some time to cut it.   It is evident that the bride fears she will make a slip of some kind with so many persons looking on, and it is plain enough that it will be easier for her if we give our attention to something else.   Therefore, I suggest that we all rise and sing the Doxology.   This will take our eyes from her and it may give her courage for what she has to do."

At once, but decorously, all the Indians stood up, and the whites who had not understood the speech were first astonished and then awed as the solemn strains of "Old Hundred" poured in a majestic unison upon them.   Before the end of the first line, the bride arose and applied the knife to the cake, and although her task was not finished with the hymn, the diversion had done its appointed work and she kept cutting in faithful observance of instructions until the last possible slice had been disposed of.

Then, as always in my association with the Ojibways, I siezed every opportunity that gave promise of bringing a previously unheard Indian song to light, and on that occasion, when it was time to disperse, I ventured to ask if the Indians would not bring the jollification to end with a rousing, old-time chorus.   By then all were in fine spirits.   We had had a number of love songs from the Ojibway men and women, all given as solo performances, and most of the whites present had contributed humorous songs or stories to the entertainment. Shyness had long since taken flight and the room was yet echoing with laughter when I made my suggestion. The Indians listened to it with customary respect, and such was the atmoswhere of perfect accord that I actually stationed myself behind a friend so that, unobserved, I could jot upon a scrap of music paper such notes of the forthcoming novelty as I could. There was no apparent consultation among the Indians. All stood up and looked at Tetebahbundung, for he was their "leading voice" that night, and it was natural that they should defer to his choice of a song. Quite in accordance with custom there was a distinct pause, impressive to me in my eager quest for new melody. Then the singing began, and nearly every voice was in with the second note. My own was added at the third and my scrap of music paper was hurriedly pocketed, for the "rousing, old-time chorus" was the Doxology!

At the end one of the Indians, who seemed to perceive that I had missed something, came to me and said, "We always close our social meetings with the Doxology." I have had many occasions since to test the uniformity of the rule. One was quite as striking as the wedding supper. I had invited about thirty Indians and a dozen whites to a camp fire on the island where I lived during the summer. It was about a mile from the mainland. The camp fire was purely a social gathering where red men and white met on even terms. There had been songs and weird dances, light refreshments and much tobacco. The moon was well up in a cloudless sky and the lake was as smooth as glass when it came time to break up.  A lady, who had been deeply impressed by the beauty of the Ojibway songs given that evening, asked the Indians if they would not sing "My Bark Canoe" when they paddled homeward.  I said nothing, wondering if they would comply and hoping that they would do so.  They did.  Paddling slowly, and keeping their canoes well together, they crossed the moonlit water singing that favorite song.  We sat by the dying fire and listened, the strains fading perceptibly as the canoes became indistinguishable in the distance; but the night was so still that the melody came back to us distinctly long after the flotilla had been lost to sight.  With characteristic faithfulness, the Indians sang the song over and over again, and if they tired of it we did not, though we wondered how long they would keep at it, and if they were standing on the mainland to sing until our fire should go out.  That they were not on the mainland was proved by a minute of careful listening, for the melody steadily grew fainter; but we knew to a certainty when they reached shore, for across the calm surface of the lake came, as a benediction and farewell, the Doxology.  The social meeting was then, and not till then, at an end.

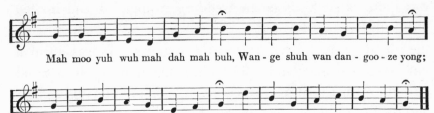

Mah moo yuh wuh mah dah mah buh, Wan - ge shuh wan dan - goo - ze yong;

Wa  yoo  se  mind wa gwiss se  mind, Kuh  ya  pah  ne  zid  oo  je chaug.

# CHAPTER VIII

## OJIBWAY VERSE

I HAVE said as unequivocally as possible that the Ojibway has not engrafted white-man music upon his own stock; that under, or despite, the influence of civilization, he has developed a distinctive folksong, Indian in character as well as Indian in the making of it. There is nothing in the observations of the preceding chapter at variance with this assertion. The Ojibways who first embraced Christianity struggled with its music, but unsuccessfully and were overcome by it. They attempted the grafting process, but eventually the hymn of civilization won its victory. There lingers in Megissun and other aged Ojibways evidence of the struggle between the two tonal systems, but the younger generation have succumbed, and the songs of the church when they sing them to-day are substantially free from the conflicts with a past style. On the other hand, what they have retained of their ancient music remains their own, resisting successfully the tendency to mix the styles, and developing to greater refinement along its own peculiar lines. Nothing could be a more convincing demonstration of the inherent strength of Ojibway melodies than this, that they retain their distinctive character in spite of the overwhelming influence of civilization which is

145

steadily destroying everything else that marked the Indian as an individual in the human family.

Inasmuch as we are dealing with a musical system that finds its expression only in songs, it is necessary to give attention to the verse that underlies or accompanies them. I have found this an agreeable necessity, for Indian verse is almost as interesting as the music; not that it is equally charming; on the contrary, it often startles and shocks not alone by its rugged form, but by the sentiment it conveys. It must be approached with patient regard for the fact that it is the expression of a primitive people; in a spirit that calmly seeks for facts and as calmly accepts them. In nowise, it seems to me, could an investigator profane his research more than by yielding to a sentimental or romantic disposition to read into his subject what, from the Indian viewpoint, is not there; but the same disposition to look the facts calmly in the face should guard him from accepting the apparent meaning of a song's words as the reality. The occasion for this warning will be clear from the illustrative examples that follow.

### COMPACTNESS.

What strikes the paleface first in his consideration of Ojibway verse is its extraordinary compactness. I am assuming that the observer has passed quickly over the stage, if he ever traversed it, where Indian verse appealed to him simply as ludicrous, or hopelessly crude. I think my conclusions in this matter would apply to most, if not all other Indian tribes, but, for the sake of safety, will limit my statements to the Ojibway. He wastes no words in his poetry, and, being primitive, he usually restricts his poem to the expression of a single thought. Now this thought may frame itself in words sufficiently clear to him and yet so few that they cannot fill out the melody to which he attaches them—it will be borne in mind that to the Ojibway all verse is necessarily music, and we must therefore keep the music somewhat in view while discussing the verse. In this dilemma what does he do? what does the civilized composer do? He repeats words and phrases in order to make them cover the entire melodic strain. The Ojibway not only does this but resorts to still another device for the completion of his tune—he runs in syllables that have no meaning.

Let us recall for a moment that one of the stock jests of the professional humorist is aimed at the mutilation of language in the setting of poetry to music. It may be doubted if any composer ever penned an anthem that obliged the soprano to sing

"Oh for a man, oh for a man, oh for a mansion in the skies,"

but the greatest masters of English song have justified the quip by constructing long arias from couplets, a process that necessitates the repetition of words and phrases to a highly absurd degree. Here are the words of an Ojibway wedding song:

*Bayzhig equayzess ne menegonun, gayget sennah negech-edaybe-ego.*

They mean: "A girl has been given to me; yes, I am glad that she has been given to me." That is to say, "I am glad because my sweetheart's parents have consented to our marriage." From our point of view this is the entire poem, but the composer of it, who, be it remembered, was of necessity also the composer of the music, was so tumultuously stirred by emotion over the great event in his life that music was awakened in him to an unusual degree, and his tune could not be confined to a plain statement of his joy and one or two repetitions of it. The paleface under the circumstances might have amplified his original thought by entering upon a glowing description of his sweetheart's beauty of face and form; he might have descanted upon her virtues and graces; or, following the immortal model set by Henry Cary in "Sally in Our Alley," he might have narrated his present relations with her and forecast the future. Not thus the Indian. That one thought of jubilant satisfaction was all that his mind could carry with comfort at one time; so, bless him! with a better sense of proportion than was manifested by the English masters, having sung his line twice, he forbears to repeat it *ad infinitum* and *ad nauseam,* but proceeds to the conclusion of his tune with "Heyah, heyah, heyah," which means nothing at all, not even to himself.

Does this literary device provoke a smile? it has never failed to when I have spoken of the matter in conversation, but was it not Shakespeare who ended the stanzas of a song with "Hey nonny, nonny?" did not the same poet piece out his comprehensible lines with "O, willow, willow?" Is there a world of meaning in these words? Doubtless as much as in "Heyah, heyah," but no more. And think of the hundreds of songs to be found in our anthologies that end with fal lals, and equally portentous syllables, and count, if you can, the English poems that end every alternate line with a meaningless "O" introduced for rhythm, or rhyme, or, at the behest of the tune, for the purposes of melody. It will do no harm, brethren, to smile at the Indian, but let us turn a fair share of the laughter upon ourselves.

TRANSLATION AND INTERPRETATION.

A better example of compactness may be found in the following to which I have previously referred as the song that awakened my interest in Ojibway music and led me to this prolonged investigation. Short as it is, the Indian does not piece it out with "heyah." The entire poem is here given as sung by the Indians, with the meaning of the words under the Ojibway equivalent:

| *Chekahbay* | *tebik* | *ondandeyan* |
|-------------|---------|--------------|
| Throughout | night | I keep awake |

| *chekaybay* | *tebik* | *ondandeyan* |
|-------------|---------|--------------|
| throughout | night | I keep awake |

| *ahgahmah-sibi* | *ondandeyan* |
|-----------------|--------------|
| upon a river | I keep awake. |

I am quite sure that this literal transfer of meanings from one language to another would convey nothing to the English paleface who knew nothing by direct contact of Indian life. His poetic fancy might evolve a meaning from it, but it is hardly likely that it would be in consonance with the Indian's meaning. I venture to take the reader over the course that was necessarily mine when I undertook to translate the song. At that time I knew not one Ojibway word. The intelligent Indian whom I asked for a translation slowly dictated the following:

"I am out all night on the river seeking for my sweetheart."

This impressed me as poetic in feeling, but I wished to get closer to the words themselves which I had carefully spelled from dictation and written as above, leaving spaces beneath for the English equivalents. I could see that there were only four words. By dint of patient, detailed questioning I arrived approximately at the English equivalents above given. Then I was puzzled and disturbed.

"Where is the word for sweetheart?" I asked.

"It is not there," replied the Indian, tranquilly.

"Then," said I, "how do you make out that the song means 'I am seeking for my sweetheart'?"

Had he been a paleface he would have smiled pityingly at my lack of comprehension, but, as he had all the traditional courtesy and dignity of his race, he put my own patience to the blush by pointing to the word "ondandeyan" which occurs three times.

"That mean," said he, " 'I keep awake.' I get tired, yes, and sleepy, but I no sleep. I keep awake. That word (tebik)

is night. Now you see. Why does a man keep awake all
night when he want to sleep?"

Like the true orator and debater, he paused for reply.

"Well," I suggested, half in weakness, and half in determination to make him work out the meaning, "he might be
hunting for deer, or something else to eat."

"No, no!" he responded gravely, "not this time. See: I keep
awake all night long on the river. Only one reason. I go
to find my sweetheart. The word is not there but we understand it. We know what is meant. Perhaps mebbe her family
has gone away. Perhaps mebbe she said she would meet me
and something happened so she couldn't. I don't know; but
we know that the man who made this song was looking for
his sweetheart, and we do not need the word there."

With this bewildering light thrown on the subject, I retired
to my own quarters and pondered. It was my eager desire
to make the attractive melody available for paleface singers.
To this end it was essential that there should be singable verses.
Observe the use of the plural. One verse, or one stanza would
not do for the demands of civilization. The Indian is content
to sing his one line over and over again, but the paleface must
have variety in his language even in so short a song as this.
I confess that my first impulse was to string together some
rhymed lines that would fit the tune, and let it go at that, as
the easiest way out of the difficulty, but it seemed a shame to
discard the suggestion offered in the Indian verse, and doubly
wrong to put forth an Indian song that should not at least
reflect the Indian thought; but so much was implied and so

little expressed! And that despairing reflection was the key to the problem. So much implied! I set myself to studying how much more might be implied than the search for a sweetheart, and it occurred to me that if an Ojibway were on the river he would necessarily be in his canoe. Here was promise of singable results and of the verbal repetition without which no representation of the original could be regarded as satisfactory. It was with conscious excitement that I hurried to my Indian friend and asked the question—would not the singing lover be in his canoe?

"Of course," said he, and then a ghost of a smile lit up his dark features; "but you don't find the word *chemaun* there, do you?" he asked.

Chemaun means canoe. "No," I answered, "but it's understood, isn't it?"

"Yes," said he, "we understand it so," and he turned away as if that settled it, or as if a continuance of the conversation would lead him to inquire sarcastically if I supposed the lover would be swimming the river all night, or balancing on a perilous, uncomfortable log?

It did settle it, and before I arrived back at my table I was humming the first of the stanzas with which the song has been identified since its publication—

In the still night, the long hours through,
I guide my bark canoe,
My bark canoe, my love, to you.

While the stars shine and falls the dew
I seek my love in bark canoe,
In bark canoe I seek for you.

It is I, love, your lover true,
Who glides the stream in bark canoe;
It glides to you, my love, to you.

### SUBORDINATION OF VERSE TO MELODY.

I was slow in coming to perception of what may be called a general principle applicable to Indian verse that accounts for its compactness and for certain negative characteristics. To summarize them: it is vague; it lacks form, that is, nothing is there that answers to rhyme, there is seldom a suggestion even of corresponding or contrasting phrases, and it is only by good fortune, apparently, that it ever assumes a metrical aspect. In other words, it is prose, for the most part, unembellished by metaphor, or any other trick of the imagination with which civilized poets enhance their expressions. This may occasion some degree of astonishment in view of the fact that all we have read of Indian oratory gives us the impression that the Indian is flowery, indulging in metaphor to such an extent as to be ambiguous, that he favors the imagination at the expense of perspicuity, caring more for striking figures of speech than for an unmistakable presentation of his ideas. This certainly was characteristic of the Ojibways. To refer to but one authority, Alexander Henry, in his *Travels and Adventures,* 1760, 1776, more than once alludes to his difficulty in following the speeches of chiefs, even after he had mastered their language, because of their excessive indulgence in flowery figures; and he says that it was a part of their education to learn to speak figuratively.   How comes it, then, that imagery is conspicuous by its rarity in Indian verse?   I think we shall find that the answer lies in the subordination of verse to melody, the Indian having no conception of poetry apart from its association with music.   In order to work out this speculation, as well as to deduce the general principle referred to, I shall dip again into narration, and not unwillingly, although one of my stories convicts me of amusing error.

It was not long after I had begun my quest for melodies that I chanced upon Tetebahbundung drumming and singing for his little son, Adamosa, to dance.   They were quite by themselves, indulging in the diversion for its own sake with no thought of spectators.   The boy threw himself into the fantastic and difficult movements of the dance with extravagant enthusiasm, and the father applied himself to his part almost as seriously as if the event signalized an important decision by a council of chiefs—almost, for he was not drumming loudly, and in his grave eyes glowed the light of parental satisfaction. By reason of his comparatively light drumming and the clearness of his voice, I heard the quaint tune distinctly and it caught my fancy at once.   I had no difficulty in notating it, for by then I had become accustomed to the alternation of triple and double rhythm, and, moreover, Tetebahbundung sang it over and over until the boy stopped dancing from sheer exhaustion.   My next consideration was for the words, and

Tetebahbundung slowly dictated them, syllable by syllable: *"Mujje mukesin awyawyon."*

Three words, the most compact poem discovered up to that moment—I have since found one that is limited to one word. I doubt whether anybody could imagine the intensity of my eagerness to learn what they meant. I was all excitement over the melody, my imagination even then leaping forward to the use I subsequently made of it in orchestral writing; and it was so individual, so perfectly rounded out, so inspiriting, that I suppose I unconsciously forecast a significance in the words that should be worthy, to say the least, of the tune. At all events it was with something like a shock that I heard the Indian's answer to my inquiry as to the meaning.

"I use bad shoes," said he.

I had no distrust of Tetebahbundung's intentions, but there was abundant reason to doubt the accuracy of his translations, for at that time he knew little English and his pronunciation was most imperfect. So I found occasion to ask another Indian about the words, and from him received identically the same answer. "I use bad shoes."

Then, as in the case of "My Bark Canoe," I withdrew to the solitude of my own thoughts. What possibly could be implied that was not expressed by these words? I asked myself. There was no faint shadow of poetic suggestion in them; they were simply funny, and I came not unwillingly at last to that acceptation of the song, for the tune itself sparkled as with humor. So I undertook to reproduce the Indian humor in English. This was easy enough, for a grotesque, or even a commonplace phrase subjected to incessant iteration becomes irresistibly laughable, and it was merely a question, therefore, of conveying the literal meaning of the sentence in words that would fit the rhythm.

Very well; the only use to which shoes could be put was for wearing, and bad shoes, from my own cornful experience, were those that pinched; but it was well nigh inconceivable that an Indian should pinch his toes in yielding moccasins, and I readily concluded that from his point of view the only bad shoes would be those that were past repair, worn out; and so a line adjusted itself quickly to the rhythm of the tune:

"Worn out shoes I am a-wearing."

I committed many absurdities that first summer among the Indians, among them being the installation of a machine that in a bygone age had been a pianoforte in my lodge. To it I took my new song, and in my confident enthusiasm I invited two or three whites and such Indians as were in call to listen. The whites responded to the humor of the piece and I was vastly satisfied with myself. Tetebahbundung was there and I asked him what he thought of it, but I am sure that my question was disingenuous. Anybody, red or white, could have seen that I expected commendation. Tetebahbundung politely gave it. Not a hint did he venture that I was in total error. His mental attitude doubtless might have been expressed thus: "It pleases him, it pleases his friends; who am I that I should presume to instruct him in the use of his own language?"

At all events no shadow of suspicion crossed my mind that I had not made a correct interpretation, and, as the song proved popular with all whites who came my way, I sang it many times, eventually to a kindergartner who begged a copy of it that she might teach it to her children. She tried it on, found that the children tackled to it eagerly, spoke to other kindergartners about it, and before very long I was in receipt of urgent re- quests from various parts of the country to print the song. I did so, and "Old Shoes" speedily found its way to kinder- gartens and primary schools, and even to the concert platform. Meantime I continued to sing it myself whenever I was in com- pany with Indians entertaining white audiences, and for a long time nobody among my Ojibway friends said a word.

One day, nearly a year after the publication of the song, Obetossoway confronted me. He is the wittiest Indian among my acquaintances, quick to see and to make a joke, but por- tentously solemn or dignified when he has something of im- portance to say to one whom he regards as his superior. At that time I was his employer, and I imagine that he must have nerved himself mightily to correct me.

"Sir," said he, in his most dignified manner, "you have got that song all wrong. It does not mean that I am wearing worn out shoes at all, sir."

"Well," I responded, "I want to be set right if I have made a mistake. What does it mean?"

"It means 'I use bad shoes,' sir."

This was almost annoying. Obetossoway speaks English fluently, and, with his bright mind, I thought he should have grasped my interpretation and not insist on bald literalness; but I was anxious to encourage just the kind of service he was trying to perform for me, and I went patiently into my argument.

"Worn out shoes are bad shoes, are they not?" I asked, and he admitted that they were. "Well," I proceeded, "in English we do not speak of using shoes, but of wearing them. Don't you understand?"

"I do, sir," said he.

"Then, if I am wearing worn out shoes, I am using bad shoes. Isn't that so?"

"It is," Obetossoway admitted, adding firmly, "but, sir, the song means 'I use bad shoes.' "

In weariness of spirit, I gave it up, silently abusing the Indian for an unsuspected blockhead, and I was so certain of my interpretation that I was disturbed by no doubt about it.

The revelation of my error came a few days after the conversation with Obetossoway. At that time the play "Hiawatha" was being performed daily in the open air. I had notated most of the songs that are introduced into the play but had not paid attention to those that figure in the gambling scene for the very good reason that I never could hear them. The drum is pounded incessantly while all the Indians dance except the few who are directly concerned in the game. Now and again I could hear the singer's voice, but never sufficiently to catch a complete musical phrase, and the words were wholly inaudible. The fact that music entered even into the gambling of the Indians suggested that it must have special significance there; and that was incentive enough for investigation. In

order to get some notion of the song, or songs, I concealed myself among bushes close to the stage with music paper on the
ground before me. From this vantage I could hear every
word and nearly every note. Imagine my bewilderment when
the gambling began, to hear Tetebahbundung sing *"Mujje
mukesin awyawyon!"* But I am not altogether blind, or deaf,
or stupid. In a moment the significance of the song flashed
upon me, for I recalled what was visible from the viewpoint
of the audience. The Indians were playing what they call
the "Moccasin Game." One player hides a small object, no
matter what, under one of three or more moccasins; his opponent tries to select the moccasin that conceals the object.
That, in brief, is the whole game, and it is said to be the origin
of that infamous swindling device known to whites as the shell
game. But it is picturesque and dramatic as the Indians play
it. The process of hiding is accompanied by a variety of confusing gestures, and it takes a long time; and while the first
player is lifting one moccasin after another, pretending to
hide the object, distracting his opponent's attention in every
possible way, the singer is industriously warbling *"Mujje
mukesin awyawyon."*

Obetossoway was right. Of course the song means "I use
bad shoes;" it can't mean anything else, but what is implied and
not expressed might be put this way: "I am using bewitched
shoes; they will fool you; you're not smart enough to get around
these wicked shoes of mine." Worn-out shoes, indeed! O, the
superior discernment of the paleface! I felt some chagrin
as I lay there in the bushes with my needless music paper

before me, but presently yielded to the humor of the event, and at the earliest possible moment after the performance I sought out Obetossoway and made amends for my obstinacy.

Before I left my place of concealment, however, I had caught another song. It is a sequel to "Bad Shoes," as the first ought to be called. When the first gambler has hidden the object and sufficiently confused his adversary, he sits back and it is the other's turn to play. Seldom is the adversary so confident of success that he indicates his choice of moccasins without delay. He first assures himself that there has been no cheating. It would be unfair, for example, if the first gambler should palm the object instead of slipping it under one of the moccasins. So the second gambler demands that the first expose both his hands and also open his mouth to show that the object is not there. When he is satisfied that nothing has been done contrary to rule, the second gambler usually makes a feint of picking out the moccasin that he thinks conceals the object. This he does by pretending to strike at it with his war club, meantime watching his adversary's eyes warily for any involuntary sign of fear or confidence. This feint may be repeated several times, or for as long as the second gambler likes, and the game does not reach its final stage until he actually strikes a moccasin with his club. That moccasin is then turned over, and if the object is found under it, the second gambler wins; otherwise he loses. The sequel to "Bad Shoes" applies to the play of the second gambler. While he is making up his mind the drummer is singing—

*Gayget wahbod nege wahbod ge,*

"Indeed! I know where it is," which is to say, "you can't fool
me with your bad shoes; I can find the thing."

A SONG OF WINTER.

A brief examination of one more song will bring us to the
principle underlying nearly all Ojibway verse to which allusion
has been made.   Early in my association with these Indians I
notated a song to the following words:

| *Kezhoyah* | *ishquandaym* | *baybogin* |
|------------|---------------|------------|
| Warm       | door          | in winter  |

Several Indians told me that it meant "My door is warm in
winter time," which is literal but not illuminating.   The young
fellows sang it with great gusto at all sorts of times and occasions, and not one of them seemed to comprehend the difficulty I had in understanding them.   I did get an impression
that it was in some way a song of hospitality, but it was not
until good fortune brought me in touch with Shingwauk that
I was enabled to look at it from the Indian point of view and
grasp its full significance.   I referred nearly all these songs
to him after they had been phonographed.   When he had listened to this one, he said:

"When I was a boy I often heard my grandfather tell the
story of that song and sing it.   The story goes that an Indian

hunter was overtaken by a furious snow storm that speedily obscured the trail and made all ordinary landmarks unrecognizable. Night fell soon afterwards and he knew that he was lost, but he kept wandering on, for it was so cold that if he had stood still he would have frozen to death. When morning came he was more bewildered than ever. The snow still fell and the wind blew a gale. He was numb with cold and faint with hunger, for his stock of food was exhausted and he stumbled on no game. All that day the north wind blew and the snow piled in such deep drifts that he could hardly struggle through them. When darkness came again he was still floundering along, almost minded to give it up, lie down and sleep the sleep of death, but in a lull of the tempest he heard the faint beating of a drum a long way off. This gave him hope, but fear, too, for how could he know that it was not the drum of an enemy? Cautiously he followed the direction of the sound which grew louder and louder until at length he discerned a wigwam from within which it came. And then he distinguished the words that the man within was singing—*Kezho-yah ishquandaym baybogin*—they were Ojibway words, and he knew that he had come upon one who would be a friend. So he went directly to the wigwam, opened the door and entered. The man who lived there stirred the fire, gave the visitor abundance of food and kept him until the storm abated.

"Near the end of the story," Shingwauk concluded, "my grandfather would pause and sing the song, though sometimes he did not sing until the story was finished."

FEW SONGS COMPLETE IN THEMSELVES.

From these examples, and many others that need not be quoted, it appears that, with few exceptions, no Ojibway song is complete in itself. For entire comprehension it depends upon something external, a story, or a ceremony. The moccasin game may be classed as a ceremony, for, in view of the regular procedure of the game, the songs that are associated with it become definitely significant. In the case of the warm door song, the story presents to the imagination a vivid picture of Winter, the sufferings of the lost hunter serving to set forth the terrors and perils of the season which the man within doors mocks triumphantly in his three-word song. The song, then, may be regarded as a mnemonic summary of several thoughts and impressions.

It is not in the manner of civilization to connect its songs with explanatory stories, though our modern lecture-recitals indicate that a greater degree of appreciation of songs is gained thereby. Is it not rather impressive to reflect that the untutored Ojibway had lecture-recitals centuries before he knew the white man? The custom of preluding every song with an explanation of the circumstances alluded to in the text is evidently as ancient as any Indian custom that survives to-day; a custom, be it understood, that was not invented for the benefit of inquisitive whites, but that was and is maintained by the Indians for themselves.

But, aside from elegance of diction, and highly developed form, and some other superficial features perhaps, the essen-

tial difference between Ojibway verse and the verse of civilization is just this: that our poetry is or aims to be self
dependent; our songs are or should be complete in themselves;
the Ojibways' are consciously incomplete statements of the
situation, feeling, or events which find expression through
them.

It must be obvious, therefore, that, in adapting these songs
to the uses of civilization, the adaptor confronts a problem
that is at once nice and complex.   He must reflect the Indian
thought, and a precisely literal translation would most effect-
ively conceal, or at best misrepresent it.   In words that fall
naturally in the Indian scheme of accents he must convey not
only an interpretation of the words actually employed, but
a sufficiently complete statement of the explanatory story, or
the attendant situation, to make the English song self dependent.

When I came to realize this principle, I saw at once that
many songs that hitherto had seemed impracticable of translation, because of the unimaginative brevity of their texts,
might be turned to account if the stories were known, and I
began a fresh pursuit with stories in view.   So, without seeking to excuse the shortcomings of the verse now linked to
these melodies, let it be understood that, in all cases where
not specifically stated otherwise, the contents of the verse have
been suggested by Indians' statements to me as to what is
their understanding of the song.   In the process by which the
Ojibway verse makes its way to English there must necessarily
be taken on some color of the adaptor's individuality; and

there is no end of liability to error. I should rejoice if other persons should interest themselves to the extent of turning the subject matter into verse more truly expressive of Indian life and spirit; in fact, one thing only would please me more and that would be the harmonization and development of these melodies by other composers.

Following is my attempt to interpret the warm door song—

Freeze, ye northern winds!
Blow, ye frosty blasts!
Here within 'tis warm
While the Winter lasts.

Whirl, ye driven snow,
Heap in smothering drifts!
Winter here lies low
Nor his cold hand lifts.

In passing this part of the subject I will allude briefly to another peculiarity of Ojibway verse that has been a troublesome stumbling-block to my work—the fact that many of the words in the songs are archaic. There is doubt among the most intelligent Indians themselves as to the meaning of some of the ancient songs, for the words have either passed wholly out of current use, or their meanings have evidently been modified with the lapse of years.

SENTIMENT AND INCONGRUITIES.

Next to the compactness of Ojibway verse the feature that most disconcerts the musical observer is the startling incongruity that is frequently manifested between the sentiment of the text and the character of the melody. There is at least one Indian, Tetebahbundung, who feels this. He came to me one day saying that he had remembered a new song, adding at once, "But it ought to be a love song and it isn't." Then he sang it, slowly, seriously, his rich voice dwelling lovingly upon the appealing phrases until the non-Ojibway listener must have felt that here was a song of human tenderness, the cry of a pure soul for affection, an expression, whatever be its detail, of the very refinement of love. The melody appealed to me instantly as the gem of the collection, and though I have found many beautiful songs since then, none, in my estimation, surpass it—but here are the words:

*Me ne nah gaynahge ne nah keewahshquaybe ah beding me ne quayon, nah suh nah gahnahway ne me shinozahme beyod goshu neen.*

"I don't suppose I'll get drunk if I take one drink; if I should get drunk, take care of me."

Comment seems unnecessary. Incongruity is the soul of humor, and a smile at this ill fitting combination is inevitable, but I confess that my smile was one of regret. I tried to comfort myself with the speculation that this was originally what the melody seemed to make it, a love song, and that some roistering scoffer had parodied it; but even if there were anything in the fanciful theory, it would not avail, for the Ojibways of to-day accept the song as it stands, finding in it merely an expression of humor. I have heard it roared by men and women, solo and in chorus, with no trace of the refined sentiment infused into it by Tetebahbundung, save that it was always sung very slowly after the usual Ojibway manner; and on one occasion, at a campfire, a clever six-year-old boy aroused much enthusiasm among the Indians by singing it with appropriate action. He staggered, hiccoughed from time to time, dwelt with extravagant emphasis on the word *keewahsh-quaybe*—drunk—and at the end of the second repetition fell full length to the ground.

### A FANTASTIC EXPERIMENT.

It may be noted that this is an exception among Ojibway songs in that it is complete in itself. I could not bring myself to profane the exquisite melody by singing it to a translation of the Indian words. Tetebahbundung had said that it ought to be a love song, and I tried a fantastic experiment, the inevitable result of which I was too optimistic to foresee. I suggested the making of a new set of words. Tetebahbundung placidly agreed, and we had several solemn pow-wows over the matter. At length, with the assistance of an educated Indian, Chief Charles Obetossoway, of Grand Manitoulin Island, brother of the Obetossoway to whom allusion has been made, we evolved the following:

*Uh pe mod dahwankah maudwazhahzhewahd shingwaukug me suh uh ne nemoshayn ne dahnadum.*

"When I am in the forest I hear my sweetheart sighing through the pines."

Then the trouble began. The new words do not fit the tune, and although Ojibway syntax permits of all manner of inversions, and the songs abound in repetitions of words and phrases, the singer could not make a satisfactory arrangement. Of course it was too much to expect that he would do so, and the song will remain a drinking song for as long as the Ojibways sing it; but for the uses of civilization I have ventured to expand the new set of words and call it "In the Forest," under which title the song may be found in the collection.

### INVERSION OF SENTIMENT.

Another instance of incongruity may be found in the song I call "Waubunosa's Longing," from the name of the man who first sang it to me. It is very popular among the Ojibways, and from their point of view it is a song of joy. The words, omitting meaningless syllables and repetitions, *Kenemashaynon dalguishid nesah wenahowquazans me sul gay galpedalguishing,* mean, "My sweetheart has returned; I am glad because she has come back to me." To the ear of civilization the song does not appeal as joyful when given in the Indian's best manner; on the contrary it seems ineffably mournful. At the last analysis this is a matter of conventional association. The melody in itself is neither sad, nor gay, the listener's characterization of it depending upon its approximation to the manner in which he has been accustomed to hear one emotion or the other expressed through the tonal art. The Indian is accustomed to express his joy in musical terms that we are accustomed to employ for expression of 'sorrow; but that settles nothing. To him it is a joyous song, and no tinge of melancholy overcasts his feelings when he sings it. It is impossible to force considerations of this kind upon a people who are just as much the slaves of tradition and convention as are the red men. No amount of philosophical argument will make this melody appeal as joyous to the average white man. Therefore, believing it to be impossible for any white singer to make the song effective with a translation of the Ojibway words, I have inverted the sentiment and arranged words that seem to accord better with civilization's sense of fitness.

Hopelessly incongruous are those love songs that give utterance only to carnal passion. The melodies are no less pure than the others, no less worthy to contribute to the delight of refined persons; and, viewed philosophically, there is nothing in the words to disturb equanimity. The Indian is frank where the white man is reserved; he does not mask brute desire under vague euphemisms; he is primitive, and honest, and speaks according to his lights. It is only when we approach the words in a spirit of sentimentalism, which is a harsh way of stating the musician's ingenuous attitude,—for this musician, at all events, was eager to find good, and good only, in all phases of Ojibway life and art—that we experience a certain pain that is not to be confounded with prudery. It amounts to this, and no more than this: that it is regrettable to find so keen a perception of beauty in one phase of the Ojibway's joint art, for such his music-poetry is, and such crude insensibility to the finer emotions in the other. There need be no pharisaical contempt for the Indian in recognizing his deficiency in this regard. Let us bear humbly in mind that no inconceivable span of years separates us from the time when English verse was open to the same criticism. There is nothing further to be said on this matter unless I need confess that I do not feel myself bound by any consideration for archæological exactness to translate verses that lie without the pale of civilization's tolerance.

Lest there be any shadow of misapprehension, I hasten to add that lewdness is by no means the prevailing characteristic of Ojibway love verse. On the contrary a large proportion of the songs appear to me to have been inspired by what we term romantic love, and my own contact with the people establishes beyond possibility of doubt the existence of romantic love among them. From a discreet distance I have watched courtships that differed from our own only as the minor details of Ojibway daily life are at variance with ours; and I have seen many instances of marital devotion, on the part of men as well as women, that would serve as high models for any people.

Returning to the discussion of verse, I would not have it understood that incongruity is universal. We must never lose sight of the difference in point of view, but in this collection will be found not a few songs in which the points of view appear to coincide; that is, the Indian's song, so far as the sentiment behind the words is concerned, is equally expressive to us and to him. For example, it seems to me that "Winter" (the warm-door song) is abundantly expressive within its narrow limits of the boisterous season and the exultation of the man who has a weather-tight dwelling and a fire in it. The two lullabies speak well for mother love that, even among civilized peoples, is usually voiced to brief phrases and meaningless syllables. In "Lonely," where the English text is, I believe, a literal translation of the original, there seems to me to be perfect adjustment of sentiment to melody.

### LACK OF VARIETY.

As might be expected there is no great variety of subject in Ojibway love verse. When it comes to the last analysis is there over much variety in the love verse of civilization? Does it not generally take on an appearance of variety from the environment of the poet? Not to make too much of this comparative observation, it is to be admitted at once that the civilized poet attains variety by the manifestation of his individuality. With the Ojibway, as, I presume, with any primitive people, individuality is not highly developed. Content to sing his one line over and over, he also is content in the making of a new song to paraphrase what has been sung before. He does not realize it, but I think that it is often the melody and not the words that individualizes his song for him. Speculation aside, there are many Ojibway love songs that speak of loneliness; usually they purport to be the wail of a girl whose sweetheart has gone to war, or upon a long journey. A class apart might be made of those that tell of being on the way to meet one's sweetheart; and it appears that the Ojibway's sweetheart was forever losing herself in the forest, which made it necessary for him to tramp, or paddle the streams and lakes all night long to find her. According to the songs he usually found her, or gave up the search, at sunrise. I have tried to avoid reduplication of thought in the English stanzas, sometimes giving to a melody words that were translated from another song of similar character. Where this occurs a special note is made of the fact.

### COMPARATIVE OBSERVATIONS.

In Ojibway music the general lack of development, speaking technically for the moment, is the chief mark of its primitive character; and it is much the same in Ojibway verse. Often is the poetic impulse plainly manifest, and with equal plainness the inability to work it out. The Ojibway is more gifted in music than in poetry; he has wrought out a type of beautiful melody, much of it perfect in form; his verse, for the most part, has not emerged from the condition of raw material. The spirit of music, struggling for expression through his primitive soul, finds its way to utterance in spite of the words with which he associates it. The Indian, like the average paleface, is incapable of grasping the conception of music as a thing of absolute beauty. Does a melody sing in his head and insist upon vocal utterance, he must forthwith invent a series of words that fit the rhythmic scheme of the tune, for thus alone can he correlate his sense of pleasure in modulated sounds with his habitual regard of other phenomena that appeal to him through the material senses as plain, comprehensible facts. We might, by strenuous exercise of the imagination, conceive of an Indian voicing a melody tentatively to meaningless syllables, and wondering as to the nature of that tonal entity that comes from—he knows not where—that allures his soul, that compels him to sing. He might wonder at it as a hermit who is visited by angels in a vision. It might awaken awe, as if it were a message from another world, the very holiest of holy speech of Gitche Manitou himself. Thrilling with the pure delight that music alone of all the arts and things upon or above the earth can arouse, he might yet hesitate to link it to words lest he offend the manitou who sent it, lest he misinterpret the message so subtly and convincingly spoken to his heart; and thus bowing in humility before the mysterious presence manifested in new melody, he might content himself and the visiting impulse with a wordless song, leaving the meaning of it to be revealed at the manitou's own pleasure.

The fact probably is that no Indian ever went so far as this in speculation. His process of composition, so far as that process can be manifested, is identically such as I have suggested. He does sing his new melody to meaningless syllables, tentatively, correcting it here and there, but meantime experimenting with words that convey meaning; and the probability is that the precise sentiment of the words finally accepted is established by rhythmic considerations, those that fall readily into the scheme of accents appealing to him as the most suitable vehicle for the melody. And, aside from dependence upon the scheme of accents, the character of the words that suggest themselves to him must depend upon his own character, his mode of life, manner of thought, the exigency of his immediate situation, whatever that may be, and not upon the unborn tune.

I am quite aware that there is room for speculation of a contrary sort on this point; that those who perceive a fixed relationship between sentiment, or emotion, and musical beauty, may assert that the words actually chosen for the song are suggested psychologically by the nature of the melody; and I am content that speculation of this kind should be carried to the end of the thinker's pleasure, but it will be well to keep the facts rigidly in view. The last fact of all is that the Indian words, from the viewpoint of the civilized observer, are often at radical variance with what would be the civilized conception of appropriateness to the melody. Let us think of this with patience and candor, for we are here considering the very beginnings of music; we gain here a glimpse, shadowy, but a glimpse, of its real relation to the human mind. The musical expression comes; the red man voices it; the form is melodic, and in all music that, at last analysis, is the potent, distinguishing factor; he must give it a name, place it somehow in a category that relates it to other things familiar and comprehensible. Hence, words; hence, from his point of view, a meaning; hence, from his point of view, the character of the composition. The words convey, it may be, ideas of repulsive vulgarity, or the driest commonplaces of life, or a rarely beautiful aspiration; it does not matter; the melody is there, beautiful, appealing to us as abstract beauty when we hear it linked to words that fortunately we do not understand. Does not this primitive method and its results suggest—if not demonstrate—that music is not only above and beyond all language, but that it is apart from any definite emotion? Observe: the melodically gifted Ojibway gives it forth and in his unreflecting way identifies it with joy; the paleface, listening but not understanding the words, in an equally unreflecting way correlates it with something heard before and identifies it with sorrow. How much truer and more appreciative of musical beauty it would be if all of us could regard the composition—simple Indian melody or complex sonata—as what it is: an appeal through tone to the very foundations of being, to that heart of the senses of which joy, sorrow, fear, love, hate, and the rest, are but ramifying manifestations!

But the ingenuous Indian does nothing in this regard that the paleface composer does not do. The Indian gives his piece a name, he undertakes to interpret its message to his fellows, and with him it is a simple matter, for instrumental music is outside his experience. In the music of civilization, discarding for the moment all the songs and hymns, do we not find pieces named nocturne, pastoral, tragic, joyous, melancholy this, that and the other? And when the composer sensibly refrains from attempting to limit the meaning of his message, there are commentators quick to discover moonlight in a Beethoven sonata, a ghastly tale of physical suffering in a Chopin prelude, and, as if this sort of thing were not enough, we have to-day a noisy prophet who presumes to dishonor the spirit of music by giving us a day out of his own inconsequential life in the form of a "Domestic Symphony!" The Indian can be forgiven the incongruities in his art, for he knows no better.

## CHAPTER IX

# INDIAN SONGS IN THEIR RELATION TO ART

W HEN we come to discuss the relation of Indian songs to art, we find that there are two distinct purposes which they may serve if, on careful examination, they seem fit for any purpose whatever. They may be used, first, as are the songs of civilization, for entertainment and the gratification of musical taste; and, second, they may furnish thematic material for (a) extended compositions, either instrumental or vocal, and (b) incidental color in works that otherwise are original and conventional.

## HARMONIZATION OF INDIAN MUSIC.

If the songs are to serve the first purpose, they must be harmonized. To me, this has always been self evident, and it is so obvious that I have hesitated to take space here to defend the practice; but I have been astonished on several occasions by protests against it, as if the harmonization of an Indian song were some sort of sacrilege, and inasmuch as there are some persons who do not approve decking out Indian melodies with the devices of civilization, it seems wise to go into the matter briefly. As I understand the objection, harmony does violence to the Indian conception of music; it was not, and could not be conceived by the Indian, and his musical output is, therefore, misrepresented when his songs are sung to pianoforte accompaniment, or in harmonic parts; and that harmony destroys the charming simplicity of the original, so that, "My Bark Canoe," for example, ceases to be Indian when it has a harmonic accompaniment.

I have considerable sentimental sympathy with these objections. I would rather, myself, hear an Ojibway sing "My Bark Canoe," in his simple way than hear it with pianoforte accompaniment; but that is because I would rather walk in the sombre forests, or guide a canoe along the wilderness waterways, than dwell in a city flat; and the circumstances of civilization having compelled me to dwell in a flat far removed from primeval forest and flashing lake, I find in the harmony added to the melody a factor for spiritual comfort that vies in sweetness with uncontaminated Nature herself. Not that the harmonies recall the forest and the lakes; not that they suggest the atmosphere of the song's origin, for music does nothing of that kind; it is that the melody, when sung under the conditions of civilization, demands the rounding out of its nature which is effected by harmony.

We are a harmonic people, we whites. We are born with appreciation of harmony, we are brought up in it, and, consciously or unconsciously, we always associate harmony with the tunes we hear, whistle, or hum. We do not sing unadorned tunes for one another's edification or entertainment; in all my concert-going, I recall but one instance where a singer sang without accompaniment, and he was a tenor of unusually appealing voice who was responding to an encore. In our haphazard social gatherings we sometimes resort to music when there is no instrument at command, but that is because we have to, not because we prefer to. The very idlers of the streets, the jovial groups in a popular excursion, aye, the family circle where refinement dwells, never resort to song but that one or more of the singers attempts to piece out the tune with an alto, or tenor, or bass part. The plain fact is that we whites cannot grasp the whole beauty of a melody unless we hear it with appropriate harmony. Therefore, if the beauty of Indian song is to be set forth to civilization, harmony must be employed in order to do justice to the Indian composer.

This is to take the objections rather too seriously, I fear. The simple truth is that I harmonized the Ojibway songs I first heard because I wanted to, which was quite enough for me, and that, if I had not done so, they would not have been heard at all outside the forest and the reservations. Therein lies the real, and whole, and unassailable justification for the employment of harmony. To hold to a fixed example, if "My Bark Canoe" had been retained in its original form, it might have been heard in the cities of civilization by a few who would have had the patience and politeness to listen to me when I sang it in the course of a lecture. That would have been the limit of white-man acquaintance with it. In its variously harmonized forms it has been sung by I dare not estimate how many thousand. It is used in many public schools; it has figured on many concert programmes; it has been and still is in frequent use as a feature of home entertainment. In these harmonized forms it has done no injustice to the Indian; rather has it exalted him, for it never fails to cause unbounded surprise that an Indian could have composed a melody so beautiful.  Thus has it served well its first purpose in art, and incidentally it has been instrumental in awakening a sane human interest in the Indian, and in inciting singers and hearers of the melody to the acquisition of some measure of truth about him to replace the ignorance and misinformation that fester in the average white man's mind with regard to him.  I believe that this little song has done more than all my writing and talking to apprise the whites of the common humanity of the red man, for the melody is obviously the creation of a human being, and, presumably, of one with a considerable gift of fine feeling.  As our ordinary estimate of the Indian is that he is a dull, if dignified, savage, such influence as the song has exerted toward a juster estimate is for the good; and so much, or so little good, whatever it may be, could not have been accomplished if the melody had been left to the occasional inspection of scientists and sentimentalists in its primitive form.

## NATIONALISM IN MUSIC.

I have suggested that Indian songs cannot be held to have any relation to art unless, on examination, they seem fit for it.  That I regard Ojibway songs as suitable for art purposes needs no other demonstration than the fact that I have given myself the pleasure of harmonizing a considerable number. It would not have been a pleasure, and I would not have taken the trouble to put them in civilized dress, if they had not appealed to me as beautiful.  It generally follows that songs fit to be sung by persons of discriminating taste are also fit for the second art purpose named in the foregoing, i. e., as the basis (a), or color (b), of extended compositions. Consideration of this phase of the matter necessarily brings up the question of nationalism in music, about which musicians are not in agreement. There are composers whose patriotism is not to be questioned who are opposed to any and every movement that tends to foster the infusion of our musical output with a distinctive character. They maintain that music is broader than the boundaries of a nation; that, in its highest development, it should and does speak to all peoples alike; that the deliberate selection of thematic material in folksongs of any type imposes limitations on the creative spirit of the composer and restricts that full and free expression of the individual which is the crowning glory of all creative work.

I am far from being inclined to controvert this view, for I am in deep sympathy with it, but it has other aspects than those indicated above, and to them I wish to invite attention. No American musician can visit Europe without suffering mortification at the estimate of our music that is held there. In a German magazine devoted to music I found, in a number published about seventy years ago, the tune "Yankee Doodle" under the descriptive heading, "Nordamerikanische Volkslied" (North American Folksong). There was a characteristically labored translation of the words into German, and a harmonized accompaniment, if you please, supplied by a man whose fortune it was to bear the name F. Schubert. I hasten to add that the great Franz Schubert died several years before the publication of the tune. The erudite editor appended a footnote to the music, the purport of which was that the song was representative of musical taste in America. Perhaps he was right, and perhaps he would admit, if he were now alive, that we have made some progress since then, although I fear he would hesitate to do so in view of the prevailing contemporary estimate of our music. A recent German critic has discovered that America's national expression in music is found in the marches and two-steps of John Philip Sousa, and our enormous output of so-called "rag-time" songs. Germans generally appear to agree with him, and Sousa's compositions, and many of the musically vulgar songs ground out by writers for vaudeville, appear on German concert programmes as American music.

In the interest of a broad view of the matter it should be noted that in the higher musical circles of Germany respectful attention is accorded to the works of Paine, Macdowell, Kelley, Bird, Hadley, and other American composers, but the fact should also be recognized that these men have spoken frankly in the European idiom. With no shadow of disparagement of their achievements intended, it must be borne in mind in this dicussion that they stand for the theory of world music as opposed to national, for the highest and completest expression of the individual as against a conscious effort to voice the feeling of their people. World music to-day is European music, and those of our serious composers who have been well received abroad have succeeded because their works approximated so well to the European conception of what music ought to be.

The question properly arises, is the world music of the future always to be European? In the days of the discussion that followed the production of Dvorak's "New World" symphony I came to this understanding of my own view: I longed for an output of music that should somehow be distinctively American; but I was convinced that such a music in our future would arise from the writings of an over-towering genius in whose certain coming my Americanism made me firmly believe. I still believe it. I must believe that the remarkable blend of many peoples that more and more is evolving the typical American will one day be distinguished by a composer who will speak to all the world through a broader, better music than ever has or will be made elsewhere; but, whether or not we believe in the coming of the over-towering genius, should we not try meanwhile to impress our European critics with a conviction that the native spirit of our country is expressible through a better medium than Sousa marches and "rag time" songs?

I think there can be no serious argument against this very general proposition. It certainly will not do to assert that America is sufficient unto itself, and that we ought not to concern ourselves with what Europe thinks of us. This attitude would do very well if we did not continue to write on European models and ape European ideas. As soon as we have really broken away from tradition, done something original and established a manner of our own, it will be time to cry indifference to European opinion. Argument aside, and taking it for granted that every American musician would like to see the musical output of his country take high rank in the world at large, let me urge upon young composers a view that combines self interest and broad patriotism. I limit my appeal to the young because their modes of expression have not become fixed, and because I recognize that it is hopeless to expect response from composers who have seen as many years, say, as I have. There is a number of such in this country who are writing beautiful music, and I hope every one will continue to do so to the end of a long life, but I have no hope that any of them could be induced to venture from his well beaten and charming path.

It is a proper wish on the part of every composer that his works might come to performance under dignified auspices. To that end the American composer toils faithfully and generally without success. If we were discussing an individual instance it would be becoming and necessary to examine his work and seek scientific reasons for his failure, and we might, of course, find that his actual accomplishments were far below his own estimates of them. Looking at the situation broadly, however, we can see one significant fact in which may lie a host of reasons for the rare appearance of American compositions on our concert programmes. Our conductors are, with very few exceptions, imported. Let them come, as I think they do, with the very friendliest attitude toward American music and its makers, they nevertheless come also with their heads filled to overflowing with the latest and, to their apprehension, the best that Europe has produced; and, therefore, they import a great quantity of European music which must be crowded into their programmes. It needs no saying that they are fixed in their admiration for European models, and that, insensibly perhaps, every manuscript offered to them is measured by European standards.

Having come thus far in the argument, the conclusion appears to be so obvious that expression of it may seem unnecessary; therefore, permit me to interject a disclaimer. I am not about to take the ground that music should be brought to performance merely because it is American in origin. I have no patience whatever with that attitude. So long as we persist in writing according to European models and seek the imprimatur of European, or European-bred conductors, we must be content to be measured according to European standards. The composer who cannot satisfy the critical taste of his time as manifested by the conductors, must be content with the joy of creative work and with oblivion as its aftermath. No, I do not raise the spoiled-child cry, but I do maintain that the study of musical theory in America to-day is so conducted as to give the rising generation of composers, say those who are still in the universities and conservatories, abundant skill in the manipulation of the means of music to enable them to write acceptably for the contemporary concert platform. I believe the failure of American composers to make themselves felt to an appreciable degree is due not to the lack of attainments but to unhappy selection of material. That material is usually, if not always, of their own invention, and very dear to them, and by so much, apparently, they are the more condemned; but it comes back to the fact that, writing with European music as their model, with European recognition as, consciously or unconsciously, their ultimate goal, they fail at present to rise higher than the contemporary and recently dead geniuses of trans-Atlantic origin. Americans who enter this race will surely continue to be out-distanced until they manage to write something that is distinctive, something that is notably different from the European output.

Here, then, comes the suggestion that, in a preceding paragraph, I called an appeal. As a patriotic American, I would still call it an appeal, believing that one end subserved would be the raising of the European estimate of our musical advancement. Merely as a musician of many dreams and some experience, let me call it a suggestion. Our alien conductors, with all their fixed ideas, are, in this period, singularly open to novelties, to innovations in the art. They hold skilful manipulation of the material as a *sine qua non* of performance, but they have no prejudice for or against any sort of thematic material. If prejudice exists, it must be in favor of the fantastic, the outlandish, to judge from some of the up-to-date monstrosities in the way of symphonic works that they display to us. Now, granting that our young men have acquired skill in manipulation, which means intelligent thematic development as well as orchestration of a high order, it seems to me the young composer would have infinitely more chance of coming forward if he would base his work on such distinctive material as is to be found in the Ojibway songs than he ever will by courageously adhering to themes of his own invention. It would be silly to prophesy that all or any manuscript thus based would be ac-

cepted by the conductor of the Boston Symphony orchestra, for
example, but I am sure that such manuscripts would be approached by the distinguished reader with a considerable degree
of sympathy, with a desire to find them good and well done.

### FLEXIBILITY OF INDIAN THEMES.

The foregoing is confessedly an appeal to individual selfish-
ness, with patriotism as a secondary thought.   Let me turn now
to another view of the general subject and urge patriotism as
the prime impulse to a consciously directed policy.   As I am
pleading for a use of Indian songs as thematic material, I must
do what I can to prove that they are susceptible of such use.
Actual examples to which the student might be referred are
rare.   If they were abundant I should feel that there was no
very good reason for writing this book.   The field is but just
opened, and few have yet ventured to cultivate it.

In view of the rather rigid formula upon which a vast number of Indian songs appear to have been composed, by which
they seem so like each other to our ears, it might naturally be
supposed that they would not yield readily to development, and
that they would therefore hinder the composer.   But it should
be taken into account that no sane musician, much as he might
admire Indian songs, would advocate building up an art that
should prove to be but a refinement of, or elaboration of the
primitive stock.   The composer who has once accepted a theme,
be it a mere motive of one or two measures, or an entire tune,
makes it his own and does with it thereafter what he pleases.

He is not concerned with what the original composer of the theme would have done in the way of developing it; he is not restricted in his extension of the material by the thought that the Indian would not have done thus or so; it is no part of his business to erect an art fabric that might be called Indian. He is concerned solely with the making of good music according to his lights; it is his business to construct a work that shall accord with his own conception of symmetry, that shall glow with color, sparkle with melody, and move to such conclusion as the inherent nature of the theme demands. In other words, having selected his thematic material, it is his right, if not his duty, to forget its origin and proceed according to the purely musical demands of the subject, guided only by his own highly developed sensibilities, and regardless of the circumstances, be they romantic, tragic, religious, or whatever, that attended the material in its primitive state.

The only question, then, is whether Indian songs are endowed with such extreme flexibility as is essential to their highest development as musical subjects.

So far as we can judge from the "Indian Suite," Mr. Macdowell encountered no serious difficulties in that regard. A criticism of the work which I have often heard runs to the effect that the music is not Indian at all; that the composer may have chosen Indian material to start with, but that he quickly deserted it for matter of his own making. Good! Why not? Analytical inspection will show that the matter of his own making was derived from or suggested by the original material.

Therein lies the triumph of the material, that, crude, imperfect though it may have been, through it, nevertheless, the composer succeeded in expressing his own individuality.

It may well be that Mr. Macdowell was not satisfied with his experiment. The raw material available to him was far from being as suggestive and interesting as much that has been uncovered since. He had not made personal excursions to the Indian country to hear the songs and absorb the inspiring atmosphere attendant upon them there. His was purely an academic view of the material, and his use of it was necessarily objective in character. The main consideration is, however, that such material as he had was made to serve his purposes in a varied and brilliant composition.

A work that adheres more closely to its thematic subject is Mr. Arthur Farwell's "Dawn," a romantic composition based upon what has always seemed to me the best song in Miss Fletcher's Omaha collection. This has been published in pianoforte arrangement and is, therefore, available to students. They will find it not only a highly developed but a remarkably attractive composition. I may add that, before Mr. Farwell's work was published, I had experimented with the same material, turning it into rather a long song for tenor voice with accompaniment for flute and pianoforte. It has not been published, and I mention it merely to show that two men working at the same material have found it sufficiently flexible for their respective purposes.

Both Mr. Farwell and Mr. Harvey Worthington Loomis have made several transcriptions of Indian songs for pianoforte, that have been published and are decidedly worth examination although they do not throw direct light on the immediate question—the susceptibility of the material to thematic development. Passing mention must be made of them, not only to complete the record as to our primitive music, but for this significant reason, also: they chose for their pianoforte pieces songs that had so little appeal for me that I had discarded them as of no artistic value. I was mistaken. These gentlemen saw better than I did. Theirs was the academic view, as was mine at the time I cast the melodies aside, for I I had not then heard Ojibways sing, and had had no association with Indians. This circumstance I regard as extremely suggestive and important. The harmonies of Messrs. Farwell and Loomis have revealed the melodies to me so clearly that I wonder now how they failed to interest me at first. The presumption is, therefore, that the entire primitive output is worth studying, and that composers will find in it somewhere a wealth of suggestion that will pay them well to discover.

I think the only other experiments in the extension of Indian themes have been my own. The "Dance of Paupukkeewis," previously mentioned, was written years before I had become an enthusiast in our primitive music. For the limited purpose it was designed to serve, the Indian theme was decidedly useful, and development was spontaneous. When the Indian play, "Hiawatha," was brought to the cities, in 1903, I was put to the hurried necessity of writing considerable incidental music for it. The several pieces included an introduction, or overture, with a long, declamatory song for bass voice, a funeral march, a set of variations (on the song, "Old Shoes"), interludes, and so forth, and a finale for solo voice, chorus and orchestra. All of these were developed from Ojibway songs. None of the orchestral pieces have been reduced to a comprehensible pianoforte version, and they are, of course, unpublished, but a somewhat compressed version of the finale is printed elsewhere in this book. I do not refer to it as a model, and if the other pieces were published I should hesitate to refer to them. Mention is made of them in order that one composer, at least, may give the tribute of his evidence to the inspiring quality of the material. It proved, so far as I was concerned, that the Ojibway songs developed themselves, and that the result was as coherent and spontaneous as anything of mine could be. I must believe, therefore, that other composers would have similar experience with such material.

### A CALL FOR SACRIFICE.

Discussion of the flexibility of Indian themes seemed to me a necessary preliminary to the appeal to patriotism. I am still addressing myself to young composers. I know their moods, their exaltation in creative work, their exuberance, their dreams, and I think no one can know better than I their firm belief in individuality, and their fondness for matter of their own making. The strains that sing spontaneously in their minds and find their way to paper are divinely beautiful. They are the very voice of the Infinite speaking through a special messenger. I know, for I have been that messenger. I have covered many pages of ruled paper with notes that represented such a stirring of the blood, such aspirations, such supreme confidence in the future, such worshipful awe, as the non-musical mortal wots not of. I know what rebellion storms in the soul when the professor condemns a melody, or runs his devastating pencil through a harmonic progression. ( For "professor" in the outside world, read critics, conductors and public.) How often have I glumly assented to the professor's changes in my manuscript in the classroom, only to restore the composition to its original form in the privacy of my chamber! My heaven-directed way was right; it could not be wrong, because that was the way the music spontaneously came; the professor's way was pedantic, rigidly correct, with no regard for sentiment. I remember very well my early contempt for that process of composition which deliberately sought folksong as thematic material. When I could not invent my own themes, I would not write. I was not so far removed from my storm and stress period when the suggestion was first made to me that my music might be joined to that of the Indians in their play. I was offended!

The purpose of this heart-to-heart talk must be obvious. I want those to whom it is addressed to realize that I am in hearty sympathy with them, and that I am conscious that my appeal for the employment of Indian themes is a call for a certain degree of sacrifice on their part. In the same spirit in which I harked back to my storm and stress period, I urge consideration of the fact that a relatively small proportion of a composer's output is as divinely beautiful as it seems to be at the time of its creation. It was all worth doing, if for no more than the compensation of the glorious moments when it took shape; it was worth doing in the light of cold, after-years judgment in that it strengthened the creative faculty by exercise. The time comes when the composer recognizes that self criticism is quite as essential to artistic success as fertility of invention, and he perceives that there is no exercise of composition better adapted to the cultivation of self criticism than the development of non-original themes. There truly is the artist at work, undertaking to get the best out of a given material; and he finds, after some initial sense of restraint perhaps, that his individuality can manifest itself in the shaping of work from given material quite as well as in the development of original themes. In behalf, then, of the desire to give our music a distinctive color, if not style, I urge that the composer sacrifice the demands of individuality for self expression and devote attention to native material of which the specimens in this book are but a minute fraction.

Here is proposed a definite policy to which gifts and attainments may properly be directed. It might be adopted from a sane desire to see for one's self what worth there may be in music sprung from our soil, and it certainly should be inspired by patriotic eagerness that our country should prove to be not behind others in melodic resources, but as richly endowed as any land that ever had boundaries. Thus I believe it to be, for, knowing that the field I have covered personally is a very small fraction of the whole, I am sure that similar investigation among other peoples than the Ojibway would be rewarded by an abundance of suggestive melody if not of pure song. The Ojibway field itself has been but scratched. Work therein remains to be done by somebody that would surely uncover not less than five times the quantity of material that I have gathered. It may be that this work will continue to be neglected, but, even so, there is already in the museums a great quantity of material on phonographic records, and this will gradually be reduced to notes. I am sure the time will come, after living Indians no longer remember their songs, when white men will turn to the phonographic records to learn what was the nature of the red men's music, and that they will certainly then regret that such a vast proportion of it should have been allowed to lapse into oblivion. And when that time comes be sure that the composers of the day will take account of such native stock as is available. It behooves the present generation of composers, and the next that is to follow, to give attention to this matter without delay.

### THE VALUE OF PLAIN TUNE.

There is one final view of the subject that requires brief presentation. The art of music, speaking generally, has been brought to a condition of artificiality that is positively unwholesome. There is need for more direct utterance, which means that pure melody, or, as I prefer to call it, plain tune, should be advanced to a higher plane than it now occupies in composition. Our masters have built a huge and wonderful fabric which called for gigantic skill in the manipulation of the material. The result is impressive for its workmanship; it amazes, startles, bewilders, and sends us homeward wondering what it is that we have heard.   We carry away little but an impression of overwhelming complexity.   The intellect admires, but there is seldom a single shred of tune to take hold of the affections.   The sincere student of composition is in real danger from the high development of technical ability that is manifest in contemporaneous works.   He feels that he must perfect himself in workmanship, and he knows, or ought to know, that it is the endless study of a lifetime.   In the striving for technical finish he is apt to overlook the fact that what makes music vital is melody; and if he be not careful he will come to despise, or distrust the plain speech of tune as something trivial, fit only for the multitude.

The time is ripe for a change that might be regarded as a reversion to an older style.   The best critics voice the demand incessantly in their comments on contemporaneous programmes.   It appears that our present day masters either dare not, or cannot write a plain tune into their works.   They appear to feel the necessity of proving their erudition by works of bewildering complexity in which the real, spontaneous musical thought, if there be any, is deftly concealed.   This is remarkable in view of the fact that the most highly esteemed concert work of our time is an example of the older style.   Apparently the significant lesson it teaches has not been so much as apprehended by the present generation.   I allude to Dvorak's "New World" symphony.   Therein is manifested superb workmanship; the themes are developed according to methods long established; no conceited innovater speaks there; within the limits of classical form the composer found the broadest room for the expression of his individual genius; and he based his entire work, every movement, upon simple, spontaneous tunes, deriving abundance of suggestion from them, and never finding that the plain melodies restricted the flow of his fancy.

I am glad that but one native American theme appears in the work. A master hand touched it and it became transfigured. So it would be with the songs of the Ojibways, for there is not one tune in the "New World" symphony that is more beautiful than are many that were created by my fellow-tribesmen. They await the transfiguring touch of a native American, one who knows his country through acquaintance with its broad plains and lofty mountains; who loves the silent rivers of its forests, and exults in the roar of its waterfalls; who has somewhat more than magazine knowledge of the conquering pioneer and the subjugated red man.

By all means let us have workmanship, let there be no end of striving for the best that can be accomplished through it; but let us be very sure that the material to which the workman lays his hand is worthy.

It is a proper objection that music of permanent value cannot well be constructed on material that does not appeal to either composer or public. I am sometimes told that the Ojibway songs seem strange. A Boston critic once wrote of them as having "exotic" interest. Their strangeness is no discredit to their beauty. It is another way of saying that they are distinctive. It is a common experience to approach something exotic with timidity and eventually hug it to the bosom as a fond possession. Time is admittedly necessary in this matter, and a beginning has hardly been made. The point for immediate consideration is this: here is good music; should we not, by putting it forward in one form and another, give the public opportunity to learn what it is, and to like it?

When all is said, it will remain for every composer to select his material according to his own predilections and taste. I do not overlook the fact that Indian songs are not the only native material available. There are American critics who have taken the "rag-time" songs into serious account as an expression of the popular fancy. My opinion is that the popularity of such music is transient, merely; it is the whim of the moment and will give way presently to something else. Meantime I can no more regard the employment of "rag-time," which is nothing but a mannerism, as expressive of our national spirit than I could assert that John Sebastian Bach's employment of syncopation, which is the technical term for rag-time, was a forecast of the grand cosmopolitanism of my people. I am much more in sympathy with those who would look to the plantation songs for distinctive color, still more with those who would approximate as closely as possible to the beginnings of an American folksong made for us by Stephen C. Foster. I do not feel that it is incumbent on me to discuss these other sources of melody, my province being that of the music that is truly and wholly indigenous to our soil; and, in bringing this part of the book to a close, I am glad to add to the record of achievements in our primitive music the fact that Mr. Carlos Troyer has published several stirring songs, the material for which he found in the music of the Zuñis. These are the people, it will be remembered, whose musical advancement is so slight that their scales are regarded as in the process of forming, and whose intervals are apparently adiatonic. It is all the more significant, therefore, that an accomplished musician has found in the material the inspiration for good, thoroughly characteristic music adapted to the uses of civili- zation. Another composer who has experimented success- fully with Indian melodies is Mr. Charles Wakefield Cad- man, of Pittsburg, and I am more than delighted to record that he has undertaken to go personally into the field for the purpose of gathering material at first hand. This is what I wish could be done by all who take interest in the subject. Academic con- sideration of the material is good, but far better is study of it in its place of origin. There insensibly the composer must find himself more closely attuned to Nature. To flee from the ar- tificialities of civilized life, and dwell for a time among the simple people of the forests and plains, is wholesome in itself and must inevitably react happily on the composer's output.

CONCLUSION.

The foregoing pages contain some facts and a good many opinions. Facts are the main thing, and what may be regarded as the report proper of my research in the field will be found in the pages that follow. Discussion of scales, rhythm, verse, and so forth, seemed to me necessary to a thorough understanding of the songs themselves. Let the opinions go; the salient fact re- mains that there is on this continent a wonderful fund of primi- tive music that is rapidly disappearing with the Indians' advance toward civilization.   It is a fact that this music deserves preservation.   It is a fact that it needs, and some day such of it as has been preserved will have, comprehensive study on the part of a competent musician, or musicians.   It is a fact that this generation bids fair to be as remiss in the matter as were the generations that preceded it.   There ought to be organized effort for the preservation and understanding of this music if for no other purpose than to make of it an enduring monument to a vanishing race.   So far as the songs that follow are concerned, the fact that they were gathered for the most part in Canada is a point of no vital importance.   This continent was the Indians' before the palefaces came to it, the Ojibways live on both sides of the arbitrary line that separates the two countries, and whatever the American Indian has to offer is our spoil of conquest quite as much as it is Canada's.   If Canadian composers should grasp the opportunity to base their art on aboriginal songs found within their borders, and thus evolve a music that should speak distinctively for their country, so much the better for them and so much the worse for us.

With this contribution to the subject I must regard my own work as finished.   It has been conducted in a spirit of love and enthusiasm, and I leave it with deep regret.   It is work that requires either the possession of independent means, or organized support, and I have had neither.   Hopeful that in the not distant future some person or persons may undertake to continue my especial work among the Ojibways, I hereby pledge myself to aid by advice drawn from experience, by introductions to Indians, missionaries and school teachers, and by any other means that lie in my power.

## CHAPTER X

## OJIBWAY SONGS AND THEIR STORIES

IT has been shown that thorough understanding of an Ojibway song depends upon knowledge of the story, ceremony, or special circumstance with which it is associated
in the Indian's mind. For this reason it seems to me that
it will be most helpful to the student to present the melodies I
have collected in connection with their stories, rather than com-
·press them into a few pages of printed music. All the melodies, therefore, will be found in this chapter, and such as I have
seen fit to harmonize may be seen also in their civilized garb in
the second part of the book.

For various reasons it has not been possible in every instance
to give the Ojibway words. Indian singers are as care-
less in the matter of enunciation as are whites. It was seldom
that I could catch all the words of a song even after several
repetitions, and when I asked that they be dictated to me slowly
I found that I was setting the Indian a very difficult task. In
his dictation he would sometimes omit words that I had plainly
heard him sing, and as frequently insert words that were not
in the song as sung. His spoken words, too, were often in an
order that differed from those that were sung, and I cannot recall one occasion where an Indian in his dictation remembered
to repeat words or phrases in the exact order, or as many times

as the repetitions occurred in the song. It might be thought, and I did think, that the phonograph would settle all doubt as to the words, but I found that that remarkable machine gives back the singer's enunciation rather less distinctly than the original, and on some of the cylinders the impressions are so faint that it is with difficulty that the melody itself can be distinguished. In every instance the songs in this collection have been referred to at least one Indian besides the singer for a statement as to the words and their meaning. The Indians, listening to the song as reproduced by the machine, often distinguishes words that are unintelligible to me, but sometimes he has to confess to missing a part of them. In such cases he gives me as nearly as he can the "general sense" of the song. Rev. Frederick Frost, of Garden River, Ontario, who has been a missionary among the Ojibways for more than thirty years, and to whom several of these songs were referred for elucidation, tells me that many of the words are archaic; that is, not in current use, and that the Indians themselves have forgotten what they mean.

Those who have pursued research among Indians will understand why, in some instances, I could not venture to pursue elusive words doggedly until the original and the correct translation had been obtained. More than once I had an Indian singing after weeks of patient waiting; he would become interested, and if let alone, would sing perhaps a dozen songs; stop him to make particular inquiry as to words, meaning, or other details, and he would almost certainly lose his enthusiasm and cease singing before he had finished his list. So, anxious

in the main for melodies, I let the Indian sing on, trusting to
the phonograph, and other Indians and missionaries for a dig-
ging out of the words.

There are a few examples where I do not care to give either
the original words, or a translation of them.  Primitive ideas
of humor and love are not always in accord with modern refinement, and I cannot see that any good is accomplished by
making permanent record of what the civilized Indian is slowly
but steadily discarding as repugnant to his awakened sensibilities.  That he is discarding vulgarity is fact, not sentimental
fancy.  Some evidence of it may be found in these songs.  I
overheard an Ojibway woman urge her husband not to let Mr.
Burton hear a certain song, because it was a "bad" song.  I
heard it, and the words are untranslatable, but the melody is
beautiful.  On more than one occasion a singer, convinced that
I wanted him to sing into the machine a melody I had heard,
complied but mumbled certain words so incoherently that the
most learned Ojibway could not tell what they were.  They
were words that gave an offensive meaning to the song.

In the translations that accompany the harmonized versions I
have tried, as heretofore indicated, to set forth the Indian's
whole thought, turning into the English text not only the words
actually sung, but others to express the attendant story or
circumstances.  I have called attention to the fact that many of
the love songs express the same thought, or deal with the same
situation, with little variation in the phraseology.  For this
reason I have ventured in two or three instances to take the
suggestion for English words from a song to which the melody

does not apply. All such liberties are acknowledged in the course of the text that follows where the songs have been arranged not in the order in which I found them, but according to classification with regard to their subjects and purpose. As it is the largest class and melodically perhaps the most interesting, I begin with

LOVE SONGS.

*My Bark Canoe.* The story of this song has been told in Chapter VIII. There is only this further to be said of it—that I reduced it to notes at a time when the Indians were putting all possible obstacles in my way. I had to hear the song from a distance, and no Indian could be persuaded to sing it to me in private. At that time the melody sounded to me as it is given in the harmonized versions. Later when the Indians willingly aided me in my work, I noticed that at the end of the first 4-4 measure there occurred a passing note over the syllable *kah*. The variation is unessential, and whether it was there in the beginning, or developed subsequent to my first hearing of the song, I do not know. As recorded by the phonograph words and music are as follows:

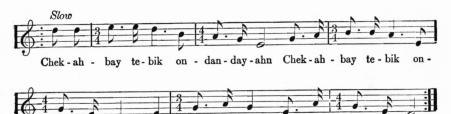

Chek - ah - bay te - bik on - dan - day - ahn Chek - ah - bay te - bik on -

dan - day - ahn ah - gah - mah si - bi on - dan - day - ahn

Translation: I am out all night on the river.

*Wedding Song.*   The attendant circumstances by which this
song is to be interpreted are suggested by the title.   See Chapter VIII.   Words and music:

Bayz - hig   e - qua - zess   ne   me   ne - gon - un   kay - get   sen - nah

neg - e - che - day - be   e - go   hey - ah   hey - ah   hey - ah   hey - ah   hey - ah

hey - ah   hey - ah   hey - ah   Bayz - hig   e - qua - zess   ne   me   ne - gon - un

kay - get   sen - nah   neg - e - che - day - be   e - go,   hey - ah   hey - ah   hey - ah

hey - ah   hey - ah   hey - ah   hey - ah   hey - ah   hey - ah   hey - ah   hey - ah

Translation:   A girl has been given to me; yes, I am very
glad that she has been given to me.

---

*Lonely.*   Two versions of this song are on the phonographic
cylinders.   The first was sung by a woman who was so dread-
fully embarrassed that hardly a word was intelligible, and
the moment she had finished she fled.   Her son volunteered to

give me the English of the song.   I copy here the translation.
he wrote in my note book:

"do not worrie When you heair that I am gon if you go⸱
away aginst my will I will have to go and my jurney will be⸱
to that island for Out in Lake I will be that loonsom loonsom⸱
loonsom."

He explained that two persons are supposed to be speaking,⸱
the first a man who announces that he is going on a journey.
Then his sweetheart breaks in with a protest, declaring that if⸱
he goes she will have to follow to the distant island, and crying⸱
that she will be lonesome.   Another Indian who heard the song⸱
as reproduced by the phonograph, recognized it as one familiar⸱
in his youth, but could not distinguish the singer's words.   He⸱
assured me, however, that the meaning, as he remembered, was⸱
substantially such as the singer's son had written.   Some weeks⸱
later a younger woman sang for me, and one of her songs was⸱
melodically a variation of this one, the words meaning, "My⸱
sweetheart is going away and I shall be lonesome, lonesome,⸱
lonesome."   Both melodic versions are given here, and both are⸱
used in the harmonized version on other pages.

*Her Shadow.* Original words uncertain. They tell of a lover seeking his sweetheart in a canoe; he sees her shadow on the beach and says that when he is sure it is she he will shout to her to await his arrival. After several repetitions of the melody the singer always concludes with a falsetto yell. The words are pieced out with nonsense syllables which, with the yell, are reproduced in the harmonized version.

*A Song of Absence and Longing.* ·I notated and published this song before the idea of making a thorough study of Ojibway music had taken hold of me. To make it more available for white singers I transposed the ending an octave. Many of the Ojibways, having heard the English version, now use the higher ending. The original form follows.

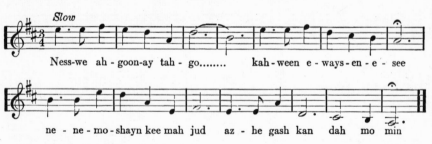

Translation: For three days I have been hungry; I have

eaten nothing. My sweetheart is absent and I am very sorrowful.

---

*Morning Tryst.* Originally another lonesome song. It is said to have been composed in the time of the great Shingwauk, the occasion being the departure of a warrior on the warpath. Another version of the melody occurs on the phonographic cylinders to words of a radically different character, unless we admit that remorse over drunkenness is at last analysis the same as grief over the absence of a loved one. The first version:

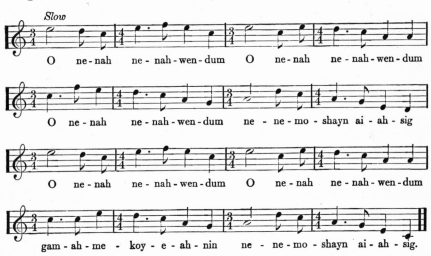

Translation: Oh! I am very lonesome; my sweetheart is absent.

Second version:

The Ojibway words of this version are not quite clear, but

they mean: Listen to me; I am full.    It is all my own fault that I am drunk.

In the harmonized version I have departed from both texts and based the words upon a type of Indian song that is frequently to be found among more tribes than the Ojibways.

---

*The Lake Sheen.*   This song was discussed at length in Chapter V, where may be found three versions of its melody and words.    It is also among the harmonized songs.    The version generally heard to-day follows:

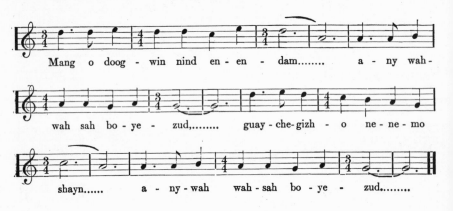

Mang o doog - win nind en - en - dam........ a - ny wah- wah sah bo - ye - zud,........ guay - che-gizh - o ne - ne - mo shayn...... a - ny - wah wah - sah bo - ye - zud........

---

*Waubunosa's Longing.*   So called from the name of the singer.    This was sufficiently discussed in Chapter VIII. Following is the phonographic version of melody and words:

*Slow*

Ah - yah!...... nen - e - mosh - ay - non de - gui - shid, Ah - yah!.....

nen - e - mosh - ay - non de - guish - id, Ah - yah! nen - e - mosh - ay - non de -

guis - hid, Ah - yah!... nen - e - mosh-ay-non de - guish - id. Ah - yah!...

nes-ah we - nah - o - we- quay-zans. ah - yah! ne sul gay-gal ped- ah-guish-ing.

---

*Midnight Tryst.* No comment or explanation necessary.

*Rather slow*

Be- jah- kah nin-de-go - bun nin-de - go-bun nin-de - go - bun be-jah-

kah niu-de-go - bun a - pe - tah ti - bi - kuk be - jah - kah nin - de -

go - bun nin-de - go - bun be - jah - kah nin-de-go - bun.

Translation: She has promised to meet me at midnight.

---

*Red Blanket*.  Although I heard this song early in my acquaintance with the Ojibways I did not put it on paper until it had been sung into the phonograph; for I had my doubt as to its origin.  It is a lively trifle that sounds as if it might have been culled from an Offenbach operetta.  But the Ojibways, men and women, insist that it originated with themselves ages ago.  They get immense enjoyment from it, apparently finding in it a meaning that is hidden from me.  As a rule a woman is called on to sing it, and she heightens the interest by dancing while she sings.  I am told that the bark referred to is the tamarack, and that the purpose of gathering it is to make a fire in the teepee.

Ay-quay-quog nin-gah - de - jah  min     ne - ne - mo-shayn nin-gah- we - je - ah

mis - koo - ah    nin - gah -mah-jah - od    wah - boy - on    nin - gah-mah - je - dun.

Translation: I will go to the edge of the forest and gather bark for my sweetheart.

----

*Waiting*:  The words as sung cannot be reproduced with certainty.  They were dictated as follows:

*Bejeenug ningahbedugweshing keegee e nen ningahdayahmah kayaygeen kaygo kewenemohkayn.*

Translated: I'll be here before long; don't get tired of waiting and don't disappoint me.

*Banished.* This is a long song for an Ojibway. It was sung with such evident feeling as to be deeply impressive. I tried to get the words but the singer dictated a few and then stopped. The phonograph does not disclose the remainder with any degree of certainty, but an Indian interpreter gives the following as the substantial meaning of them all:

There is a hill to be climbed, and you must keep climbing if you want to get home. Take a knife to defend yourself. The way is long and you will weary, but you must keep going.

The song becomes clear in the light of an old custom. A young man's parents exercised absolute authority over his marriage. If he brought to the parental wigwam a bride of whom the old people did not approve, they refused to receive her, and he had to send her back whence she came. This song, then, is the heart broken lament of a lover who brought home a wife from a distant village and was compelled to send her away.

*An Odowah Song.* The Ojibways of the Lake Superior region refer to certain Indians who live on or near their reservations as "Dowahs," or "Odowahs." They are presumably Ottawas, a branch of the Algonquin stock, whose language few Ojibways understand. The man who sang this said that it was an "Odowah love song," and it is therefore included among the love songs although nobody to whom it has been submitted can get any meaning from it.

*No. 31 (b).*  This, and similar designations, refer to the
number of the phonographic cylinders whereon the song may be
found.   The words, many times repeated, mean: "I am going
far away, my swetheart."

*No. 32 (a).*   Untranslatable.

*No. 33 (c).*  From the spirit with which men sing this the
listener might suppose it to be a war song.   The words as dictated: *Jangwayshequess ne dahguahdahmad go ne ningeyah-
gah me ahgo.*  Translated: They say I took away another
man's sweetheart, but this is jealous gossip.

No. *39 (a)*. The only words that are audible mean, "I can see his face."

No. *39 (b)*. The words mean: "I don't see why you disappoint me. I have kept my promises to you, but you have disappointed me."

No. *39 (c)*. The interpreter surmises that this is the utterance of a man who has been rejected. He gives this as the meaning: "I am going to leave you; no use in staying any longer."

No. *41 (a)*.  Untranslatable.

No. *41 (b)*.  The words as dictated: *Megowahbung cheb-oyean asahkomik chinahdead mahmoway waynezesing ningah-nahdeod wenzesing nin bedenwah nenemoshayn.*  Translated: "Early in the morning I will take my canoe to go and gather the moss I am asked to get, and I will get the best I can find. Afterwards I will bring it to my sweetheart."

The moss referred to is a kind used by the Ojibways for wrapping babies in.

*No. 42 (b)*. This song is interesting as an example of Indian humor. Early in the summer of 1904 I became acquainted with a woman who was said to be a good singer, but I could not induce her to go near the phonograph, or sing to me alone. She put me off with one excuse or another, always good humoredly and with so much joking that we never failed to laugh when we met. Often she declared that I never would persuade her to make a fool of herself by singing into "that thing," meaning the phonograph. One evening I joined a social party around a campfire. Songs were sung, stories told, and there were several general dances. At the height of the fun I managed to bring her to the centre and make her dance alone. Then she insisted that I should dance with her, which

I did to the best of my ability, and much to the amusement of the crowd. There was no end of fun over it, and when I saw her next morning in the cabin where I kept my phonograph, knowing that she would be unusually good natured, I decided to make another try for a song. I strolled in and the customary bantering began. Bringing the talk around to music, I declared it to be my conviction that Ojibway women knew only one cradle song, "The Naked Bear." She promptly denied it, saying that she knew another herself.

"What good does that do," I asked, "when you don't know how to sing it?"

"I do know how," she cried indignantly. "I sang it times enough to all my children."

I laughed at her, saying that what she sang was "The Naked Bear," and that she didn't know the difference. With a contemptuous exclamation she ran to the phonograph and demanded that I set it going. I complied with a fine air of indifference and she proceeded to sing the cradle song I call "Sleepy Time," which will be found in its appropriate place. Then she said, "Now I will sing you a song all for yourself," and she sang the following melody:

[a laugh]

I was not sufficiently versed in Ojibway to follow it closely, but when I referred it later to my interpreter he laughed heartily. It seems that the melody is that of an old time love song, but that the singer had extemporized words that applied wholly to myself. It was her joke on the notator, and she was much put out when she learned that I had discovered the trick. I may add here that extemporizing words, especially names of persons, in songs to give them an immediate application is not at all uncommon at Ojibway social gatherings.

*No. 29 (b).*   The singer announced that this was a love song, but the words are indistinguishable and no interpreter has hazarded a guess at their meaning.

*No. 35 (a).*   The words are not clear but the interpreter gathers that the song is a lament over the prolonged absence of somebody.

*No. 35 (b).*   The words appear to mean "I come from the mountain with my sweetheart."

SOCIAL SONGS.

Under this caption are included not only songs that seem to be used only at social gatherings, but cradle, humorous and drinking songs.

*Parting.* To me this is a most lugubrious tune, but it represents the Ojibway's conception of a jovial song. It came to light under romantic circumstances. While the Indian play, "Hiawatha," was running during the summer of 1902 at Desbarats, Ont., Tekumegezhik Shawano, who played the title role, was married to Margaret Waubunosa, the Minnehaha of the cast. As the wedding day approached it was suggested to the Indian actors that they take note of the event by introducing a festal song in the scene known as "The Wedding Festivities." The word "festal" was not used in conveying the suggestion, but pains were taken to impress the Indians with the fact that what was wanted was such a song as they would sing on a jolly occasion. They were asked if they had any song of that character and replied that they knew many; they would think it over and select one. After three days of thinking it over they announced that they had decided on a very ancient song that was just the thing for the occasion. When I heard it roared forth by forty powerful voices at a solemn adagio, I thought there must have been some mistake, but when I understood the words I knew that, from the Indian point of view, nothing could have been more appropriate.

Am - bay - ge - way - do...... che - wah - de - bah - bun kee - gah - gee -

kay ne - me - go - min...... ka - hen - ah kon - e - gay - aung.

Translation: Let us go home before daybreak or people will find out what we have been doing.

---

*Winter.*  The story of this song was told in Chapter VIII.

Ke - zho - yah 'shquan-daym ke - zho - yah 'shquan-daym ke - zho -

yah 'shquandaym baybogin 'shquandaym. Kezho - yah squandaym ke-zho -

yah 'shquan-daym, bay - bo - gin 'shquandaym ke-zho - yah 'shquandaym.

Translation: My door is warm in winter time.

*Forest Song.* See Chapter VIII for story and revised words. The tune is varied slightly by some singers, the variants being indicated here by small notes, the large notes indicating the version reproduced by the phonograph.

Me - ne nah - gay nah - gay...... ne - nah kee - wash -
quay - be...... ah - be - ding me - ne quay - on nah suh nah gah -
nah - way ne me shin o zah me be - yod go shu neen.

Translation: I don't suppose I'll get drunk if I take one drink; if I should get drunk, take care of me.

---

*Old Shoes.* Originally a gambling song but often sung now without reference to its application. See Chapter VIII.

Muj - je muk - e - sin aw - yaw - yon muj - je muk - e - sin aw - yaw - yon
muj - je muk - e - sin aw - yaw - yon muj - je muk - e - sin aw - yaw - yon.

Translation: I use bad shoes.

*Gambling Song.* A sequel to the foregoing, sung only in the course of the moccasin game with direct application to a turn in the play. See Chapter VIII.

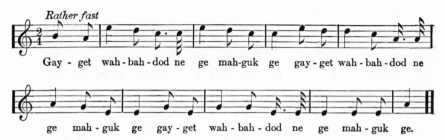

Gay - get wah - bah - dod ne   ge   mah-guk   ge   gay - get wah - bah - dod ne   ge   mah - guk   ge   gay - get   wah - bah - dod   ne   ge   mah - guk   ge.

Translation: Indeed, I know where it is.

---

*In the Sugar Camp.* The Ojibways knew the delicious merits of maple syrup and sugar long before the paleface came to them. Alexander Henry tells of one April during his captivity when he and the Indians with him had nothing but maple sugar to eat during the entire month. At this day even the civilized Ojibways lay in a stock of birch bark every June to be fashioned into pans for catching sap at the end of the following winter. It is a season to which they seem to look forward with great joy. At the right time whole villages move into the forest and pitch camp among the maples. There follow days of toil, men, women and children sharing in the work. At length all the sap is taken, much of it already has been converted into sugar, and time begins to hang heavy on idle hands. As evening comes on and all are resting, the young men take empty pans, and, headed by a drummer, dance grotesquely from one family shelter to another, singing this

song.  They hold out their pans for contributions of syrup
or sugar, and though their words are not explicit their actions
say "give, or we will take by force."  Usually the contributions are forthcoming good humoredly, but when they are not,
the young men invade the shelters of the niggardly, drive
out or overpower the occupants, and take as much sugar as
they think will teach the owners to behave more hospitably
in the future.

Translation: We look as if we could eat.

---

*A Drinking Duette.*   This was sung by a man and a woman,
but the result on the phonographic record is far from what was
designed.   It is a song with action, a dialogue with music.
The mechanical arrangements destroyed all freedom on the
part of the performers and embarrassed them so sadly that
even the musical phrases are undoubtedly distorted.   It is unlikely that anything of melodic value was lost, but I should
need to hear the duette several times to make sure of repre-

senting correctly a form of entertainment out of which the Indians get much pleasure. In the dialogue, fragments of which are spoken but most of which is sung, it appears that two lovers have been drinking and that the supply is exhausted. They lament this state of things, and the man interrupts his singing abruptly to exclaim, "I wish I had just one drink!" The response is to the effect that one drink would not be enough for two, and after further lamentations over their enforced sobriety they conclude: "It would do if we had one drink between us." The following melody is what the phonograph reproduces of the attempt to give me the duette:

Realizing that the effort was a failure from their point of view, the man then sang the following, repeating most of the words that had occurred in the dialogue:

*No. 20 (b):* This melody is often sung in the most spirited manner to meaningless syllables throughout. It has drum accompaniment of a regular character, the beats falling on the eighth notes. As a rule the song is used for an old time dance. I am not clear as to the meaning of the few words that sometimes appear in the first two measures.

Ne - mosh-ke-nug we - we - se se - ne - wug hey - ah hey - ah hey - ah

hey-ah hey-ah hey - ah hey - ah hey-ah hey-ah hey-ah hey hey-ah hey.

*Carousal.* Another song of the empty drinking cup. The usual explanation given to justify the odd words is that a party of young men undertook to have a drinking bout, but neglected to provide enough liquor to bring on a satisfactory condition of inebriety. Hence, the flask being empty, there was nothing for it but to go to sleep.

Kah nin-dah-ne- bah se- neen kah nin-dah-ne - bah se- neen ke tah- go- go-

bah gaun- je nan-ka ma min ne - quay aung kah nin-dah-ne - bah se-neen.

Translation: I wouldn't go to sleep if there was anything left to keep me awake.

*Visiting Song.* This was discussed in Chapter V.

Hey - ah   hey - ah   hey - ah   hey   hey - ah   hey   ah   hey -

ah   hey - ah   hey - ah   hey - ah   ah!   hey - ah   hey   hey-ah   hey - ah

hey - ah   hey   hey - ah   hey - ah   hey - ah   hey - ah   hey - ah   hah.

O - git - ko......   nem - ah - dah - bit......   nin - gah-nom - dog......   hey -

ah   hey   ah   hey - ah   hey - ah   ah   hey - ah   hey   hey-ah   hey - ah

hey - ah   hey   hey - ah   hey - ah   hey - ah   hey - ah   hey - ah   hey - ah.

Translation: Who sits on the ice can hear me singing.

*The Naked Bear.* It is this song from which Longfellow (through Schoolcraft) derived the line in "Hiawatha,"

"Hush! the Naked Bear will get thee."

It is explained in the glossary that is appended to most editions of the poem, that the Naked Bear is a mythical creature invented by Indian mothers to frighten their children into good behavior. The full text of the song shows that the screech owl was used in the same way. See Chapter VI.

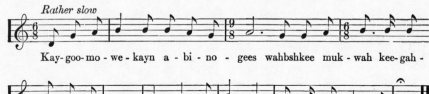

Kay-goo-mo-we-kayn a-bi-no-gees wahbshkee muk-wah kee-gah-

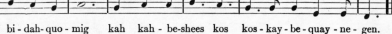

bi-dah-quo-mig    kah    kah-be-shees kos    kos-kay-be-quay-ne-gen.

Translation: Hush, little baby, go to sleep; do not cry, or the naked bear will eat you.

---

*Sleepy Time.* A cradle song made up almost wholly of meaningless syllables, "ayah, ayah" and so forth. In this respect it resembles many a lullaby that may be heard in civilized nurseries, and I may confess that melodically it appeals to me more strongly than any lullaby of paleface creation that it has been my fortune to hear. For the sake of making the little song of possible use to my own people I have ventured beyond the suggestion of the few Ojibway words, and, taking my cue from the Naked Bear and the screech owl, have invented a spider to figure in the harmonized version.

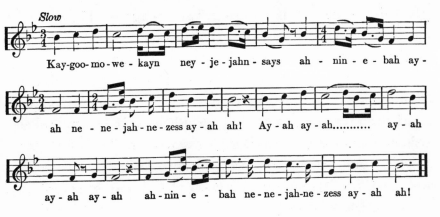

Kay-goo- mo -we - kayn    ney - je - jahn - says    ah - nin - e - bah ay -

ah  ne - ne - jah - ne - zess ay - ah  ah!    Ay - ah ay - ah............    ay - ah

ay - ah  ay - ah    ah - nin - e - bah  ne - ne - jah-ne - zess ay - ah  ah!

Translation: Don't cry, little one; go to sleep, baby.

---

*Firefly.* This is a song I hunted for in vain. Schoolcraft heard it about eighty years before my visits to Ojibway land. He set down the words and declared that they were the "wild improvisations of children in a merry mood." Schoolcraft further wrote that "in the hot summer evenings, the children of the Chippewa Algonquins (Ojibway) along the shores of the upper lakes frequently assemble before their parents' lodges and amuse themselves by little chants of various kinds, with shouts and dancing." That is, the children began early to entertain themselves after the manner of their elders, and there were songs for children as well as grown-ups. The historian was undoubtedly mistaken in assuming that the words of the Firefly song were wild improvisations of children. Had he been musician as well as historian, the tune would have told him that the words had been carefully arranged by somebody who had rudimentary poetic talent. But no matter. Longfellow turned the words to excellent advantage in "Hiawatha," and I was very desirous of coming upon the tune which I sought for in the precise neighborhood where Schoolcraft heard it. I was not successful. Nobody thereabout remembered the song, but a missionary among the Ojibways of Minnesota heard it and reduced it to notes which he sent to Dr. Baker while the latter was preparing his essay. Dr. Baker included it in his publication, and, with his permission, I include it here, also, for I think any collection of Ojibway songs would be incomplete without it.

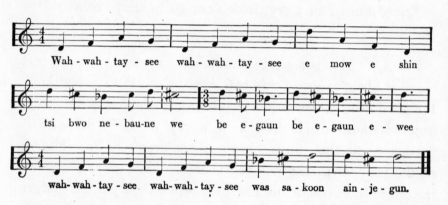

Wah - wah - tay - see    wah - wah - tay - see    e    mow    e    shin

tsi    bwo    ne - bau-ne    we    be    e - gaun    be    e - gaun    e - wee

wah- wah - tay - see    wah- wah - tay - see    was    sa - koon    ain - je - gun.

Translation: Flitting white-fire-insect, give me light before I go to bed. Light me when I go to sleep with your bright candle.

---

*Confession.* This endless song is immensely popular with the Ojibways. I have heard children sing it by the hour, but its main use is in social gatherings when some singer, usually a woman, sings it with a different proper name in each repetition, and with gestures to give unmistakable point to the words. The words here given are for a man to sing. *Kennamahshaynon Quakahbahnokwes* means, "You're my sweetheart, Quakahbahnokwes," the latter word being a girl's name. A woman, singing it, would use a man's name, and Ojibway women arouse much laughter by pointing to one man after another and calling his real name, or identifying him by some phrase the application of which is understood by all listeners. During a series of entertainments I gave with Indians in eastern cities I had a young woman sing the song and made a point by following it with a translation, accompanying it with gestures like her own. For the purposes of the entertainment my translation ran, "My sweetheart sits just over yonder." On one occasion the young woman staggered me and convulsed the Ojibways on the platform behind her by concluding the song with a gesture toward a man in the front row and singing the equivalent of "My sweetheart is that bald-headed man!"

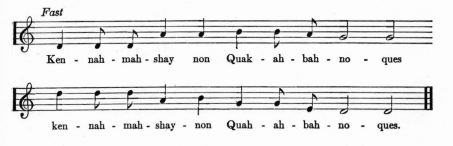

*The Forest Choir.* It is with deep regret that I find myself unable to set the Ojibway words of this song under their corresponding notes. One of the oldest Indians of my acquaint-

ance sàng it.   His name is Sagachewiose, but he is generally
known by the easier, less impressive name of Clark.   For a
long time he was averse to singing for me, but at length,
persuaded by his wife, who has been the Nokomis of the Indian
play from the beginning, he sat down before the phonograph
and in a businesslike way delivered sixteen songs to its cylinders.   Of course there was no stopping him till he had done,
and at the end I could get no assistance from him in the translations, for it is with difficulty that he sustains the simplest
conversation in English.   Some of the Ojibway words are perfectly distinct, others are hopelessly blurred, but Shingwauk,
who remembers the song from his boyhood, tells me that it is
an address partly to the singer's human friends, and partly to
the birds of the forest.   According to Shingwauk, "Listen
friends," the singer says, "our neighbors, the birds, are singing.   Pleasant are the sounds.   Let us sing with them."
Then, speaking to the birds, "Listen friends; you will enjoy
the sounds we make."

*No. 26 (a).* The words mean: "What are you looking around here for? I never had a call from you before. I believe you are coming to court one of my daughters."

*No. 17 (a).* To the eye this song seems to be barren of melody, and, reproduced upon the pianoforte, it is undeniably dry and monotonous; but, as sung by Tetebahbundung, it is decidedly impressive. The man's rich voice sounds to better advantage in this song than in any other. All whites who hear him sing it are charmed, and they usually ask for a repetition. The charm is undoubtedly due to the quality of Tetebahbundung's voice and the appearance of deep feeling that he manifests in all his vocal work. It is the feeling of the artist, merely; the natural emotion of one who loves music and exults in the beauty of his own tones. I am hazarding no sentimental guess here, for the song is calculated to arouse only laughter or disgust on the part of those who understand it, according to their respective conceptions of humor. It is a ballad, and the story it tells is vulgar to the last degree. There is especial interest to the musician in its ending brilliantly on a long sustained high note, contrary to the Indian custom of ending in the depths.

No. 29 (d). A drinking song. The words mean: "I don't think I ought to be drunk; I didn't drink enough; I had only one glass."

### SACRED SONGS.

Civilized man divides his songs into two great categories which are readily distinguishable: sacred and secular. In general, the sacred song has to do with the church. The line cannot be drawn in exactly the same way when Indian songs are under discussion. Any that had to do with religious ceremonies should undoubtedly be classed as sacred; but we have seen that, from the Indian's point of view, certain other songs were equally sacred. In this group, therefore, I include not only ceremonial songs and prayers, but such hunting songs as appear to have been used as prayers in the old days. There are other songs of animals that may have been regarded as sacred, and which even to-day serve for general dances, but as their character is obviously open to doubt, they will be found classified by themselves.

*A Song of Faith.*    This song and the one that follows were sung by the good pagan, Inniquahung, of whom some account was given in Chapter VI.

Hey - ah hey - ah hey - ah hey  hey - ah  ha...... hey - ah ha

hey - ah hey - ah  ha  hey - ah  hey - ah  ha  Un - je - du......

ma - ni - to  nin-ga - nom - dog  hey - ah ha  ?  hey - ah hey - ah

hey - ah  ha  hey - ah......  hey - ah ha  hey - ah hey - ah

hey - ah hey - ah  ha  hey - ah hey - ah hey - ah  ha  hey - ah

hey - ah  ha  hey - ha,  Un - je - du......  ma - ni - to  nin-ga-nom-dog

hey - ah ha  ?  hey - ah hey - ah hey - ah ha  hey - ah ha.

A—Syllables and notes are doubtful here, and at the corresponding place—B

Translation: Surely the spirit will hear my prayer.    Literally, will hear me singing; but the deep significance of the verb *nogom,* to which attention was called in a previous chapter, justifies the translation, prayer and song being inseparable; and, moreover, every Ojibway to whom these words have been referred for interpretation has indicated in one way or another that prayer is implied.

---

*The Omen.* Ojibways tell of a bird larger than the largest eagle that used to be seen in their country. It is possible that they have reference to some creature now extinct, but whatever it was, its appearance under certain conditions was regarded as an omen. For convenience the name of the bird may be translated "giant eagles." With that allowance, the song, literally translated, means, "While I was crying, the giant eagles lit on the sky." Exactly what this implies only an Indian could say, and I have found none who will hazard more than a frank guess. "Lit on the sky" probably is an expression for the poising of a bird in mid air, apparently motionless. One Indian guess as to the significance of the song has it that the author was in trouble, either personal or tribal, for he may have been a chief in doubt whether he should lead his people to war; that, in his grief, he sought for an omen to guide him and found it in the appearance of the great birds. In such case he would likely sing the song to his people as a prelude to announcing what he drew from the omen. Another Indian has told me that in the old days this song was sung on the eve of battle, the inference being that the appearance of the birds was a sign of victory.

Mayg - wah mah - we - od    ki - ne - wug  pe - boo - ne -

wug  ke - zhe-gung    mayg-wah mah-we - od    ki - ne - wug  pe - boo - ne -

wug  ke - zhe-gung,    mayg-wah mah-we - od    ki - ne - wug  pe - boo - ne -

wug    ke - zhe-gung    ki - ne - wug  pe - boo - ne - wug  ke - zhe-gung.

*A Song of Trust.*  No comment is required upon the words of this song which, translated literally, give an unmistakable expression of the singer's faith; but attention may be called to the fact that the significant words are interrupted by meaningless syllables.  My inference is that, crude though the melody is, the Indian had a definite conception of its form to which his significant words could not be adjusted; therefore, after the word *manito,* spirit, he injects *ayah hey* to fill out the musical phrase and then proceeds with the statement of his creed.

Hey - ah   hey - ah  hey - ah....  hey - ah  hey - ah  hey - ah  ha   ha

hey - ah  hey - ah  ah  hey - ah  hey - ah hey - ah ha hey - ah  hey - ah

hey - ah  hey - ah  hey - ah  ha  hey - ah  hey - ah  ha.

Kez-he - gung bay- mo - sed  ma - ni - to  a - yah hey ke - no - ah  bah -

me-nung hey - ah  hey  hey - ah  hey - ah  hey - ah  hey  hey- ah  hey  hey

hey - ah  hey  hey-ah  hey - ah  hey-ah  hey-ah  hey  hey- ah hey- ah hey.

Translation: The spirit walking in the sky takes care of us.

---

*The Morning Star.* Among the ceremonies of the ancient Ojibways was one that took place at daybreak and is often referred to as the "Morning Star." I have not come upon anybody who could describe the ceremony, but Mrs. Sagach-ewiose, who is remarkably well versed in Indian lore, and an adept in everything pertaining to the ancient mode of life, as-sures me that this song was an important feature of the ceremony, and that the words here given were the ones used in it. The civilized Ojibways retain the melody and sing all manner of words to it. The tune occurs several times on my phonographic cylinders, and no two sets of words are alike.

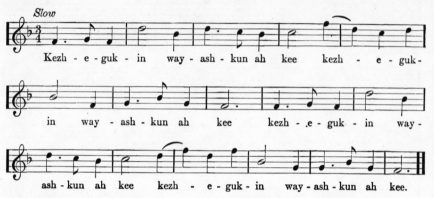

Translation: when it is day the earth is illuminated.

---

*All Birds Follow Me.* The title is a translation of the text and conveys all I know with certainty about the song save that it is widely popular. Melodically it is interesting on account of the apparent lack of relationship between the main part of the song and the ending. I have heard it at least one hundred times and have wondered often what tonal instinct it was that led the singer unerringly back to the initial tone after he had come to the end. Not only does no singer ever fail to hit the first tone squarely in a repetition, but every singer drops a count from the fourth measure, as indicated in the musical text. This appears to be one of the ancient religious, or mystical songs, the full significance of which has been forgotten.

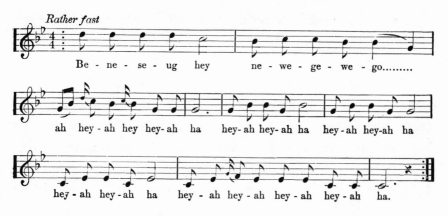

*Wabeno Song Cycle.* There are three classes of mystery men among the Ojibways, of which one is known as the Wabeno. W. J. Hoffman, writing on the "Grand Medicine Society" of the Ojibway, in the seventh annual report of the Bureau of Ethnology, has this, among other things, to say of the Wabeno: "The term has been explained by various intelligent Indians as signifying 'Men of the dawn,' 'Eastern men,' etc. Their profession is not thoroughly understood, and their number is so extremely limited that but little information respecting them can be obtained. . . : From personal investigation it has been ascertained that a Wabeno does not affiliate with others of his class so as to constitute a society, but indulges his pretensions individually. A Wabeno is primarily prompted by dreams or visions which may occur during his youth, for which purpose he leaves his village to fast for an indefinite number of days. It is positively affirmed that evil manitous favor his desires, and apart from his general routine of furnishing 'hunting medicine,' 'love powders,' etc., he pretends also to practice medical magic."

During my last summer with the Ojibways I became acquainted with an aged Wabeno from whom I obtained this cycle of songs and the mnemonic chart which is always used when they are sung. He pledged me most solemnly not to disclose his identity, for he was certain that trouble would come to him if I should do so. Just what the trouble might be he would not say, but another well informed Indian with whom I talked about Wabenos in general assured me, contrary to Mr. Hoffman's opinion, that there was a time when the Wabenos were affiliated in a society of some sort; that their incantations were profound secrets; and that betrayal of them was punishable with death. I asked him what would happen if a Wabeno should give me his hunting prayers.

"Well," he replied gravely, "there are a few Wabenos still left along Lake Superior, and if such a fact should come to their knowledge I think they would find some means of putting the traitor out of the way."

There may have been some vain imagining on the part of both Indians, possibly they sought to impress the paleface inquirer; but the fact is sufficiently established that these are peculiarly "sacred" songs. The man who gave them to me is nominally a Christian, but he never sets out upon a hunt without secretly saying these prayers to Nanabozho, the mysterious being about whom cluster all those stories that Longfellow told under the Iroquois name, Hiawatha. Their phraseology will not appeal to the civilized reader as prayerful, but it must be taken into account that the Ojibway prayer comprises more than words; there is ceremony of some kind, usually, as in this instance, a dance. Altogether it is a religious service which, taken as a whole, constitutes a petition, and the songs with their few words are but imperfect details.

The Wabeno, with evident reluctance—it had taken him weeks to consent—gave me a copy of his "prayer board." The original was probably drawn upon birch bark, but this was scrawled in pencil and subsequently burned with a hot iron on two thin cedar slabs. The grotesque figures on the prayer board do not constitute any sort of musical notation. No device for preserving their tunes was known to the Ojibways, charts of this kind serving simply to remind the singer of the words. No Indian could interpret this board unless he were himself a Wabeno, and the one I dealt with had great difficulty in making the matter clear to me. The central figure in each picture is Nanabozho. Observe that he is of gigantic stature as compared with animals and human beings. Tradition says that early in the days of the human race he called all the animals and birds together and informed them that thenceforth they must be subject to men. I have not been informed as to what Nanabozho told his creatures in detail, but it is fair to presume that he did not base his edict on hostility; for with all the Indian's reputed savagery, there is deeply ingrained in him a sentimental regard for animals that is manifested at times oddly, and at times with wisdom that shames the enlightened paleface. From the Indian's simple point of view the animal has the same right to life that man has. It is necessary

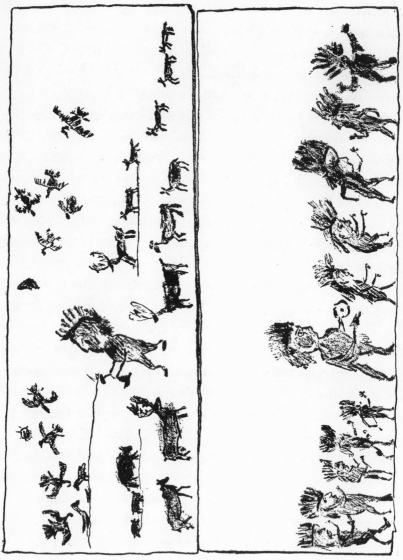

WABENO PRAYER-BOARD.

to use the animal for the subsistence of man, but the animal is sacrificed regretfully for this purpose. Henry tells how the Ojibways of his day offered a prayer of apology to the bear before going upon the hunt for him. They had ceremonies to propitiate the spirit of certain animals slain by them. The Ojibway of that time and the present does not hunt for the mere pleasure of killing. That he will pursue his game relentlessly, resort to any device to lure it to ambush, track a frightened deer for days over the treacherous crust and at last knock the exhausted animal on the head without a qualm of squeamishness, is true; and it is doubtless equally true that he exults in overcoming the forest beasts, big and little, that the death throbs of his prey awake a responsive thrill of joy in his breast; but the Ojibway does not kill more than he needs. When he has all that he can carry home, the slaughter ceases. It was not the Indian, and it never would have been the Indian, who destroyed the buffalo. It is not the Indian to-day who threatens to exterminate all the beautiful wild life of the Canadian forests.

But, to return to the prayer board, Nanabozho summons the animals and birds by beating a drum of the kettle type. An indulgent imagination will enable the reader to identify many of the beasts and birds pictured in the upper half of the board. It will be seen, too, that Nanabozho faces the rising sun. In the lower board are represented Nanabozho's favorites, the Wabenos, to whom he has given especial power over animal life. They are dancing while Nanabozho leads with a drum of the usual type, the dance and song being a grateful acknowledgment of Nanabozho's benevolence. As I understand it, this part of the prayer board has direct reference to the fifth song in the cycle.

Melodically these songs are of the slightest value. Owing to the drum strokes by which they were accompanied they are rhythmically distorted, and bar lines cannot be drawn with certainty. Neither the vocal nor drum scheme of accents was maintained rigidly in any of the songs. A most interesting feature of the performance was the fact that no drum was used. The Wabeno had instead a pair of "prayer sticks," pieces of cedar about eighteen inches long, slightly tapering, whittled smooth and charred by fire until they were black. With these in his hand he sat before the phonograph and rapped them together while he sang. Some idea of their rhythmic relation, or lack of it, to the song is indicated in the music text. At first he sang from memory, but he missed his words at the beginning of the third song and had to refer to the prayer board. I was unable to see how he contrived to correct himself from a consultation of the chart, but he did so and then went on steadily to the end.

The first song is merely a summons: *Wabeno ondass,* "Come, Wabenos."

A. From this point time values are approximate. The stick-beats continue without appreciable accent to the end.

In the second the summons is made more definite: *Wabeno ondass gaygo keeweewindumon,* "Come, Wabenos. I have something to teach you."

The waved bar lines indicate the probably correct division of the melody into measures. The stick-beats cannot be counted at first, but there are 14 in section A and 32 in B.

The third: *Nimbahbeog endenukongay ishkooday,* "I am waiting for you all by my campfire."

In section A there are 24 stick-beats.    At B the sticks coincide with the voice for a moment and then are beaten fast again.

The fourth: *Nendonayego,* "I am looking for you all." This song is sung much faster than the preceding three.

The triplets are clearly defined, but time values are approximate throughout.    At no point can the ratio of stick-beats to voice be established by counting.    These remarks apply also to the fifth song in the cycle.

The fifth: *Nendomogwah mojegisewod gahinohmojekisewug anishinabeg,* "Indians rejoice over what they have learned." This was sung at an exceedingly rapid tempo and with an appearance of considerable excitement.

*Buffalo Songs.* The Indian who sang these for me evidently believed that he was making a great concession and contributing something of rare importance. It had taken him a long time to decide that he would do so, and at the last moment he threatened to back out because a young man happened to pass the house. "I don't want any of the young fellows to hear these, or know that I sing them," he growled. Assured, at length, that no one was in hearing, he sang, but refused to dictate the words. Other Indians to whom the cylinders have been submitted say that the songs are prayers. They claim to understand the general purport of the songs but are not certain of all the words. According to Indian interpreters, the first song means: "I hear the tread of the buffalo in the distance; I wait for him in ambush."

The interpreter explains that this is a prayer that the buffalo may not smell the enemy and turn aside. Second song: "I have found the tracks; all are going around this way; we will go around, too, and head them off."

Third song: "I've followed him so far that his tongue is hanging out; he will have to go to the river to drink, and there I will kill him."

*Beaver Songs.* Although this interesting cycle was sung for me without any pretension of mystery or reluctance, it is probable that in the old days the songs were regarded as prayers. From our point of view the words have a decidedly secular character. The Indian singer was much wrought up as he approached the climax, and he finished with excitement that was infectious. As the songs give a coherent and rather vivid description of a beaver hunt, I will treat them as a whole rather than separately. In the first the singer is calm and sings as slowly as if the song were a hymn. He says: "My fire is burning bright before which I am sitting." That is, he has gone into the forest for beaver and pitched camp near a dam. He waits patiently and confidently for some sign of his game. The second song tells us that he has seen a beaver, but the animal dived quickly and the hunter had a glimpse only of his tail. He philosophically sits down again and resumes his waiting. In the third, where the words are so blurred that they cannot be set down under the notes, he has seen the beaver again. The speed of the song increases, but "while I was looking he went down and I lost him." The last, very rapid, is a song of triumph. "I got him by the back of the neck and I threw him into my canoe."

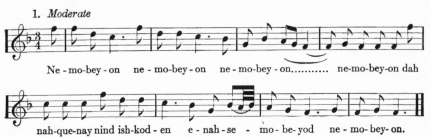

1. *Moderate*

Ne - mo-bey - on    ne - mo-bey - on    ne - mo-bey - on........... ne-mo-bey-on dah

nah-que-nay nind ish-kod - en    e - nah - se - mo - be- yod    ne - mo- bey- on.

**2.** *Faster*

Ay - ah yo ki - ne may mo kay - ah may ay - ah yo ki - ne

may mo kay - ah may zheg - wo - mo - kwah nind e - ge - non - day

ko nind e - ge - non - day e - ge - non - day.......

**3.** *Still faster*

Words uncertain

**4.** *Very fast*

Ne - nah - wod e - nah o - quay-gon - o - ning ne - nah - wod e - nah

o - quay - go - no - ning che - maun nin - gah - pu - ge - nah che-maun

nin-gah-pu - ge - nah ne - nah-wod e - nah o - quay-go - no-ning ne - nah-wod.

*No. 35 (c).*  The melody is the same as *No. 35 (a)* which was given under the love songs where it appears as a lament over an absent lover.  Here the words concern the ill luck of a hunter who was on the track of game and missed it.  "Let us be more careful," he says; "You can see the tracks again."

---

### SONGS OF ANIMALS AND BIRDS.

Here are included songs about which there is doubt whether they ever had any religious significance.

*Caribou Dance.*  Often sung on social occasions.  The caribou dance is an old time religious ceremony, a prayer for plenty. Caribou antlers are used by the leaders in the dance, the significance of which is derived from the fact that to the Ojibway the caribou is the most useful of animals.  From it he obtains some of his food, he makes garments from the skin, and he used to turn the antlers into household utensils.  An Ojibway proverb has it that "there is nothing wasted about the caribou."  When Christianized Ojibways give the caribou dance, as they often do for the entertainment of themselves or white visitors, they usually dance to this song; but the words are so frankly humorous that I infer that the real dance song was some other, perhaps the caribou song designated *No. 27 (c)*, the precise words of which I have been unable to obtain.

In winter the caribou finds food in a gray moss that grows on the rocks.  It appears to be abundant enough, and the animal browses upon it through the snow, but from the words of this

song the conclusion is inevitable that the moss is not over nu-
tritious.

Kah - ne' - tah we ne - no - see kah - ne' - tah
we ne - no - see wah - be - kuh mah - me zhey - ah min.

Translation: I seldom grow fat eating this gray moss. Following is another version of the same song:

Ka - ne - net - ah we ne - no - see kah - ne - net - ah
we ne - no - see wahb' kuh me mah - me zhey - ah min hey oh!

*Skunk Song.* The characteristic head dress of the Ojibway
consists in a skunk skin worn as a fillet with two feathers attached over the forehead and pointing horizontally in opposite
directions. I have often heard this garment referred to as a
cap. The skunk is taken in traps for the sake of its fur, and
this jolly song has to do with the method of taking the catch
home. For once the singer does not piece out his jubilation
with heyah heyah, but repeats his two words till the melody ends
and then begins again with the utmost enthusiasm. *Shekog-*

*quean baydahbahnug,* "I drag the skunks behind me," means that the trapper has found his traps well filled on a winter morning. He has occupied himself as long as need be in killing and skinning the animals. Then he takes one skin, or more if necessary, and makes a sled of it, packing the other skins upon it, attaches a thong to the load and proceeds cheerfully homeward drawing his catch behind him and, theoretically at all events, singing the song as he goes.

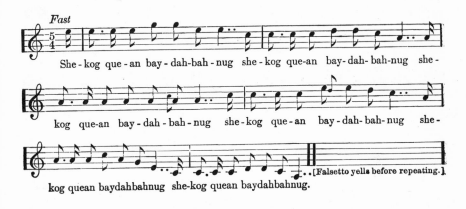

She - kog que - an bay - dah-bah - nug she - kog que-an bay- dah- bah-nug she -
kog que-an bay - dah - bah - nug she - kog que - an bay - dah- bah- nug she -
kog quean baydahbahnug she-kog quean baydahbahnug. [Falsetto yells before repeating.]

*No. 27 (c).* A caribou song, alluded to in the foregoing; words uncertain. The meaning is said to be: "There he is, right there! Let us go and look."

*No. 34 (d).*    A hunting song which the interpreter thus translates: "I shan't be gone long, and when I come back you can help me carry the meat home." The interpreter explains further that the singer is courting, and the meat is a love token by which he hopes to gain his sweetheart's favor.

*The Witch.* An old woman undertook a prolonged fast. In the course of time hunger overcame her will and she asked for food. Her people refused to give it to her. For two days she pleaded with them, threatening, if they persisted in refusing, to turn herself into an owl and haunt them. At the end of the second day she put her dire threat into execution, flying suddenly in the form of an owl to a neighboring tree where she perched and caused no end of annoyance by incessant hooting.

Kezh - e - guk - in    te - bi - kuk - ee........    ne   bay - zhe - non -

gay   baybah ko ko      o   moy - on   baybah ko ko      o   moy - on.

Translation: By day and night you can hear my solemn voice crying ko! ko!

---

*No. 36 (c).* Another owl song. The interpreter understands that it is sung by a little boy to his sister. He says the words mean: "It is getting dark; let's go home. See the owl in the way! We'll tell father and he will come and kill it."

---

## WAR SONGS.

*The Bravest.* There is only one significant word in this song: *Ungitchedah.* It means, the bravest man. By implication it conveys the utmost boasting of which any warrior could be capable. The Indians say that it might be used either as a boast, in which case it should be interpreted "I am the bravest of all men," or as a compliment to another, when the meaning would be, "He is the bravest of all men." In a general way, therefore, it is the laudation of a warrior, and the application varies with circumstances.

Un - git - ched - ah......... hey - ah hey - ah....................................

hey - ah hey - ah  ah  ah  hey - ah........ hey - - ah......... ah

hey - ah hey-ah  hey - ah...  hey - ah  hey - ah  hey-ah hey-ah hey - ah hey.

*Song of a Coward.* A party of warriors set forth to meet the enemy. One of the number sneaked away from the column and went back to the place where the women and children were hidden for safety. The song is in derision of him. An aged woman tells me that this is only a fragment of the song. She refers, of course, to the words which presumably told what happened to the coward; but she cannot remember the story and I have not found anybody who can supply the missing lines. The song as here given is often sung at social gatherings and is very stirring when given by a large number of men's voices.

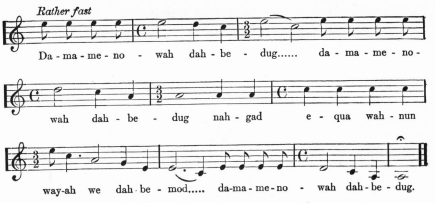

Da - ma - me - no - wah dah - be - dug...... da - ma - me - no -
wah dah - be - dug nah - gad e - qua wah - nun
way-ah we dah·be - mod..... da-ma-me-no - wah dah-be - dug.

Translation: See him sitting there among the women.

---

ₙ - *Sole Survivor.* This and the following were sung by a woman, and both are distinctively women's songs. The words as reproduced by the phonograph are not clear and do not seem to agree wholly with the dictated version which is as follows:

*Wesahquodayweinini ogeetahkobenung omahmequa ogeepozaybenung chemaunaysing ogee kahnjaybenung chebahmah bomowid:* All the men were lost; one woman only was saved; she was tied up in a canoe, set adrift, and picked up by people of another tribe.

*Apprehension.*   Dictated words: *Pahbahmahdaymowun we-nemoshayn wan nayndoobunejig koonemahdensahme:* I am crying about my sweetheart who is fighting the enemy.

*Small-Legs.*   A hero song of which both words and music undergo variation with different singers.   The general character of the words, however, is always the same, and they mean: "See that man with the small legs, the son of Always-flying; he is the best among us for he is the bravest."   The version on the phonograph follows:

A more frequent version is the following which I never chanced to hear when the phonograph was within reach.

*Song of a Scout.* The words mean: "I was alone when I found the teepee and feared to attack lest they overpower me; so I waited for the others to come to help me."

*Before the Battle.* It is said that this was composed in the time of the great Shingwauk when, under his leadership, the Ojibways joined the British in quelling some local disturbance. The chief had been making an address to his people after which he stepped into his canoe and sang: "*Kahkeenah wahweengay ne mozho kahwah kahkeenah wahweengay anishinahbeg ne mozho kahwah.*" I bid farewell to all my people as I go forth to battle."

*No. 5 (b).* The singer of this song knew no English. Neither from him nor any other could I get further meaning from the words than is conveyed in a literal translation.

Nim-bah-bah me-wi-ne-go ne-me-quah-nug... nin-gah-kee-way

we-ne-go hey-ah hey-ah hey-ah hey-ah ha hey...... ah ha

hey-ah hey-ah hey-ah ha hey-ah hey-ah ha hey-ah ha hey-ah ha.

Translation: They are taking me away, but my feathers will bring me back again.

SONGS OF TRAVEL AND DEATH.

Inasmuch as the Ojibways were great travellers in the old days, and no journey ever was begun without an appropriate song; and inasmuch as every Indian is supposed to have a death song that he means to sing and does sing if possible at the supreme moment, it should follow that this class would be represented numerously in a collection. I was surprised and disappointed while at work in the field that I did not come upon more examples. I was forever asking for death songs, and whenever it seemer possible to jog an Indian's memory, I suggested that he sing a travellers' song. Until recently I was unable to account for the scant result of this special search, and I do so now only by theory, but I believe the theory is sound.

My contact has been in the main necessarily with Indians more or less civilized. The Ojibways are still fond of travel, but habituated now for a generation or two to the restraints of reservation life, they have discarded the traveller's songs with so much else that pertained to the older manner. That is, the songs of this type have been forgotten. Furthermore I am almost convinced that the traveller's song was usually a familiar tune to which words were extemporized to suit the occasion. In that case it would be small wonder that the Ojibway singers failed to give me songs of travel, for, with their keen sense of appropriateness—which is manifested in such a marked degree by the names they give their children and adopted members of the tribe—it would not occur to them to invent a set of travel words to a melody which they were accustomed to singing to words of another character.

The argument is much the same with regard to death songs. As indicated in the foregoing pages, the habit of using a death song persists in a modified fashion, but the song chosen for the occasion does not appear always to have a special bearing upon the event, or special application to the dying man. So far as I can learn, the Indian who had forethought to his last hour selected a song that should be his and made words for it; and it is hardly supposable that such a man would make public his song while yet he felt that death was afar off. It is probable, too, that in many instances the death song was extemporized, words and music, under the pressure of the awful occasion. Such a song would necessarily perish with the individual unless some friend were near and remembered it. Army officers have told me of hearing death songs when Indians were led to military execution. From their description it would seem that the words vaunted the victim's courage, his prowess in battle, catalogued his heroic deeds and expressed savage confidence that in spite of death he would yet exult over his enemies; and musically they must have been little more than a highly dramatic chant. Finding the Ojibways so much more highly developed than other Indians in most of their songs, I had naturally hoped that in the death songs, incited as they would be by circumstances of such profound import, I should come upon melodies of rare pathos and majesty; and I frankly confess my failure, although the example known as "Hiawatha's Death Song," quoted below, is to my mind, the finest aboriginal song that has been preserved.

Whatever may be the merit of my theory, the fact is that I

have taken but one death song that was admitted to be such by the singers. And it seems to me significant that this song, so far as the words go, is not at all of the type that would be expected; for it does not boast of the past or tell of confidence in the future. On the contrary, it expresses the gloomiest doubt as to what the future has in store. The Indian words cannot be given exactly, but, according to an interpreter who listened to the phonograph, they mean: "I am dying, but I have my doubts as to whether I shall go where the good spirits are." The melody follows.

*Prince of Wales Song.* About forty years ago Edward Seventh, King of England, then the Prince of Wales, visited Canada. He went, among other places, to Sarnia, at the southern end of Lake Huron. At that time the chief of the Ojibways was the great Shingwauk who lived at Garden River, some dozen miles east of Sault Ste. Marie. Shingwauk, selected twenty warriors who sailed the length of the lake with him to meet the Prince. When the party left home, Shingwauk sang this song, and I am told that it was later sung before the Prince at Sarnia. As indicated on a preceding page, the tune was an old war song to which the chief adapted words of his own appropriate to the occasion. I heard the song first from Mrs. Sagachewiose, a granddaughter of Shingwauk, who remembers well how she stood on shore with all the village and watched the warriors set forth on their journey  I have referred the song to other Indians who were alive at that time, and all remember it.  Melodically it is of little value, but its historical interest makes it worth preserving.

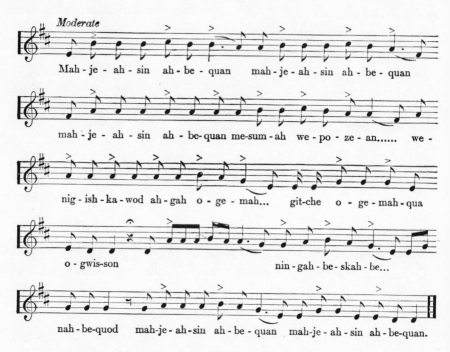

The words in the above are what I hear from the phonograph, the blank spaces indicating that I cannot distinguish the syllables.  Mrs. Sagachewiose dictated the words with evident care, but she did not sing them in the same order.  The dictated words and translation follow:

*Mahjeahsingabequan mesumah wepozean wenukwayshkowug ogema kitcheogemahqua ogwisson ningabeskahbe nahbequaning bemahsing nahbequod:* The ship sails away in which I embark to meet the chief, the great woman-chief's son. I shall return in the ship when the ship sails back.

---

*Hiawatha's Death Song.* When the Indian play was in process of making, Mr. L. O. Armstrong, who originated it, had the Indians sing many songs for him and selected those that were used in the first performance. Most of them, like "My Bark Canoe," "The Naked Bear," and this one, have been retained in the play and probably will always figure among its charming features. The song now to be quoted was chosen as especially suitable for the departure of the prophet, a scene which was so well managed when the play was given at Desbarats, Ontario, that it warrants sufficient digression to describe it. The play was presented in the open air on the shore of Lake Huron, most of the action taking place on a tiny island a few yards from shore. The final scene began with an address by *Hiawatha* to his people. He bade them farewell, prayed to the four winds, and stepped into his canoe. Raising his paddle in air he said: *"Kabeyaynung,"* (westward) and immediately the canoe started in a westerly direction. Without visible means of propulsion the canoe glided along the gleaming path of the setting sun, for the play was given in the afternoon so that this scene came when the water glowed as with fire. As he traveled thus mysteriously across the lake, the Indian actor sang this song, and his fellow actors, left on the island stage, shaded their eyes with their hands and watched his progress. When he had finished the song, the people on the island repeated it in resonant unison. Then *Hiawatha* sang it again, and by this time he was so far away that his voice was perceptibly fainter. The antiphonal finale was continued until the Indian prophet disappeared in the shadow of the two small islands nearly half a mile distant. It was a wonderfully poetic, impressive scene, realizing, in fair weather, Longefellow's fanciful and glorious description of the prophet's departure; and the emotional force of the episode was strongly enhanced by the noble, dignified strains of this song.

It is not, strictly speaking, a death song, and I am responsible for its somewhat misleading title. Long after the play had become established I came to have some share in its development. The song was there and I was deeply stirred by it. That it should be called "Hiawatha's Death Song" seemed to me a matter of course, and I so named it when I offered it for publication among the six songs from the play with which I sought to learn whether others would hold Ojibway music in the same estimation that I did. It is a matter of course now that the name should stick, but after I began to study Ojibway music in earnest I found that originally it was a traveller's song, and that it was always used for the journey from Sault Sainte Marie rapids to the place where Detroit now stands. This, for the Indian in his rude Mackinac boat, was a long voyage and justified the solemnity of the parting song. The Ojibway word

for Detroit is *Wahweyahtenung*.   Originally, then, the song
was as follows:

> *Mah noo ne nah ningamahjah*
> *Mah noo ne nah ningamahjah*
> *Wahweyahtenung ningadejah*
> *Mah noo ne nah ningamahjah*
> *Neen Wahweyahtenung ningadejah.*

Do not be anxious; I am going very far away,
Do not be anxious; I am going very far away;
To Detroit I am going.
Do not be anxious; I am going very far away;
I to Detroit am going.

The Indian actors, to adapt the song to the purposes of the
play, left out *Wahweyahtenung* and inserted *Hiawatha*.   I understand that the Indian who did the adapting incorporated
more new words than *Hiawatha* in the text, and I should be
surprised if such were not the case, for the words as sung to-
day are not, grammatically speaking, good Ojibway.   Some
carelessness crept in with the numerous repetitions of the song
called for in the performances of the play until the present
version seems to be fixed unalterably.   The actors are conscious
of the false syntax, but, as one of them said to me, "What does
it matter? the white people do not know one word from another."   Inasmuch as I never have heard the song in its original version, I give here the form which is used in the play.

Mah-noo ne nah nin-gah - mah - jah mah-noo ne nah nin-gah - mah -

jah...... Hi - a - wa - tha ne nin-gah-de - jah mah - noo ne nah

nin - gah-mah - jah neen Hi - a - wa - tha neen nin - gah - de - jah.

In the harmonized version will be found an interpretation of the words that accords with the idea of the scene in which the song is used. Many persons have remarked upon the fact that the melody is strongly suggestive of the music of the Roman Catholic church service. My own first impression of it was that the song had taken on this color from contact of the Ojibways with Jesuit missionaries, but I have found no evidence to support this view. Analysis shows that it is Indian from beginning to end. Its ecclesiastical manner is no more significant of white-man influence than is the "Scotch snap" which occurs repeatedly not only in Ojibway songs, but in the songs of tribes remote from them. It is shallow wisdom that would jump to conclusions from such coincidences as these; and at the last analysis this song remains a noble melody, as individual as any in the realm of music, that was found among Indians, used by them alone, utterly neglected and unappreciated by whites until a wandering enthuiast had committed it to print.

## MISCELLANEOUS AND UNCERTAIN.

*Vanity.* According to some Indians this is supposed to be sung by a woman, but Shingwauk interprets it as the utterance of a vain man who has arrayed himself in his best finery and is annoyed by the inconsiderate crowding of family and neighbors to look at him. It is a popular song. I have heard it from many singers. There are two songs to the words on the phonographic records, and the words reappear to the tune of the Morning Star song.

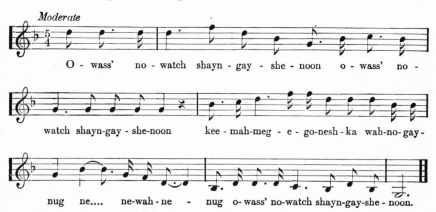

O - wass' no - watch shayn - gay - she - noon o - wass' no - watch shayn-gay - she-noon kee - mah-meg - e - go-nesh - ka wah-no- gay- nug ne.... ne-wah - ne - nug o - wass' no-watch shayn-gay-she - noon.

Translation: Better stand further off or you will crush my feathers.

Another melody to the same words:

First time        Second time

Allusion has been made more than once to the survival of melodies originally associated with ceremonies now obsolete, and the Morning Star song has been instanced as an example. It may, therefore, be interesting to glance at another set of words to that tune. The following may be found on phonographic record No. 10 (c):

*Nenemoshayn kahkeekedud, nekonahsass ningahnahdin koneemahdah keesenah nenemoshayn kahkeekedud:* My lover says it may be cold to-night, so I'll get my little blanket.

---

*My Big Lover.* The words as dictated: *Ningitchenenemoshayn dush wid nindenahbun ahbetah tibikuk ne gahgaydalgueshin nindenahbun ningitchenenemoshayn:* I have told my big lover that I will meet him at midnight.

*No. 13.* Sung by a woman who covered three quarters of the cylinder with false starts, giggling, and exclamations expressive of extreme embarrassment. Encouraged by another woman who stood by she at last mumbled the following melody and fled, her mind apparently in such disorder that she could not gather her wits sufficiently to dictate the words which are almost wholly inaudible on the cylinder. The woman who stood

by said they meant: "My lover and I are going around drink-ing."

*No. 20 (a).* Sung to meaningless syllables throughout and often used in this form for dancing. Shingwauk says that originally it was a canoe song, the singer telling of going to meet somebody, presumably a sweetheart.

*No. 27 (a).* Supposed to be a Menominee song, for the words are untelligible to Ojibways and the singer had lived among the Menominees.

---

*No. 29. (a).* This is another "Odowah," or Ottawa song. The singer's interpretation of the words is to the effect that a chief's daughter had two suitors; before setting out on the warpath each of them called and proposed to her; she remarks upon the fact that each of them said identically the same thing, and she concludes, "You can't believe what the men say."

*No. 29 (c).* This was one of a series that I did not venture to interrupt for the purpose of making sure of the words. An Indian who stood by when it was sung told me afterward that this was the meaning: "A gentleman calls to see the daughter; the mother meets him, and he says, 'What are you making eyes at me for? It is your daughter I came to see!'"

*No. 30 (a).* Untranslatable.

* Out of tune.

*No. 34 (a).* Words indistinguishable.

*No. 34 (b).* Supposed to be a Menominee song.

*No. 34 (c).* An interpreter hears the following words on the cylinder: *Kahwin nindekayndezin kaheegowanen;* I cannot remember what was told to me.

\* Out of tune.

*No. 37 (a).* According to Shingwauk, the singer says: "I don't know what to make of this man; I used to think well of him, but he disappointed me."

*No. 37 (b).* A man has come to a river and wishes to cross. Standing at the edge, he sings, "Come and get me; I've no way of crossing; come and get me."

*No. 37 (c).* Supposed to be a woman's song accusing a faithless lover of broken promises. Shingwauk thus translates the words: "You are walking around trying to remember what you promised, but you can't remember."

*No. 38 (c).*  Menominee song.

---

LIGHT ON A CONTROVERSY.

While I find that most persons are ready to áccept these songs as genuine products of Indian imagination, there are those who profess to discriminate and assert that some of them have undoubtedly been affected by civilization. Among the songs given in this chapter are many so crude that civilization balks at assuming any responsibility for them; and I observe that the only melodies believed to be the result of paleface influence are those that are well formed and beautiful. That is, civilization is quick to claim credit for what is good in Indian music, and equally quick to disclaim what is crude. I do not purpose to enter upon further argument in the matter but hope that the two songs that follow will throw some light on it.

I have alluded to the struggle that took place between Indian and civilized music when the Ojibways were converted by Protestant missionaries. The two styles did not mix well or permanently. The hymn tune could not be grafted on the Indian stock, nor the Indian melody on the hymn tune. Shingwauk has told me that the chiefs tried to make over the tunes taught them by the missionaries, seeking to adapt them to the Indian

manner.  He and other Indians believe that some of the tunes
still used in the church service are "half Indian and half white,"
and he sang several to me as examples.  I reproduce one as ac-
curately as may be from the phonographic record. (No. 22.)
The words are a translation into Ojibway of the hymn beginning,

> A charge to keep I have,
> A God to glorify.

Our notation is incapable of expressing with absolute exactness the manner of singing the hymn.  It is so slow that it seems
to be drawled rather than sung; time values are disregarded, and
the voice slurs up and down from one tone to another in the
most extraordinary fashion.  I have tried to suggest the extreme portamento by a generous use of slurs and small notes.

This may, or may not have some similarity to an ancient
Ojibway tune.  With patience there may be dug from it a
melodic outline that certainly resembles one of our own old
hymn tunes.  Having heard the version above indicated, I

would not need to be told that such a mixture of styles could not survive. It has not. As a rule the tunes of the Protestant service are now sung by the Ojibways substantially as the white congregations sing them, and songs of purely Indian origin, concerning Indian subjects and expressive of Indian thoughts, survive in their proper form, characteristic and distinct in type.

Contrast this deliberate attempt to graft one style upon another with the following. I was told by his friends that Jacob Akwenzs was a good musician, and of course I sought him out. After considerable persuasion he sang. Hardly had he begun before I knew that he was not giving me aboriginal material. The words were Ojibway, but the tune, poor as it was, disclosed its foreign character at once. When he had finished, I asked him who taught him the song.

"Nobody," he replied, "I made it."

On further inquiry it proved that he had been to school and had worked somewhere on the eastern shore of Lake Huron. Most of his life had been passed in close contact with civilization, and he had risen so high as to play second cornet in a brass band. Here, then, was an example not of what might happen, but of what had happened when a musically inclined Ojibway yielded to the influence of white-man music. The tune reveals no trace whatever of its Indian origin. Instead of a native theme developed more or less according to the style of civilization, or instead of the native manner refined by perception of form, there is neither native theme nor manner. The tune is simply a weak dilution of civilized commonplace. The inference is inevitable that when the two musical styles clash, one or other succumbs utterly.   The Ojibway who is really influenced musically by civilization simply abandons his native art; he who feels the force of his native music, clings to it.

Akwenzs made the words of his song as well as the tune.   It is a sea song, telling of a young man who saw a schooner coming into port.   He asks his employer for his "time," says farewell and sails away.   Here is the melody:

# PART II.

## TWENTY-EIGHT OJIBWAY SONGS, HARMON-IZED AND PROVIDED WITH ENGLISH WORDS.

The Ojibway words are spelled phonetically. Consonants have their normal English sounds, but g is always hard, soft g being represented by j. Singers are cautioned not to give the "continental" pronunciation to either vowels or consonants. M-u-d in Ojibway is *mud,* not *mood.* Broad a is represented by ah; without the h, pronounce a as in mate. Pronounce e as in see, i as in it, o as in rose, u always as in tub. The sound of i in night is represented by ai. Sound ay as in say. The diphthong ch is soft, as in church; ng is not strictly a diphthong in Ojibway, both consonants being pronounced nearly as in finger. Exception: at the end of a word, ng sounds as in sing.

# My Bark Canoe.

In the still night, the long hours through, I guide my bark canoe, My bark canoe, My love, to you. While the stars shine, and falls the dew, I seek my love in bark canoe, In bark canoe I

Che-kah-bay teb-ik on-dan-day-ahn Chekah-bay teb-ik on-dan-day-ahn Ah-gah-mah sib-i on-dan-day-ahn.

seek for you. It is I, love, your lov-er true, Who

glides the stream in bark ca-noe, It glides to you,— My love, to you.

## Red Blanket.

**Allegro.**

My red blan-ket I will put on And to the edge of the for-est rove,
*Ay-quay-quog nin-gah de-jah min— ne-ne mo-shayn nin-gah-we-je-ah*

Where my knees I will fall up-on And pick up sticks for my la-dy love.
*Mis-koo-ah nin-gah-mah-jah-od wah-boy-on nin-gah-mah-je-dun.*

# Carousal.

**Allegro.**

Ham-mer on the drum, pound it! Sit-ting by the
*Kah nin-ah-ne-bah se-neen, Kah-nin-ah-ne-*

fire, round it; Start a live-ly song, sound it!
*bah se-neen, te-tah-go-go-bah gaun-je*

What shall be the theme? found it! Gloom-y is it, con - found it!
*nan-kah-mah-min-ne quay-aung, Kah-nin-ah-ne-bah se-neen.*

All the liqu-or's gone, well, oh! Let the thirs-ty mob bel - low,

4

Full is ev-'ry man, mel - low, Jol-ly is the tight fel-low,

Full of fun the tight fel-low. At the emp-ty flask, blink-ing,

*poco meno mosso*

Eyes are drow-si - ly wink-ing, Got to go to sleep think-ing

How I'd ra-ther be drink-ing; In my dream I'll be drink-ing.

# Waubunosa's Longing.

**Andante.**

Long moons have passed since she de - part - ed
*Ah - yah! ___ ne - ne - mo-shayn-on de -*

from me, Long moons, Ah! will she come a - gain to
*guish - id, Ah - yah! ___ ne - ne - mo - shayw - on de -*

greet me? Wea - ry, I wait for her, my ab - sent
*guish - id, Ah - yah! ___ ne - ne - mo - shayw - on de -*

sweet-heart. Soft blows the south-wind, blows at ear - ly
*guish id,* Ah - yah! — *ne - ne - mo - shayn - on de -*

morn - ing, Soft blows the west-wind with the sun de -
*guish id,* Ah - yah! — *ne - suh we - nah - ow - e -*

scend - ing; Up - on their breath I hear her sigh - ing for me.
*quay - sans,* Ah - yah! — *ne sul gay - gel pe - dah - guish - ing.*

## Sleepy Time.

Andante.

Close your bright eyes, _____
*Kay - goo - mo - we - kayn* _____

my __ ba - by __ dear, __ The spi - der with his web is
*ne - ne - jahne - ses __ Ah nin - e - bah ay -*

here, He'll spin it 'cross your eyes, ba - by dear.
*ah - ne - ne - jahn - e - zess ay - ah ah!*

Ay - ah ay - ah _____ go sleep, my ba - by, go sleep,
*Ay - ah ay - ah _____ ay - ah ay - ah ay - ah*

The spi - der with his web is here, ba - by dear, ay - ah ah.
*ah - nin - e - bah ne - ne - jahn - e - zess ay - ah ah.*

# Song to the Morning Star.

# Wedding Song.

There's a girl whose par - ents have con -
*Bay - zhig e - quay - zess ne me ne -*

sent - ed, That is why you see me so con -
*gon - un Kay - get sen - nah ne - ge che day - be*

tent - ed.
*e - go.*
Hey - ah, hey - ah, hey - ah, hey - ah, hey - ah,

*Copyright MCMIX by Frederick R. Burton.*

hey-ah hey-ah  hey - ah.
*Bay-zhig e - quay-zess ne me ne-*

To my life great hap - pi - ness she's

bring - ing,  There - fore I can't  help my joy - ous  sing - ing.
*gon - un  Kay - get sen - nah  ne-ge-che-day-be  e - go.*

Hey-ah hey-ah  hey - ah  hey - ah hey-ah  hey - ah hey-ah

hey - ah  hey - ah hey - ah  hey - ah.

*p*

# Lonely.

Go not, my sweet-heart, Vain - ly I cry;—

To — yon far is - land Yearn - ing — I sigh.

Thith - er — must I go, Sad - ly I moan;—

Heav - y — my — woe,— Left — here a - lone, Left here a - lone.

# Midnight Tryst.

## A Song of Elopement.

Here a - lone    wait - ing the    hour,    Here a -
Be - jah - kah    nind - e - go - bun .    Nind - e -

lone_ I    wait the bless-ed    hour,    Wait - ing    lone,
go - bun    nind - e - go_ - bun,    Be - jah - kah

14

# War Song.

war, war-riors all.
*wah dah-be - mod.*

Forward to the fight, war-riors all, _____ forward to the fight, war-riors all.

Let the cow-ardshide with women, yah! let them hide _____ for-ward to the fight, war-riors all. _____

# Parting.

Ahm-bay-ge-way-do ___ che-wah de-bah-bun kee-gah-gee-

kay ne-me-go min ___ ka-hen-ah ko-ne gay - aung.

Let us go home 'tis near the break o' the ___ day, If

we should be seen, what would the peo-ple say.

# Doubt: a Death Song.

# In the Forest.

In. the for - est, lone - - ly, I hear my sweet-heart sigh-ing through ___ the pines, ___ — As she gent - ly whis - - pers, my heart o'er flow - ing, breathes a sigh ___ back to her.

# Winter.

# In The Sugar Camp.

good. _____ Come! give us a sup _____ of syr _ up or
geen.

cake _____ Ob-serve us dance up _____ our por-tion to

take; _____ What is it we want? _____ some syr - up, of -

course! _ Give free -ly, or we _____ will take it by force. _____

# The Lucky Trapper.

Now gay - ly will I dress my head, For
She - kog - que - an bay-dah-bah-nug She-

furs a - bun-dant have I found; I'll make of one a han - dy sled To
kog-que-an bay-dah-bah-nug She - kog - que-an bay-dah-bah-nug She-

drag them o'er the whit-ened ground, To drag them o'er the whit-ened ground.
kog - que - an bay-dah-bah-nug She - kog - que - an bay-dah - bah - nug She-

kog-que-an bay-dah-bah-nug.

It caught its prey, each clev-er trap, It

caught its prey, and held it fast Oh! there will be full many a cap To

wear when winter moons have passed, To wear when winter moons have passed.

# A Song of Absence and Longing.

Sweet - heart mine, I im - plore you, Speed your com - ing to me. All the day long be - fore

you, My lone heart longs to be ____

Three days long have I fast - - ed

Since my love went a - way; ____

Hun - - gry on - ly to see her, For

her re - turn I pray. _____

*molto legato.*

Lone in for - est I call her,

Lone, I glide on the lake. _____

Fear - - ing what may be - fall her, My

long - ing heart will break _____ will

break. _____

# Her Shadow.

Out on the lake my can-oe is glid - ing, Pad-dle dip-ping
*Ay-qua-nah-quog pe - ah be - dah - go jing, Kee-gah wah-bah-*

soft lest she should take al-arm Ah, hey - ah hey - ah
*mah non kee mah shay mi nay ay hey - ah hey - ah*

ho, hey-ah hey-ah ho, thus I go! Some-where a - long shore she is
*ho, hey-ah hey-ah ho, hey-ah ho.*

*Copyright MCMIX by Frederick R. Burton.*

hid - ing She is shy to yield to love's al - lur - ing charm, Ah,

hey - ah hey - ah ho, hey - ah hey - ah, love will win, I know.

There is a

shad - ow swift - ly steal - ing! Should it be her

own, soon I will end the race, Ah hey-ah hey - ah

ho, hey-ah hey-ah ho, I think it is! Will she but turn, her-self re-

veal - ing, I will shout a-loud when e'er I see her face, Ah!

hey-ah hey - ah ho, hey-ah hey-ah ho, There she is! Hal-loo!

*falsetto.*

# Old Shoes.

**Allegro moderato.**

Worn out shoes I am a-wear - ing, worn out shoes I am a-

wear - ing, worn out shoes I am a-wear - ing,

worn out shoes I am a - wear - ing,

## Confession.

**Allegro.**

You are my sweet-heart, you o -ver yon - - - der,

*Ken - nah-mah-shay - non Quay- kah-bah - no - - ques,*

*mf*

you are my sweet-heart, you o-ver yon - - der,
*ken - nah-mah-shay - non  Quay - kah-bah - no - - ques.*

you are my sweet-heart, you o-ver yon - - der,

you are my sweet-heart, you o-ver yon - - der,

**Last time.**

you are my sweet-heart, you o-ver yon - - der.

# The Forest Choir.

Hark! list-en well! All the birds, our neigh-bors, sing-ing loud and clear! Let us join our voi-ces in their song. Their's a song of peace, let ours give them no

fear,                    To      us      me -

lo - dious songs be - long;          Feath - - ered

friends, en - joy        all   the sounds you   hear.

# The Lake Sheen.

Shim - mer - ing sun up - on the lake,

Is it my sweetheart beck-'ning me?

Does it not bid my soul a - wake.

Rise from its dreams and thit - her flee?

Rip - ples with sun - light there at play,

This, and no more is what I see

But I will dream that o'er the bay

It is my sweet-heart beck-'ning me.

# The Naked Bear.

Kay-goo-mo _ wek-ayn ah-bi-no _ gees wahbshkae muk-

wah kee-gah-bi-dah-quo-mig kah kah-be-shees kos

kos-kay-be-quay-ne - - gen Hush, lit-tle babe, go to sleep, lit-tle

one, Hush-a-bye, ba-by, don't cry_ I pray,

Or the great Nak-ed Bear will come and take you a - way.

## Gambling Song.

Allegro.

I'm the man who can __ find it, I
Gay - get wah - bah - dod ne ge mah - guk

know where 'tis hid, yes, I __ do, You can't
ge gay - get wah - bah - dod ne ge mah - guk

fool me no no, you cant __ fool me, I'll bet! I'm the
ge gay - get wah - bah - dod ne ge mah - guk ge. Gay - get

End.

# Morning Tryst.

44

She who will come to meet me; Earth has no
O ne-nah ne-nah-wen-dum ge-mah-me-

vis-ion rar-er Sweet-heart come to greet me.
ko-ye-ah-nin ne ne-mo-shayn ai-ah-sig.

## Banished.

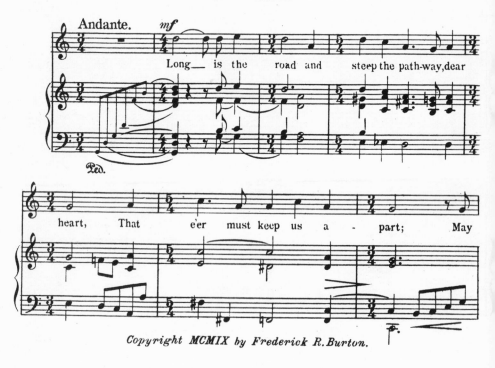

Andante. *mf*

Long is the road and steep the path-way, dear

heart, That e'er must keep us a-part; May

spir - its give cour - age to thee, dear heart, Fare thee

well, Oh, fare - well! My eyes are blind - ed, my

grief I can - not tell, ___ God grant thee His care in the

depths of de - spair! Good - bye, then, dear heart, fare thee well!

# The Beaver Hunt.

### Originally a cycle of four songs.

Be - side my camp - fire's flar - ing light, Here
Ne - mo - be - yon ne - mo - be - ' yon Ne -

will I pass the night, _____ the gloom - y night. Not
mo - be - yon _____ ne - mo - be - yon dah

far - a - way my longed for prey Is hid - ing __
nah - que - nay nind ish - ko - den e - nah - se -

on-ly see his tail go un - der, tail go un - der.
*ko nind e - ge - non-day e - ge - non-day.*

Tempo Primo.

Allᵒ molto.

※ Where now is my skill? *Ay - ah!* I shot a - gain, shot to kill,

※ Some of the Ojibway words in this section cannot be distinguished on the phonograph record. These are clear: *aynahbeyon keenundaygogee menon*, meaning "While I was looking he went down again."

Took care-ful aim while he stood still, Where now is my skill? *Ay -*

*ah!* Where is my skill? Down he went in - to the wet,

down he went in - to the wet *Ay - ah!* I'll get him yet, see 'f I don't

I'll get him yet, get him yet!

Tempo primo.

Allegro.

*mf*
While I watched, up he
*Ne - nah - wod    e - nah*

rose from out the drink. While I watched, up he
*o - quay - go - no - ning   Ne - nah - wod    e - nah*

rose and gave a wink; Then I shot him in the
*o - quay - go - no - ning   che - maun   nin - ga - pu - ge*

head, Pad-dled to him found him dead. While I watched, up he
*nah che-maun nin-gah-pu-ge - nah ne - nah - wod e - nah*

rose from out the drink, gave a wink, ha! ha! ha! ha! ha! ha!
*o - quay-go - no - ning ne - nah - wod.)*

ha! Now there's noth-ing else to do But take him home in my ca -

noe! Ha! ha! ha! ha! ha! ha! ha!

# Hiawatha's Death Song.

_nin-ga-de - jah._ ———   Mourn ye not o'er my de - part - ure,

Mourn ye not; I   go up - on a jour - ney,   I, Hi - a - wa - tha,

soon will have de-part - ed. Mourn ye   not; my   jour-ney is e - ter - nal.

I  Hi - a - wa - tha, soon   will have gone for - ev - er. ———

# My Bark Canoe.

### Quartette, unaccompanied.

# A Song of Absence and Longing.

call her, Lone, I glide on the lake, _____

call her, Lone, I glide on the lake, on the lake, ___

call her, Lone, I glide on the lake, _____ Fear ___

call _____ her, _____ Lone, I glide _____ on the lake, ___

Fear - ing what may be - fall her, My long - ing heart will

Fear - ing what may be - fall her, My long - ing heart will

_____ ing what may be - fall her, My long - ing heart will

Fear - ing what may be - fall, be - fall her, My long - ing heart will

break, _____ My heart will break.

break, My long ___ - ing My heart will break.

break, _____ My heart will break.

break, My long ___ - ing heart _____ will break.

# The Lake Sheen.

# Hiawatha's Death Song.

### Finale to Hiawatha, The Indian Play.

**Andante maestoso.**

Mourn ye not o'er my de - part - ure,

Mourn ye not; I go up-on a jour-ney, I, Hi - a - wa - tha,

soon will have de-part - ed. Mourn ye not; my jour-ney is e - ter-nal

I Hi - a - wa - tha, soon will have gone for-ev - er

Fare thee well, then, Hi - a - wa - tha! Fare thee well, Oh!

Fare thee well, then, Hi - a - wa - tha! Fare thee well, Oh!

Far thee well, then, Hi - a - wa - tha! Fare thee well, Oh!

Fare thee well, then, Hi - a - wa - tha! Fare thee well, Oh!

fare thee well for - ev - er! Sinks the sun, our pro-phet go-eth on-ward.

fare thee well for - ev - er! Sinks the sun, our pro-phet go-eth on-ward.

fare thee well for - ev - er! Sinks the sun, our pro-phet go-eth on-ward.

fare thee well for - ev - er! Sinks the sun, our pro-phet go-eth on-ward.

Fare thee well, May stars shine on thy jour-ney, O, Hi-a-wa-tha, through

Fare thee well, May stars shine on thy jour-ney, O, Hi-a-wa-tha, through

Fare thee well, May stars shine on thy jour-ney, O, Hi-a-wa-tha, through

Fare thee well, May stars shine on thy jour-ney, O, Hi-a-wa-tha, through

shad-ows ev-er-last-ing. Fare thee well, Hi-a-wa -

shad-ows ev-er-last-ing. Fare thee well, Hi-a-wa -

shad - ows; Fare thee well, Hi-a-wa - tha! fare thee

shad - ows; Fare thee well, Hi-a-wa - tha! fare thee

**64**

go - eth\_ on - ward, on - ward.

go - eth\_ on - ward, on - ward. fare - well

on - ward, on - ward.

Mourn ye not, I go up - on a jour - ney, fare-well then for - ev - er

Sinks the sun, our pro-phet go-eth

Sinks the sun, our pro-phet go-eth

Sinks the sun, our pro-phet go-eth

Mourn ye not; my jour-ney is e - ter-nal, Sinks the sun, our pro-phet go-eth

fare - well!

wa - tha!

ev - er, fare-well!

well   Mourn ye not; my jour-ney is e - ter-nal.

Fare thee well, Hi - a - wa - tha

Fare thee well, Hi - a - wa - tha

Fare thee well, Hi - a - wa - tha

Fare thee well, Hi - a - wa - tha

O Hi - a - wa - tha, fare - well, fare - well for - ev - er

O Hi - a - wa - tha, fare - well for - ev - er

O Hi - a - wa - tha, fare - well for - ev - er

O Hi - a - wa - tha, fare - well for - ev - er

fare thee well _____ fare thee

fare thee well _____ fare thee

fare thee well _____ fare thee

fare thee well _____ fare thee

# GENERAL INDEX

Abbreviations: ph., phonographic record; H.v., harmonized version. The page references are to Parts I and II respectively.

ABSENCE AND LONGING, a song of, Ojibway: I, 42; ph. 206; H.v., single voice, II, 26, quartette, 57.

AKWENZ, JACOB, Ojibway musician: I, 280–281.

ALL BIRDS FOLLOW ME, Ojibway song: ph. I, 240–241.

AMERICAN MUSEUM OF NATURAL HISTORY: I, 1, 15, 68.

APPREHENSION, Ojibway song: ph. I, 260.

ARISTOXENOS: I, 33, 36.

ARMSTRONG, L. O.: I, 140, 267.

ART VALUE OF INDIAN SONGS: I, 2; 18, and Chapter IX, 178–200.

BAKER, DR. THEODORE: I, 7–8; 36, 69, 228.

BANISHED, Ojibway song: ph. I, 211–212; H.v. II, 45.

BARK CANOE, MY: Ojibway song: I, 19, 42, 90, 96, 119, 121, 139, 144; account of the translation, 149–153; allusion to in argument for harmonization, 178–179, 267; ph. 203; H.v., single voice, II, 2; quartette, II, 55.

BEAVER SONGS, Ojibway: ph. I, 251–252.

BEFORE THE BATTLE, Ojibway song: ph. I, 261–262.

BIRD, ARTHUR: I, 182.

BOAS, DR. FRANZ: I, 15, 37.

BOY TURNED TO EAGLE, The: a Pawnee song used to illustrate the discussion of conflicting rhythms, I, 52–57, 61.

BRAVEST, The, Ojibway song: ph. I, 257–258.

BUFFALO SONGS, Ojibway: ph. I, 249–250.

BUKWUJJININI, TECUMSEH: I, 120.

BUREAU OF ETHNOLOGY: I, 13, 15, 241.

CADMAN, CHARLES WAKEFIELD: I, 198.

CARIBOU, Ojibway dance songs: ph. I, 253–254–255.

# GENERAL INDEX

CARNEGIE INSTITUTION: I, 15, 44, 70.
CAROUSAL, Ojibway song: ph. I, 226; H.v. II, 4.
CARUSO: I, 17.
CARY, HENRY: I, 148.
CAUGHNAWAGA, Iroquois reservation: I, 77.
CHIBIABOS: I, 129.
CONFESSION, Ojibway song: ph. I, 230–231; H.v. II, 34.
CORDER, FREDERICK: I, 49.
COWARD, Song of a, Ojibway: I, 42, 105; ph. 258-259; H.v. II, 16.
CRINGAN, A. T.: I, 77.
CURTIS, MISS NATALIE: I, 14, 17, 27, 28, 36, 37.

DAKOTAS: I, 37.
DANCE OF PAUPUKKEEWIS: I, 19, 47.
DANCE: significance, I, 58–59.
DEATH SONGS: I, 137–139. See also pp. 132–137, and " Hiawatha's Death Song," 263–270.
DESBARATS, place where the Indian play was first given: I, 220, 267.
DETROIT: I, 268.
DORSEY, DR. GEORGE A.: I, 44, 53.
DOUBT, Ojibway song: ph. I, 265; H.v. II, 19.
DOXOLOGY: use at Ojibway social gatherings, I, 139–144.
DRINKING DUETTE, Ojibway: ph. I, 224–225.
DRUM: I, 22, 46, 80, 109–110, 125–127, 130–131.
DVORAK: I, 11, 183, 195, 196.

ESQUIMO: I, 15.

FAITH, A song of, Ojibway: ph. I, 236.
FARWELL, ARTHUR: I, 14, 189, 190.
FIELD COLUMBIAN MUSEUM: I, 1, 44.
FIELD OF RESEARCH: I, 3–6.
FILLMORE, JOHN COMFORT: I, 11, 36, 37.
FIREFLY, Ojibway song: from Dr. Baker's collection, I, 229–230.
FLAGEOLET: I, 83–86.
FLETCHER, MISS ALICE C.: I, 8–11, 17, 18, 36, 37, 116, 189.
FLUTE: I, 83–86.

# GENERAL INDEX

# GENERAL INDEX

IROQUOIS: I, 1, 73–77.

JONES, WILLIAM: I, 70.

KELLEY, EDGER STILLMAN: I, 182.
KWAKIUTL: I, 15, 19, 47, 48.

LAKE SHEEN, The, Ojibway song: I, 96–100; ph. 208; H.v., single voice, II, 38; quartette, II, 60.
LANGUAGES: fifty-eight ethnic families of aborigines, I, 4.
LECTURE-RECITALS among Ojibways: I, 163.
LONELY, Ojibway song: I, 42; 170; ph. 204–205; H.v., II, 12.
LONGFELLOW: search for originals mentioned in his "Song of Hiawatha," I, 108, 229–230; use of Ojibway traditions, 113; his characterization of persons and country, 128–129; 242, 268.
LOOMIS, HARVEY WORTHINGTON: I, 189, 190.
LUCKY TRAPPER, Ojibway song: ph. I, 254–255; H.v., II, 24.

MACDOWELL, EDWARD: I, 12, 182, 188, 189.
MEGISSUN, Ojibway singer: I, 133–136.
MENOMINEE songs: ph. I, 274, 276, 278.
MIDNIGHT TRYST, Ojibway song: ph. I, 209; H.v., II, 14.
MINNEHAHA, personage in the Indian play: I, 140, 220.
MISSIONARIES: 270, 278–279. See also Frost.
MONOTONY of Indian music: 89–92.
MORNING STAR, song to the Ojibway: I, 42, 104, 271; ph. 239–240.
MORNING TRYST, Ojibway song: I, 41; ph. 207; H.v. II, 14.
MOSQUITO, The, Iroquois song, I, 73–75, 77.
MY BARK CANOE: see Bark Canoe.
MY BIG LOVER, Ojibway song: ph. I, 272.

NAKED BEAR, The, Ojibway song: I, 42, 108, 217, 267; ph. 228; H.v. II, 42.
NANABOZHO, chief figure in Ojibway mythology: I, 242–246.
NATIONALISM in Music: I, 11–12; 180–187.
NEW WORLD SYMPHONY: see Dvorak.
NOKOMIS, personage in the Indian play: I, 232, 266.
NONSENSE WORDS in Indian verse: I, 147–148.

# GENERAL INDEX

# GENERAL INDEX

# GENERAL INDEX

VANITY, Ojibway song: ph. I, 271.

VARIETY and lack of it in Ojibway songs: I, 5–6, 171–173, 202–203.

VERSE, Ojibway: I, 145–177; its compactness, 146–153; subordination of verse to melody, 153–165; verse a mnemonic summary, 163; sentiment and incongruities, 166–172; inversion of sentiment, 168–172; lack of variety, 171–173 and 202–203.

VISITING SONG, Ojibway: I, 95, 100–103, 116; ph. 227.

VOICES, Indian: quality, compass, and so forth, I, 78, 79, 80.

VULGARITY in Ojibway songs: I, 166–171, 202.


WABENOS, Ojibway mystery men: I, 241–249. Song cycle, the same.

WAITING, Ojibway song: ph. I, 210–211.

WAR SONG, Ojibway: II, 16. Other Ojibway war songs, I, 257–262.

WAUBUNOSA's LONGING, Ojibway song: story, I, 168; ph. 208; H.v. II, 6.

WEDDING SONG, Ojibway: I, 147–149; ph. 204; H.v. II, 10.

WINTER, Song of, Ojibway: I, 42; story of the song, 161–162; versification, 165; 171; ph. 221; H.v. II, 21.

WITCH, the, Ojibway song: ph. I, 256–257.

WOOD, WILLIAM: I, 79.


ZUNIS: I, 15, 25, 32, 35, 107.